Also by the Author

Hairdresser to the Stars

Dear
Vivian
I'll miss
you my very
dear friend
Have fun
I love you
Ginger

Ginger Blymyer
131 8th Street (6)
Hermosa Beach, CA, 90254
www.flyingintothesun.com

FLYING INTO THE SUN

GINGER MARYCE BLYMYER

ISBN 0-7414-4387-2

Published by:

INFINITY
PUBLISHING.COM

1094 New DeHaven Street, Suite 100
West Conshohocken, PA 19428-2713
Info@buybooksontheweb.com
www.buybooksontheweb.com
Toll-free (877) BUY BOOK
Local Phone (610) 941-9999
Fax (610) 941-9959

Printed in the United States of America

Printed on Recycled Paper

Published August 2008

To my husband Pat

I am fortunate to be alive at the same time
and share this life with you.

To Adi Da Samraj,

Without Him, and what He does for the Whole Universe, I don't believe I would be here.

Because of Adi Da Samraj, my Teacher, my life is full of love and feeling. I am never alone. He makes it possible for me to live in this world in spite of what is happening, and to know that there is Prior Unity, and a Reality that we are all one, no matter what we believe.

.

FLYING INTO THE SUN

The sun you see in the sky

Is imitative and metaphorical;

There is a far more real Sun that is manifesting everything.

Everything is one of its rays,

Everything is born from this Sun and dies back into it.

It is this Sun you should yearn for so that you can come into more than just sense-objects.

And so your knowledge can go on growing and growing.

There is another Sun, apart from the sun of physical form,

A Sun through which inner truths and realities are unveiled.

Any partial Knowledge that enthralls you is a branch of that

Great knowledge and a ray of it.

And this ray is summoning you to that Great Knowledge

Sun of Origin

Rumi

PROLOGUE

CHIANG MAI, THAILAND

Muggy skies loom above the city clinging like a damp, woolen blanket. A small red vehicle called a tuk-tuk weaves through the mayhem. The driver tries his best to negotiate the onslaught of traffic and humanity. It is a three-ring circus. If there is truly "order in chaos," the streets of Chiang Mai are a perfect example.

The tuk-tuk driver leans back and angles his right ear toward the passenger seat. He barely understands his passenger who shouts wildly in a British accent. "Faster! Faster! I must get to the temple before I lose my mind! I can't wait a moment longer!"

The passenger in a state of madness does not behave with the customary cool British attitude. "Sorry to be such a problem. I know you do not understand. I'm not sure I do myself, but if I don't do this now, it will be the end for me. "Hurry, hurry"

The road to the top of the mountain is steep. At the summit stands an enormous Buddhist temple sparkling in the sunlight, glowing with a golden radiance. The road curves back and forth, confirming that one must struggle to reach the Buddha. The driver pulls up to the bottom of the steps. A small red cable car travels down the incline. The British man leaps out of the tuk-tuk, almost falling on his face. He hastens up the steps, unwilling to wait for the cable car to empty.

"Sorry, sorry," he mutters, as he bumps into one of the orange-garbed monks walking down the steps. The other monks rescue their brother. They glare at the Brit. He climbs to the top of the steps and hurries past a long line of immense brass bells bordering the path.

At the second level, he kicks off his shoes, and places them alongside multiple shoes piled by the entrance to the temple. Rituals are the same. He tosses a handful of bhats, the currency of Thailand, to a small wrinkled old woman. She smiles an appreciative, toothless grin. In return, she hands him incense, a candle and a small gilt paper. He holds his hands together and bows to her. "Namaste."

The light in the temple is dim. He slows, lights his candle, and places it along side others burning on the table. He ignites the incense in the flame, holds it up, and offers it to the Buddha. Lastly, he rubs the gilt on the belly of a small statue of the deity. He walks deeper into the cool hall. The great Buddha gazes down upon him.

The moment he comes to a stop, sweat begins pouring down his brow, his spine, it is as though he has stepped into a shower; one does not usually hurry in weather like this. At last, he is still. He has reached his destination. Quiet for a moment, he begins to pray.

"I surrender. I give up control. There is no other way. I understand."

He kneels in front of the Buddha, holding his hands open wide. He prostrates himself. His places his head on the cool tile as he surrenders.

"Please send the woman. I need her. She is my inspiration, my muse. I cannot do this without her. I will do whatever I can to make this work. Show me the way. Send her in any form. I will do anything you ask. Thank You in advance."

He lies there; his body absorbs the coolness of the tiles. A short time later, he gets up, and looks directly into the Buddha's eyes.

"I'm counting on YOU. This is the rest of my life."

He has never prayed like this before; never asked for so much.

Surely, the Buddha will answer his prayers.

THE TRAIN RIDE

A train flies swiftly along the tracks, through a violent storm heading toward Wales. Trees bend to the ground, whipped by driving winds, lightning shoots across the sky in jagged bolts, thunder rumbles and reverberates overhead.

Snug inside the train a woman fascinated by the storm. brushes her hair back so she can see the storm more clearly. Her eyes widen in amazement as she enters this new world. It occurs to her that she is saying yes to a new life. A sensuous, earthy woman of fifty, Katherine is at home in her body. Strands of white are beginning to appear in her dark curly hair. Light blue eyes crinkle at the edges and her smile surfaces readily.

For the first time in twenty-five years, she is no longer needed as a mother. Her children have gone off to college. The only plans she has for her future are to spend time with her husband Bernardo, a successful movie director shooting a film in Wales. Until now, she has taken it for granted that like her parents at this age, she will settle down. Although her life has been full of travels and changes based upon her husbands work schedule, she has never needed to make any major decisions on her own. Her husband, always the director, has automatically cast her in many different roles. She has played them without question.

I wish someone would sit beside me so I could share my adventure.

"Is this seat free?"

She glances up, pulled from her thoughts.

"Yes, of course."

A tall man, dressed in worn tweeds, sporting a scruffy beard, tips his hat to her, and places it in the overhead compartment along with his overcoat and bag. His deep green eyes are extraordinary in an ordinary face. When he speaks, his voice is deep and sexy, with a lovely Welsh accent.

I hope he is friendly and wants to talk. One never knows with strangers, especially the British.

Her wish is granted immediately.

"Are you reading Dylan Thomas?" He asks, glancing at the book in her lap.

"Yes. I loved <u>A Child's Christmas in Wales</u>, but I don't know if I can get through this book of his letters," she sighs. "It's so heavy, the weight of the book I mean, and truthfully the content of the letters. I'm hoping it might help me understand the Welsh."

"Maybe," he replies, doubtfully. "But remember, not all Welshmen are as self-destructive, nor as talented, as he was. His whole life was a drama, and yet he wrote some wonderful things."

"You may be right."

He fixes his deep green eyes on her. She feels an instant attraction causing her heart to beat rapidly. She is surprised by the intensity of her response.

"Where are you off to?" She asks, trying to break the depth of her attraction toward this stranger.

"Asia," he replies.

"Aren't you heading in the wrong direction?" She jokes, now more at ease.

"Right, it might take years."

He sits back in his seat and begins to explain. "It may sound crazy but I've been given a chance to live my dreams."

"What do you mean?"

"I've wanted to be a writer for a long time. Unlike Dylan Thomas, I've had to wait a while; there was always my family to support. Suddenly, things changed. My dreams were granted in an instant. Today, I'm on my way to say goodbye to some old friends, and then I'm off."

"Are you actually off to Asia?"

"It may sound strange, but that's where I'm headed," he laughs.

She senses his excitement. It is as though he is intoxicated and Katherine is inhaling the fumes. Only moments before, she made a wish for someone to appear. Now her wish has turned out to be better than she could have ever imagined.

"Lunch, my lady and gentleman?" the sandwich seller interrupts

"Two ploughman's lunches, and tea, please." They order quickly, both wanting to continue the conversation

"What are you doing in Wales? Have you ever been here before?"

"No," she shakes her head. "I've come to join my husband." *I hope that makes me sound a little saner. I do not know if he notices my reaction to him. I am not used to behaving like this. Am I being too friendly?*

She sits back and looks out the window for a few moments. She swallows a mouthful of her sandwich and continues. "My husband is shooting a film on location in Llandudlow. I am not sure what I shall end up doing. My children just left for college, so this is first time I have ever had an opportunity to be able to spend as much time with him as I would like.

"Ahh, it's a lovely place when the sun shines, a real vacation spot. Tell me, what sort of work does your husband do on the film?"

"He's a director. Right now, he is looking at the locations. They are getting ready to shoot in a couple of days."

"Where will they be shooting?"

"I'm not sure. He said something about working at the copper mines and the slate mines."

"Those mines are fantastic. I am familiar with that area. The slate mine looks like outer space; I imagine they will look rather futuristic on film."

"We'll be here for a week, and then we return to London, where they'll continue to shoot at Leavesdon studio for a few weeks. The sets are being built right now."

"It all sounds very exciting."

"So...where do you live?" Katherine asks curiously.

"I was born in Wales, but I've lived in London for more than thirty years. I'm visiting old friends today, and then I shall be off to the Far East to seek my fortune."

She smiles as he continues.

"At last I will be able to write my book," he says enthusiastically.

She cannot help but respond. "That is exciting."

It occurs to her that is unusual for a British man to show so much unrestrained enthusiasm. She can feel it bubbling up inside of him. *He is as pleased as I am to find someone with whom to share his thoughts.*

"I've had this dream for so long. I was about ready to give up on it, to let it go, when everything became possible. I wish I had more time to explain how it all happened, but sadly, my stop is next."

Katherine wants him to remember her. She reaches into her pocket and closes her fingers over a small rose quartz stone a friend has given her. She takes it out of her pocket and places it in his hand.

"Here, this is for good luck. It is a touchstone and I want to share it with you."

He closes his hand over the stone. "It is deliciously warm, thank you."

"Good luck to you too. Even though our time has been so short, I am ever so happy we've met."

He stands up and puts on his coat and hat. "I shall always remember you."

With that, the train clunks to a stop. He reaches for the rest of his things, and ads, Good luck with that book. It may be one of the unreadable books, like most Russian literature. Then again, remember not all Welshmen are like Dylan Thomas."

He walks toward the end of the car, and steps out onto the platform into a light rain. Katherine watches him, not wanting the moment to end. He opens his umbrella, and glances back in her direction. Their eyes meet for a moment, and then he is gone. She does not even know his name.

As she sits back in her seat, Katherine recalls a time when she was seven years old. Riding on a merry go round. She was so happy. She went round and round, and reached for the ring, hoping to catch the gold one in her small hand. Silver, silver, silver. Then suddenly, for the first time ever, she saw that she had caught the gold ring. She held the ring tightly in her hand for a moment. She was thrilled. But as she opened her hand so that she could see its brightness, the ring fell from her hand and dropped through the cracks in the floorboards. She never found it.

Don't worry about saving these songs!

And if one of our instruments breaks,

It doesn't matter.

We have fallen into the place where every-
thing is music.

The Essential Rumi

ARRIVAL IN WALES

"Llandudlow!"

The train pulls into the station. Katherine fetches her luggage, stowed in the compartment at the end of the car. The train comes to a thunking stop. She steps out onto the platform, glancing nervously around, filled with relief when she sees a driver holding a large card with her name written upon it.

WELCOME KATHERINE

"You found me." Tension drops from her shoulders as she smiles.

The driver speaks. "No problem."

"This is a wild storm." Katherine tries to make conversation about the weather, but the driver is busy with her luggage and only nods his head in agreement.

It is nearly dark by the time they are ready to leave the station. Katherine peers out the windows as they slowly circle through narrow streets, past picturesque cottages with soft lights gleaming in the windows. It reminds her of illustrations from books she had read to her children. The main part of town borders the sea, and the shore is resplendent with huge, old Victorian hotels that look like giant wedding cakes. Llandudlow has been a vacation spot for more than a hundred years.

The driver pulls up to a magnificent hotel. Refurbished, it retains the elegance of the original Victorian period. Wide steps invite her toward the etched glass doors that open to the lobby. Enormous logs burn in a huge fireplace, and offer welcome warmth on this stormy evening. She rubs her hands together in delight.

The driver deposits her suitcases at the front desk. "Will you need anything else? If not; I'll be at your disposal tomorrow morning."

She tries to hand him a gratuity, but he refuses it. "I'm with production. It is not necessary."

"Thank you. I doubt that I'll want to go anywhere tomorrow." She is too weary to make plans at the moment. Utterly exhausted, she turns to the woman at the desk, who is ready to direct to her room.

"The bellman will show you to your room. Don't worry about anything. You are all checked in. Your husband's secretary has seen to everything." The woman proffers a room key.

The doors of the suite swing open. Tall windows overlook the sea. She can hear the pounding surf, but can barely see white the caps tossing in the dark water. Victorian furniture is complemented by deep red flocked wallpaper. An enormous bouquet of autumn flowers sits grandly on a table at the entrance, reflecting a second bouquet in a gilded mirror. A card from Bernardo expresses his love. Beside the card is a note from Emily the secretary. "Please relax, Bernardo may be working late. Not to worry."

Katherine, never at her best after a long flight, sighs with relief. Time to herself is precious. She unpacks what she needs, and orders room service.

"Cucumber sandwiches, oysters on the half shell and a glass of Chardonnay."

Always a cure for her ills, a hot steamy bath is in order. Hyacinth scented bubble-bath, poured into an immense tub fills the room with a glorious scent. Room service arrives and she immediately places the tray on a stool beside the tub. Casually dropping her clothes in a heap, Katherine slides down into the hot steamy water. The weariness accumulated by her travels drains from her body as she sinks in.

She lies back, relieved by the fact that she has no need to go anywhere this stormy night. After a sip of wine, and a taste of the sandwich, she begins to reflect upon her day. Thoughts of the stranger on the train return. She knows she will never see him again. Still… closeness developed between them during the hour they were together on the train.

After a lengthy soak, she climbs out of the tub and wraps herself in a soft towel, and sits quietly taking time to cool down. She slips into a brand new powder blue flannel nightgown; a gift from her children. It has the special smell of new flannel nightgowns and feels wonderful. The cozy bed beckons her. She crawls between the soft cotton sheets, covered by a velvet quilt, and snuggles down, enveloped in clouds. She attempts to read for a few moments, but quickly looses the battle, and switches off the bedside lamp.

****

The smell of coffee permeates her dreams. Even before she slowly opens her eyes, she is aware of the sun streaming through the windows. Bernardo is already dressed for work. He smiles, and walks over to the bed and embraces her. Bernardo is twenty-five years Katherine's senior, but one would never know it. Born in Italy, he is a mix of Burl Ives and Federico Fellini, with the vitality of a much younger man.

"Welcome, my, darling," he says, warmly against her neck. He looks at her appraisingly. "You must have been exhausted. You were sleeping so beautifully last night; I couldn't bear to wake you. "

He sits on the bed beside her. Katherine loves this bear of a man, who bubbles with the warmth of his Italian heritage. He has retained his accent and loves the dramatic. Their relationship remains romantic, even after all their years together.

She holds up her face for a kiss. "Good morning, my love."

As always, Bernardo is totally involved with his current project. Excited, he races on. "We're off in a few moments to scout the rest of the locations. We begin shooting tomorrow. This is my last chance to get everything all set up. I must lay out the shots. You'll have to come out and see these fantastic places where we are shooting. It is spectacular." He gestures widely.

Katherine is used to his nonstop announcements. This morning she is too lazy to wake up completely. She sips her coffee and watches him through sleepy eyes, doing her best to take in all he is saying, nodding agreement to his suggestions. In reality, she cannot imagine leaving her bed at the moment.

Bernardo walks to the window, and throws it open so she can get a feel for the day. He never gets enough fresh air. Today the storm has passed; the sky is bright, blue and clear. He kisses her goodbye, and a moment later he is out the door.

She is accustomed to his ways and she knows how to take advantage of the quiet moments. She dozes for a couple of hours.

KATHERINE'S DIARY WALES, OCTOBER

It feels so good to lie here in bed. No place to go. I've ordered more coffee, and now I'll take the time to write in my diary. I need to put my thoughts in writing, before I can understand just what is going on in my life. It's sort of, like I have to bring my thoughts outside to really understand them. Ever since I began to write, I have kept some sort of journal, and I've loved this process. Maybe I will even write a book someday. I picture my children, after I am gone, trying to go through all of these journals looking for important things I might have said. Therefore, I try to make it sound more like a book, just in case that does happens.

I love the starched sheets. I will allow myself to be lazy this first day. I've been rushing for so long, closing the house, and getting the twins off to college in Hawaii was lots of work. I feel the toll it's taken on me. I'm not as young as I think I am. I don't think I forgot anything and all will be fine at home. Come on, you worry wart, of course it will be.

The Trip

New York was great. I love my friend Franko. It's great to have a gay friend because Bernardo isn't jealous of our relationship. Franko gave me a beautiful purple journal with huge pages for the trip. He knows I keep a journal.

Franco's apartment is gorgeous, just redecorated. Again! He changes it according to his moods. Franko has a view to kill for overlooking Central Park.

He is affectionate and honest. He knows me so well, sees me so clearly and consoles me in my times of need.

Forthright, and outspoken he was just who I needed to talk to at that moment.

It's a time of a great change in my life, a little death they say. All will be different from this time forward. The kids are gone; they don't really need me anymore. That is as it should be. I've been happy to devote my life to them, but what should I do now? I'll still oversee the care of the house. The accountant pays the bills. At this moment, life seems simple. I never felt the need to make plans for the future.

I decided to ask for Franco's take on that. After he finished with me, I wasn't so glad I had asked. The first words out of his mouth gave me a start. "So who is the newest Katherine going to be?" He asked, in a nagging voice he saves for times like this. "Has Bernardo cast you in a new part yet?"

I actually blushed when he said that. Trying to defend myself, I have to admit I am a somewhat of a people pleaser, but am I so obvious? "Give me a chance, the kids just left for college."

"Ahh, yes, the empty nest syndrome will follow now." Franko can be sarcastic.

I defended myself. "I'm just starting to figure out what I'm going to do. I've always thought that when the kids left for college, I would be there for Bernardo. He's getting older, and I have to face the fact that he can't go on forever."

Franko knows me so well. He went deeper and then said, "I don't want to upset your applecart, but I'm not sure you're needed. Bernardo has his film crew. You know they have always served as his family while he is away from home. People in the movie business live in two separate universes running parallel to each other."

His crew likes me; at least I think they do. But then, I think about Emily. She is Bernardo's new secretary and very possessive. Will I be in the way?

Finally, I got what Franko was trying to tell me. He kept saying in different ways that I couldn't continue to live in Bernardo's shadow.

Do I really do that? Franko has seen all sides of Bernardo because they worked together for years before I met him. He loves Bernardo, but he always says Bernardo is so powerful that he doesn't leave any room for others. There is no space for anyone else. It is all about him, his current project. I don't think he means to do it, he just does. His energy and excitement draw people to him. We all want what he has, we love him, but I must admit, Franko is close to the truth.

I have to agree with Franko about the fact that I have no idea who I am. In truth, I am a reflection of my family. I'm not a wimp, I'd do anything to protect them, but still I wonder if I really have the courage to investigate who or what might be lurking inside of me, just waiting to appeal? It terrifies me. If I ask too many questions, I may not like the answers.

Back to yesterday and that man. Just imagine what it would be like to be as free as he is. I couldn't conceive of throwing everything to the wind. What gives a person the courage to go for what they desire? Do they have more passion than others, or do they finally give up doing what they should, and just go for what they desire? I must lack passion; I can't think of anything for which I would throw my present life away. My righteous friend at home marches for her beliefs. I have never been inclined to do anything like that. All of a sudden, I wonder what might make me change. All my needs have been met and have been all my life. I never had to work, really. I loved being a photographer for films, but it never felt like work. It might be scary to make changes now. Why do it, anyway? I believe we start to look inside when something really difficult happens to us. When we get cornered, we find a new dimension within and learn to change.

We talked long into the night, and, after what seemed only few minutes, the alarm went off. It was time to go.

At the airport, Franko advised me. "It's time for you to go a little bit crazy. Try not to worry about anyone else for a change." With a last, "I love you," he kissed me and gave me a big hug. "Keep in touch." He watched me as I got on the plane.

I rushed to London where I dropped my extra baggage. Yesterday morning I got on the train to Wales. I'm exhausted. It is nice to have time to let everything that has happened sink in.

It's time to get up and out of this stuffy room. I'll go outside and start (Dare I say it?) the first day of the rest of my life.

The world rushes on
And now spring is over.
It seems that only yesterday
Everything I saw
Was in full flower.

<u>The Ink Dark Moon</u>.

LLANDUDLO

The dining room is extremely proper. Meadows of white tablecloths await her; silverware gleams, crystal vases, each containing a single red rose, sit pertly in the center of each table. The stiff-necked, Maitre D' looks down his nose at her as he asks, "Your name, Madame?" When she tells him, he leads her to a table in the back of the dining room. A sign on the table says, "Reserved for Movie Crew." She sits alone at the huge table.

Pen in hand, the waiter awaits her order.

"I want to enjoy that English breakfast I've read about in books. I imagine sideboards of fish, bacon, broiled tomatoes and dry toast in a silver rack. It doesn't seem to be here."

He acts as though he hasn't heard her.

"Toast with marmalade, coffee and orange juice first, please." She adds, smiling.

"Sorry, Madame is too late for breakfast. The buffet has been put away."

Put in her place, Katherine is disappointed and chastened.

"Tomorrow, I will have to get up earlier," she says, coloring slightly.

"The lunch buffet is almost ready. I can bring you some tea for starters, if you wish."

"That's fine; I'll just have a tomato sandwich instead," she snarls at him. By now, all she wants to do was to get out of there. Her stomach is in knots. She wonders why snooty waiters make her feel so uncomfortable. She eats quickly.

The door opens toward the sea. Her scarf blows across her face as she walks toward the beach. Seagulls dart up and down, screeching loudly. Angrily, they dive into rubbish and dead fish blown onto the beach by the savage storm. Shrieking like banshees, they challenge each other as they fight over fishy treasures.

Vacationers, sensibly bundled up, stroll as though it is summer day. Nobody appears to be bothered by the weather. A breath of ocean air opens Katherine's lungs and clears her head. It is stuffy in the hotel in more ways than one.

Turning the corner, she comes to a busy street lined with a bonanza of tiny gift shops. She loves window-shopping. This is a tourist town all primped up to lure tourists' pounds out of their pocketbooks. Store windows are filled with elegantly displayed clothes, jewelry and other expensive gift items. Katherine gazes into the bookshop window. She has to remind herself that she will have plenty of time in London to shop for books. The trouble is books put some sort of a spell on her. If she actually steps across the threshold of a bookstore, she is unable to leave without an armful of books. She pulls herself away from the shop proud that she has purchased not even one book. As she glances across the street, she is pleasantly surprised to find Marks and Spenser, one of her favorite department stores. She enters through the street floor basement and finds a grocery selection that astonishes her. She grabs a wire-shopping basket from a pile and strolls up and down the aisles. Licking her lips as she observes the wares, she chooses from among amazing displays of sweets, puddings of real cream, Scottish Shortbread, plus perfect salads and fruits lining the shelves. Everything looks delicious. By the time, she has checked out, her arms are laden with bags of goodies.

Back at the hotel, she fills the refrigerator with her treasures. Still weary from her trip, she decides to lie down for a few moments. In what seems like only minutes later, Bernardo awakens her with a kiss.

"The light goes so quickly at this time of year; our days may not be too long on this location, my dear."

He kisses her on the neck the way she loves him to do. "We have reservations for dinner tonight," he reminds her. He lies down beside her and holds her close for a short time. She enjoys his closeness and warmth as she began to wake up.

"Um, that sounds good," she murmurs. "You go ahead and take your shower first, while I wake up. I never imagined that I could sleep so much."

"You must need it." He heads for the shower.

The car awaits them as they step out of the hotel. The air is nippy. Wearing his black cashmere overcoat, Bernardo looks very handsome. A beret tops his wavy silver hair, and a silk scarf is wrapped around his neck. He slips on soft leather gloves. As he does, he wiggles his fingers, proudly showing off the gloves to Katherine. "A gift from my producer."

She strokes his hands. "They are soft as a baby's bottom. I want a pair too."

Bernardo, being Italian born, has never forgotten his heritage and loves all things Italian. The restaurant is divine. Wine bottles line the walls, giving the effect of mosaic tiles. Traditional red and white checkered cloths cover the tables adorned with candles floating in glass vases. For a moment, they are able to imagine that by some mistake they have left Wales and ended up in Italy.

The waiter, who appears to be Italian, greets them with a Welsh accent, bringing them back to reality. They burst out laughing. "No time travel, after all," says Katherine.

Bernardo takes Katherine's hand in his and begins to tell her about his day's work.

Dinner is tender veal picatta, pounded to perfection, fresh vegetables al dente, pasta, and a large bottle of red wine suggested by the waiter.

After they enjoy their meal and pay the check, Bernardo suggests, "Let's walk back to the hotel." He is a vital man for his age. He walks fast and greets people on the street with charm and energy. He believes they will appreciate his greeting.

They have been married for twenty-five years, but have not spent that much time together. With Bernardo on location, and Katherine home with the children, they have often been apart for months on end. Each time they reunite, there is a delicate time of re-entry into each others lives that needs to be slow and gentle rekindling between them. Often, when Katherine visits Bernardo on location with the kids, they scarcely have a moment to themselves. When that happens and there is no time to get reacquainted, it is as though they remain proper strangers who sleep together.

Katherine appreciates this time alone with Bernardo. When they return to their room, she slips on one of Bernardo's favorites, a black cashmere robe over a red silk nightgown. Bernardo loves silk and often gives her beautiful lingerie as a gift. He is already in bed. She pulls back the sheets and snuggles into his arms. He holds her tight, as though he wants to devour her, his hands softly touch her body in places he knows so well. They lie there, talking, happy to be close and intimate. Soon they are wrapped in each others arms. Katherine feels at one with Bernardo now. When he makes love to her it seems to be the one time he is able to forget his work, and give her his all, his full attention. He has always been a romantic lover. They fall asleep in each other's arms, reconnected.

Early the next morning, Bernardo is off to work. Katherine, content from the night before, studies the brochures she found at the kiosk across the street.

TOUR SNOWDONIA PARK, SEE MOUNT SNOWDONIA

Once again the stranger with the green eyes comes back to haunt her. These are the places he suggested she see. She makes reservations for the following day. Today with the company car at her disposal, the driver is waiting for her in the lobby. He is a local fellow and often takes people on tours. He knows the area and she wants to see places tourists seldom go. He makes some suggestions that sound ideal. She orders picnic lunches for the driver and herself.

"Which is your favorite place around here?" She asks.

"The Swallow Falls, Betws-y-coed," he tells her as they drive along.

"Never be able to pronounce that." She laughs.

The craggy mountains make Katherine imagine King Arthur and his men galloping across boulder-strewn slopes. She expects to look up and see them at the crest of the hill. They arrive at a grassy glen where Ben, the driver, leads her down a path through the forest. He carries the picnic basket. Water dances over the rocky riverbed and sprays their faces. It feels heavenly. The day is deliciously warm. Trees, still green, line the edge of the river. No autumn changes here. After a leisurely lunch, they hike beside the water, and stop to rest. Katherine leans back against a tree trunk, and before she knows it, she is dozing in the gentle sunlight.

The following days are busy, filled with tours. Castles and more castles, each superior to the one before. Katherine is impressed with the workmanship, and wonders how everything could have been created, hundreds of years ago without the power tools available now. At home in Connecticut, it had taken over a year to remodel her kitchen.

She shivers while walking through the cold, damp castles, unable to imagine spending a winter there. The only heat would have been from the fireplaces. On the day she takes the tour of Snowdonia Park, she rides up the narrow gauge railway to the top of the mountain. She thinks her green-eyed friend would have been proud of her.

Having seen enough castles for a lifetime, she visits the set where Bernardo is shooting a scene in an apple orchard. He is directing an actor picking apples. The actor ascends the ladder that leans on the branch of the tree. He picks one apple and drops it into a metal bucket. It thumps loudly as it hit the bottom of the receptacle.

"No! No! That's not the way to pick apples!" Bernardo shouts in frustration. He walks over to the tree and looks up at the actor

"You bruise the apples when you drop them like that. You must caress them the way a woman caresses a man's balls. Gently, let them roll slowly into the bucket."

"Never done that myself but I think I get the picture," replies the actor.

Katherine laughs as she overhears a crewmember standing beside her remark. "Bernardo does have a way with actors." The next take is perfect.

Bernardo comes home late that evening. Location daylight is limited, and he has to get all the filming done in a short time. By the end of the day, he is cold, stiff, and in need of a hot shower before he rushes off to see the dailies. Katherine has been through this before, and had no desire to accompany him. In the meantime, she has given in to temptation and walked through the door of the bookshop. Her night table is loaded with wonderful treasures. She plumps up the pillows, snuggles down under the comforter and reads until she falls asleep.

The day before location is finished, Bernardo suggests that she go ahead to London and get situated in the house. He knows that his last day in Wales will be very busy saying his goodbyes; he will have no time for her. It sounds like a good plan, so Katherine packs and travels to London the next day.

LONDON

The movie company has chosen an impressive manor for Bernardo. Gigantic grey stones piled one upon another give way to leaded glass windows. A tall chimney towers above the slate roof. Smoke curls up, rising into the foggy sky. The grounds are bare, but Katherine can see remnants of a flower garden. Here and there, a brave snapdragon pokes up from beneath leaves that have fallen to the ground. It is bleak, yet charming, somewhat mournful like a description from an old English novel. Katherine tries to imagine the people who might have lived in the house centuries before.

She doesn't have a key yet, so she knocks on the door, a little nervous. While she waits for someone to answer, she recalls some of the fabulous houses that had been rented for Bernardo when he went on location. The director is always king and production wants him to be happy. Emily has hired all the servants.

The door swings open, and a round-faced woman with bright red cheeks appears; a Dickens character, no less. She pushes her blonde curly hair back from her forehead.

"Oh, hello, Ma'am," she exclaims, wiping off the moisture sparkling on her brow.

"Welcome. My name is Mary. Come in." Suddenly Mary realizes she is not dressed properly. "I'm baking a pie for dinner, and the kitchen was very warm."

"That's fine." Katherine reaches for her hand and shakes it, introducing herself. "I'm Katherine, Bernardo's wife. It smells wonderful in here."

Mary smiles in relief.

Katherine explains. "I stopped on my way to Wales last week. It must have been your day off, so we never met."

"Oh yes mum. Max was here that evening. Here, please, let me take your things to your room. Sit here for a moment, while you have some tea. I must turn on some lights." The immense cavernous house is dim, the lamps not yet lit.

"Sorry, I thought you would be here a little later." Mary apologizes.

"Not to worry, as you say here."

The tea is perfect and refreshes her.

Mary makes her feel welcome as she leads the way up the stairs to the bedroom. "Just ask for whatever you need, at any time. I'm the cook, there is a housekeeper that comes in daily, and Max, my husband and handyman will be your driver while you are in London."

When Katherine enters her room, she is amazed at the contrast to the rest of the house. It is cheery and warm. The night she spent here before her trip to Wales, she had been very tired, affected by jet lag and had not taken notice of much. Now she sees her room is spacious and lovely. Antique furnishings stand like little children awaiting her approval, each piece of furniture with its own character. To her delight, there is a resting couch, covered in flowered chintz, placed in front of the hearth where a fire is crackling. Mary has anticipated everything. Stained glass lamps light the room with pools of golden light. It is perfect.

"Thank you, Mary, I'll be fine. I'd like to rest. What time is dinner?"

"Is seven all right for you?'

"Great."

Katherine settles in and stretches, trying to get rid of the stiffness that has affected her during the long trip. She walks through an open door that leads to another bedroom with a masculine feel. *Must have been the master's bedroom in times gone bye.* She muses. It is a perfect setup for Bernardo who sometimes works late into the night and hates to keep her awake.

The tub in the bathroom is deep and inviting. Large fluffy towels hang on shiny pipes, drawing warmth from them. From her window, she can see the grounds, with lovely trees everywhere, and a pond in which two swans glide gracefully beside each other in perfect unison.

By the time she has finished her investigation, she has lost the desire for a nap. Instead, she draws herself a bath, and pours bath salts, that smell like spring, into the hot water. When the tub is full, she lets her self down into the hot water and opens a book. Water has a healing effect on Katherine and always cures her ills.

By the time Bernardo arrives the next day, Katherine has begun to make the house look like it belongs to them. Vases are filled with the special spring bouquets that flowers he loves. Mary has been to the market and shopped from a list Katherine has given her. The fridge is now full of Bernardo's favorite snacks. Katherine has unpacked his trunks and all his clothes hang in the walk-in closet. His favorite books are placed beside his bed, and his computer is on the desk in the adjoining den. A deep green leather chair sits by the fireplace, a soft maroon blanket draped over the arm. His slippers are on the footstool. His shaving things are set out, just as he likes them, in the bathroom.

Mary surprises them with an Italian feast the first night. Katherine is pleased to discover that Mary is such an amazing Italian cook. Bernardo too is delighted. Through the grapevine, Emily had heard about Mary's talents, and hired her on the spot. Emily will live with them, in an apartment over the garage. Always available for Bernardo, she will be able to have her own privacy, and so will they. Bernardo does not start shooting in London for a few days. Over dinner, he shares his plans, and they talk long into the wee hours of the night.

Late the next morning, Bernardo is off to the studio to see the new sets, and to talk to the writer about some changes he wishes to make. Rehearsals have been set for the next day. Before he leaves for work, Katherine asks him about the upcoming party that he plans to give that weekend. Traditionally he throws a party before filming begins so the crew can get acquainted. Proudly, Bernardo tells her. "You won't need to lift a finger. Emily has arranged everything. It is all under control"

Suddenly, Katherine feels left out. "Ah yes, the ever-competent Emily."

Bernardo is taken by surprise. "My dear, it's your birthday this weekend, I don't want you to have to do any of the work. All you need to do is to show up, and be the belle of the ball."

Katherine feels strange, and she is unable to hide her disappointment. It is time to be truthful. "I appreciate that, but I also need to be a part of your life now. Somehow, I feel left out, diminished. I know it sounds silly, but I need something to do"

Bernardo is taken off balance, confused, not quite sure what to say. He has never considered what Katherine would think; she has never acted like this. It is time to leave so he holds her, and kisses her goodbye, hoping the moment will pass. "I'll be home as soon as possible."

After he has gone, and Katherine has some time to think about the situation she finds herself amazed by her reaction. She should have realized that she would not be asked or needed. Emily, or someone, has always taken her place when Bernardo was on location. Katherine has always planned the parties at home. She hadn't meant to reveal her feelings. She understands that Bernardo is only trying to do something special for her. Later she calls him to apologize, and tells him that she is excited about the party.

The night of the party Bernardo presents Katherine with a lovely Kashmiri sapphire necklace. The blue jewels are fabulous. She loves it. There is a huge sour milk chocolate cake, her favorite. Everyone sings Happy Birthday to her. The party is a success and the crew stays until dawn. English people love their parties, and they are excited about working with Bernardo. The stars are polite. They talk to Katherine, expressing their delight about their roles. As usual, they talk primarily about themselves.

For Katherine, the highlight of the evening, is meeting Murphy, the producer's wife. They immediately sense they are kindred spirits. Both are married to successful men with powerful drives who love to make movies. They sit in front of the fire, sipping wine, and take time to get acquainted.

Murphy is a lovely woman, tall with bright white hair, and a full figure. She glows with a sense of happiness and as her blue eyes dance. Katherine is immediately drawn to her.

"Murphy, you make me feel so good. You must have experienced all the things I am going through right now." Katherine is honest about her feelings. She senses that Murphy will understand because she must have had the same experiences during her marriage. She must know how it feels to be at loose ends.

"I'm so glad to finally meet you, Katherine. I've wanted to for a long time." Murphy leans closer. "I will be forward. I know you and Bernardo haven't had much free time together yet. That won't change during production. I've seen this happen too often. It did to me also. So I understand. It isn't easy. It sounds great to be here on the whole location, but if you aren't working on the set, it can get pretty lonesome. There is just so much you can do to entertain yourself."

It was as though she has read Katherine's mind. "You are so right."

Murphy is like a doctor, able to give her the perfect prescription. "I'm sure if he has any free time, you will be his priority, but don't bank on it happening often."

Katherine agrees whole-heartedly. "I know."

If you have any questions, or want to see the sights, just give me a call. Don't hesitate; I'm free most of the time."

"Oh Murphy! You showed up at the perfect time."

"I have lots of time to myself too. My husband some-times forgets I'm around. Through the years I have learned to entertain myself, to do what works for me."

Katherine smiles, Now that it is out in the open, the elephant in her room is no longer to be avoided. "I wanted so much to come to London, to be with Bernardo, but traveling around a new country by myself, even if they do speak English, can be intimidating."

"Let's make some plans tomorrow then." Murphy says as they hug goodnight. "Give me a call."

Although Katherine's necklace is spectacular, Murphy's friendship is the present she most appreciates.

KATHERINE'S DIARY

I have to admit the party was a success, in spite of my having no input. Once I met Murphy, I really began to enjoy myself. In the beginning, I felt left out. Emily is so...capable of handling "everything." Sometimes, I'm surprised at my reaction to her. She acts so superior, such a proper little miss. I get the feeling that she wants to prove that she is more useful to Bernardo than anyone else is. I've noticed this happening at times when I've gone to visit Bernardo. Sometimes women on the set look at me like I am an intruder. Maybe I'm being too sensitive, or am I becoming really bitchy? This may be a good time to discover the darker side of myself, which I usually stuff right back inside. I don't allow myself to go there; on the other hand, I don't think I am all wrong about this.

Bernardo leaves very early in the morning and I seldom see him because I'm still asleep. Maybe I should get up with him, but I know he prefers his quiet time in the morning. At night, when he returns exhausted, I'm awake. I try to stay occupied while I wait for him. I've read so many books. I want to be here for him, but I wonder if that is what he needs. He is often preoccupied although he tries to be polite, when what he really needs is his sleep. I can remember, years ago, when I worked as a set photographer. By the end of the day I was so exhausted I had no room for anyone else in my life. In fact it seemed like a miracle that Bernardo and I ever found time to get together when we did. It was only while we were traveling, scouting locations together; before he started to shoot the film that, we had time to grow close. The truth is once he begins a film; he is in his own world and remains there until the film is finished. If he has to come back to earth to deal with ordinary matters, it takes a great deal of effort. I can sometimes feel him straining at the bit, like a horse that wants to go faster. He is polite because he loves me but I must admit it is a strain for him.

More and more, I have begun to realize that, at seventy-five, he is no longer as young or vital as he used to be. He needs to be able to focus more, to conserve his energy for work. I understand. I don't have the energy I used to either. I tire more easily. I am sure the excitement of the work on the film carries him through the day, filling him with energy, but at the end of the day, he is ready to drop. I'm beginning to feel that I am somewhat of a burden just by my being here. Maybe I require some energy that he doesn't have to spare. I know he worries about my being happy. I am beginning to understand that I must find something to do, to find my own passion. What can it be?

With that in mind, I decided to take Murphy up on her offer. We have begun to explore the country. Our first trip was to Stonehenge. Enveloped in fog, the stones were mysterious and mystical. The energy of those huge stones penetrated me. I could feel ancient spirits dancing in the mist and I had an urge to join them. Maybe I have been here in a previous life.

Later, the same day, we went on to Bath, an old city that looks like a Christmas card. I kept thinking Scrooge might still live there. I wondered if he might show up and chase me through the Roman baths.

The Roman baths are two thousand years old, an ancient place. I descended into the earth below the building and felt drawn back two thousand years. Some of the remaining baths are part of the original building. I could imagine Roman soldiers returning from battle, filthy, full of lice, undoubtedly itchy, anxious to soak in those steaming hot baths. I can't understand why, when the Romans left, people went back to living in dirt-floored hovels, covered in lice, never bathing. I can't imagine being unable to bathe.

Dinner was delicious, which was fortunate, because the ride home was incredibly slow. The roadway was packed with cars heading back into London. Fortunately, we had Max to drive us.

A few days later, we visited Windsor Castle. Our group gathered outside the castle, and as the tour guide pointed to an airplane in the sky, one of the tourists piped up. "Why did they build the castle so close to an airport?" We all smiled.

During the changing of the guard, they played Hollywood tunes. Did they know where we came from? An immense church held tombs of important Kings and Queens. When I entered the castle, I immediately got a lonely feeling in the pit of my belly. It is too big, too elegant, too formal, and so cold. I could never be happy living there. I felt sorry for the King and Queen of England and their children having to endure the place. The guide said they had their own apartment. I hoped it was cozier. I did like the dollhouse. It was a replica of the whole castle.

Later, after our tour, we walked up the street to have lunch with an old friend of Murphy's. She owns a thriving business, where they serve lunch to tourists. They offered croissant sandwiches filled with ham and cheese, delicious broccoli cheese soup, and tea. Her friend was originally a neighbor, in Los Angeles.

After a trip to Scotland, and to the Tor near King Arthur's digs, it was time for Murphy to leave for home. It was also time for me to get my Christmas shopping done. I cried when we said goodbye. Murphy had become like an old friend. I feel a deep loss. We plan to meet in Thailand, after Christmas.

The way I must enter

Leads through darkness to darkness….

Oh moon above the mountains rim

Please shine a little further

On my path.

<u>The Ink Dark Moon</u>

THOSE ARE MORE THAN PRETTY CARDS

Katherine feels left out of Bernardo's life in London. She needs something to fill her time, so she decided to come on this trip after much thought and doubt. It is a long trip up to the north of England but she promised Franko that she would do this. A few nights before, Katherine had called him and confided in him. She told him about feeling so very lonely after Murphy left for home.

"I know I sound like one of the kids, but I can't help it."

Franko understood, he had been worried about her. He had warned her that this might happen, but until now, she hadn't really understood what he meant. He didn't want to remind her that he had told her so.

"You must promise to do this for me. "He gives her a number to call. She makes the appointment.

It is time to grow her backbone. Katherine makes a reservation for the train, declining Max's offer to drive her up North. The train flies past lakes, streams, meadows, and soon the countryside becomes less settled. A rental car is waiting for her at the train station. She asks for directions.

The approach to the house is lined with a variety of flowers that she recognizes as herbs. An array of plants, small bushes, and vines, grow up and cling to the side of the dark brown-shingled house. The cottage blends in with the forest, as though it too has grown there.

Small pots line the steps, and are filled with lavender and sweet smelling herbs. Gardening tools rest beside the pots. A wooden rocking chair sits on the porch. Katherine is tempted to sit down and enjoy the garden. Beside the chair is a small table covered with notepads and books. An occasional bee buzzes over the blossoms.

Katherine begins to feel comfortable now; this is her kind of place. She slowly moves up the steps. The front door appears to have come from a centuries old castle; the hinges black wrought iron, large and strong. The doorknocker is an angry looking bronze bear. What signal does this give? For an instant, she wonders if she should knock at the door, or turn away. Katherine lifts the heavy knocker, and is startled when the door suddenly opens.

Esmeralda's appearance doesn't disappoint Katherine in the least. Franko had warned her. She is very tall. Her long dress is purple velvet adorned with shiny moons and silver stars. Katherine has an insatiable urge to touch the material, but restrains herself. After all, she has never met this woman before.

Esmeralda's long curly hair falls to her waist. Her huge beautiful eyes look directly into Katherine's. They are the color of violets. Her mouth is large and generous. Her lips are full and she smiles exposing bright white teeth. Her smile makes Katherine comfortable. She visibly relaxes.

I'm glad you found your way. Please come in."

"I'm so proud of myself. This is the first time I've driven on the other side of the road."

Esmeralda smiles, and leads Katherine through a large room; a combination living, dining and kitchen. Comfortable furniture is piled with pillows of every size, color and texture. Jars filled with dried herbs line the kitchen shelves. A blue table aged with nicks and scratches holds a bowl of fruit and a vase of wild flowers.

"Follow me." They walk through the large room into a small dark chamber lit solely by candles. An altar draws Katherine's eyes. It is lovely, covered with a velvet cloth. Blue glass vases hold flowers, surrounded by clear crystals. A goblet of deep, red wine sits on the altar, along with flower-scented candles. Incense burns sweetly and there is a large statue of some sort of goddess.

Esmeralda reaches for a crystal bell, and rings it. "This will clear the air."

She motions to a table with two chairs. Two large candles are the only illumination. "Sit down please. Have you ever had your Tarot cards done before?"

Katherine shakes her head, "No."

"I use the Mother Peace cards. They are feminine and round. They are perfect for a woman's reading. The most important thing to remember is to let in your first impression. Do you have any questions?

"No. I don't think so."

"First we go through a meditation to quiet your mind."

Next, Esmeralda instructs "Think about how your life looked to you beginning three months ago? Try to remember what important event took place at that time, and try to relive the following three months, like a movie running through your mind."

Katherine closes her eyes and thinks back. A pause.

"Now project that movie from your mind and into the cards."

Esmeralda waits for a few moments. "Make your questions very specific."

Katherine hesitates for a few brief moments. She wants time to think about all of this, but it doesn't take long for a question to arise.

"I want to know what I should be doing with my life right now. I have no idea what to do, but I am open to what may come up."

Esmeralda cuts the round cards to the left three times, and piles them back in a different order. She shuffles and cuts the cards again; offering them to Katherine, face down.

"Without looking, you will pick a card that will be used as the Significator. It will represent the present situation, the Querent, the person the reading is for, the here and now."

Katherine picks a card and turns it over to find Temperance. It indicates that she is working to harmonize, balance and blend the elements of her personality.

Her next pick is Covering, or strong energy, which promotes the situation. She picks Oppression. It shocks her. The card is full of flames, a wolf howling, a woman dead on the ground, covered with huge rocks with men's faces on them.

"What can this mean?" she asks.

"You are bound to physical concerns to the exclusion of your spirit or feelings."

The Crossing card appears next. She selects the Star. It is lovely; a woman is floating above the world. In the heavens, water pours from a vessel, stars sparkle in the sky.

"That feels better."

"It indicates that you will feel good, and experience the refreshing energy of the star. You might want to sing and dance."

It doesn't feel like an obstacle to Katherine, although Esmeralda notes that this is its position.

"This card is the root, the base of the reading, the Foundation card." Katherine chooses Life Weaver, Spider Woman.

"This is about a sudden shift. It appears that fate will step in and bring a whole new set of circumstances into your life."

The General Sky, the mood or energy of the situation, is Mawu, a woman on an elephant, giving birth to a child. Her head surrounded by white light, full of life, positive. "She is the Great Goddess, Supreme Power that creates all. Mawu is about looking for power within, instead of looking toward others. It is also about creativity, healing, expansiveness, fertility, and overflowing abundance."

Happy now, Katherine states. "I like this more all the time, but how do the cards know?"

"Your energy is picking the cards. All I do is interpret them for you. You will learn to understand what the true meaning is for yourself."

For the Recent Past, Katherine pulls The Lovers. "This card is about remaining free of oppressive patterns in love, while continuing to honor the sacredness and life-producing effects of one's passion."

The Immediate Future (the next six weeks) produces Amaterasu, The Sun, huge with oriental eyes, full of life and nourishing. "When the sun comes out, you can laugh and play. It is a little tilted, signifying there could be a delay to your rebirth." The Source of Strength card shows The Amazon driving her chariot. It is also tilted. "That means you should be careful, seeing as the two horses pulling the chariot can go in different directions, and the chariot might be torn in two. It could be that you need to discipline yourself to achieve results and inner peace before attempting to drive the chariot."

The reading amazes Katherine. So many of the questions in her mind are now answered, along with some things she doesn't yet understand.

"Just a little more." Esmeralda says, as she picks The Phoenix, which is about the situation or question. The Phoenix is upside down, an angelic creature with flaming wings and a white flowing dress, rising from the ashes.

"She is about a rebirth, after a death, rising from the ashes. Perhaps because it is reversed, you might resist or block the energies. "

For Hopes and Fears, Katherine picks Strength. It is about what one hopes for and fears at the same time. It is also reversed.

"Are you out of touch or in disharmony with your powers? It is time, and very important to take your own power, to take control of your own destiny."

The last card to be drawn is the outcome of the situation. Katherine draws The Moon, Yemaya. It is a watery card, glimmering. The moon is big and bright, surrounded by circles and more circles of light and shimmers. The dark water beneath the moon is lit by its glow.

"She is about intuitive power and the knowledge of how to live. The moon signifies a slow voluntary change, which is self-initiated and gives time for clear transitions. It is a time to affirm changes and channel them creatively into your life."

The reading is finished. "You have quite a life ahead of you." Esmeralda smiles and asks, "Do you have any other questions?"

"This is better than turning to the pills that so many of my friends use for depression. If I have the courage to go for it, my life sounds like it will be exciting."

At the end, Esmeralda extinguishes the candles; the reading is officially finished. She offers Katherine fragrant tea, made from herbs grown in her garden.

"Remember that the answers may mean different things in the future. It will be up to you to decide. You can always listen to the tape I made for you. "

Suddenly, Katherine feels much better about her future. She understands that she must be the director of her life. She is very pleased that she knocked on that door.

KATHERINE'S DIARY

I read my horoscope each day. It gives me sort of a general idea of what might happen, but this Tarot reading goes so far beyond anything else I have experienced. It is so personal, all about me, no one else. It's almost scary, the way it touches on all the points I personally need to consider; things I've never allowed myself to think about.

I'm glad I made the trip on my own. I've begun to feel helpless since I came to England, diminished in some way. Maybe it's because I have nothing worthwhile to do. I am at loose ends. At home, my life was full. I hate to admit it but now I am bored. All the things I do to entertain myself are just distractions. The Tarot gave me some direction. I certainly need it. The thing Franko said, about Bernardo giving us roles, is truer than I realized. I've seldom had to make a major decision on my own.

I've listened to the tape, over and over. I hear things I didn't remember her saying. There is so much to take in. I have to call Franko to thank him... at least I think I should thank him, but I'm not ready to explain anything to anyone yet.

It is definitely time to make changes in my life. The twins are gone and I am not sure which way to turn. I'm so happy for them and I won't allow myself to feel sad although I am going to miss them. They are having their first great solo adventure and that makes me very happy. They are independent. I have to trust that something will happen to enlighten me. The Tarot reading teaches me to pay attention, and to trust my feelings. I don't need to go too fast, but I need to pay attention to my own needs. It sounds selfish, but sometimes selfish is important.

Bernardo can't help casting us in our parts, we tend to enjoy acting out whatever role he gives us. He is a born director, but now, I can see that if I don't take the reins of my life, I'll go on living the life someone else planned for me. How did I let this happen?

I understand that Bernardo wants to me to be happy. During our life together, I always sat back and let him do that. I never took responsibility.

I am not needed here. I wanted to be helpful while Bernardo was working, but Franko was right, in gently warning me about how his film family takes care of everything. Emily loves that role. Before, when I had my hands full with the kids, I never noticed how much Bernardo's secretaries did for him. To be truthful, I didn't really care. I didn't have the time.

It's just… that I thought once the kids were gone, I could step into a whole new role he would give me. Now I have no role assigned, and I don't know what to do. This is tough but truthfully, I have nothing to complain about. I'll keep working at it.

LOOSE ENDS IN LONDON

For obvious reasons, Thanksgiving is not celebrated in England, but the American crew deserves a holiday. They were away from home and working long hours. The producer agreed... to a point. Always business-minded, he doesn't give them the whole day off; instead, he throws a party for them on Thanksgiving night. They have the following three days off.

The Bell Inn, located near the studio in Watford, is utterly charming. The innkeepers agree to serve a traditional American Thanksgiving dinner. Katherine leaves for the party early. She has no idea what time the crew will arrive. In England, she feels comfortable sitting in a pub by herself. She sips a glass of ruby-red wine while she waits. She is beginning to feel slightly more independent. She shopped and found a dress of luscious, deep red velvet; perfect for the holidays. Her new necklace compliments her outfit. She hasn't planned any social events during this location. She understands that all day long people make demands on Bernardo. By the end of the day, he appreciates peace and quiet. Her gown, soft and slinky, puts her in a romantic mood. She orders a second glass of wine.

By the time the crew arrives, she is quite relaxed. The door opens, and in walks Bernardo, his energy still intact. "Ahh, my lovely wife." He draws her close and gives her a sexy kiss. "You look beautiful, my darling, like a Christmas present."

They enjoy another glass of wine, and then Bernardo gently helps her from the stool. He escorts her to the charming dining room. The table is set with bright fall flowers. Everything glistens in the candlelight. Crewmembers, Katherine has met through the years, are already seated. Many have flown their families to London for the holidays. Katherine greets them. She is introduced to some people, and reunited with others.

The ever-efficient Emily flits here and there, making sure everything is done to perfection. Katherine has to admit Emily has outdone herself.

A flawless American-style Thanksgiving dinner is served; roast turkey, stuffing, and small new potatoes, asparagus tied with a bow, tasty gravy and fresh cranberry sauce. The food is elegant, the conversation, friendly and warm. Although far from home, everyone appears to be enjoying themselves.

Katherine is very happy too. She looks forward to the next three days she will be able to spend with Bernardo. At the end of the evening, with stomachs too full, a little tipsy, they walk to the car. The limo driver takes them home. Content, Katherine snuggles in Bernardo's arms.

The short holiday flies by all too quickly. They enjoy some sightseeing, but quickly Bernardo is back to work, and the long hours resume.

It was time for Katherine to buy books for Thailand. They will continue filming in Thailand at the beginning of the New Year. She has been forwarned that in the city of Ayutthaya, an hour north of Bangkok, there will be few books available in English. In fact there are few books written in English available anywhere in Thailand.

"If you want to stock up on books, you must go to the open air book market on the Embankment by the South bank complex," the English prop man informs her. "Be sure it is a sunny day when you go."

Upon arrival at the market, she immediately understands why it should be sunny. It is a magical setting outdoors, the largest bookshop she had ever seen. Thousands of books are displayed on huge tables, along with maps, prints and magazines. She circles the tables and discovers the books to be in surprisingly good shape. The sunshine slants under the Waterloo Bridge, spreading patterns and shadows of light and darkness. As the shadows fall and quiver across the books, they seem to come alive.

Katherine joins the casual browsers who wander around during their walks by the river. Little by little, she fills the first of three canvas bags she has brought in anticipation of many purchases. Max lingers nearby, waiting to carry anything heavy. She finds books by one of her favorite authors, Gearld Durrell. He was the brother of Laurence Durrell and loved animals so much that he even created a zoo on the Isle of Jersey. His stories are most entertaining. She fills three bags before she is finished, and is thankful that Max is there to lug them for her.

After her book-buying spree, she sends Max home. Katherine wants to find her own way around the city. The Film Café is nearby. She sits outside and orders tea. She watches a crackerjack juggler put on his show, and marvels at how he is able to catch all the flying objects without dropping them.

During the next few weeks, she attempts to amuse herself by keeping busy. She sits on the bench in Leicester Square, and makes conversation with other tourists. She pets dogs, and begins to miss her two Goldens Retrievers at home. The Square is a bustling place with a large grassy area surrounded by iron fences and buildings. A MacDonald's stands nearby, but she is not tempted. She prefers to buy fish'n' chips wrapped in newspaper from the local shops.

Bernardo and Katherine attend a film premiere. Afterward they join the film director along with his friends for dinner. Katherine enjoys being with Bernardo for the evening, even if she must share him.

On the bright side, she muses, "At least I am getting acquainted with London. I always wanted to do that." When she gets an urge for ice cream, she stops at the Hagen-Das Café where there is always a queue. She watches people have their portraits painted on the spot. An artist asked her if she wants her portrait done, but she says no. She doesn't wish to remember herself feeling this lost.

Katherine takes her camera with her. It gives her reasons to watch the street musicians, the rappers, and dancers. When she first met Bernardo, she had been a successful still photographer. Now as she photographs people hawking their wares, she began to think about something she can do with her photography. She realizes she needs a theme, a story, a direction. Maybe she can do a photo book of her travels.

The weather turns cold. Aches and pains come quickly with the damp weather. Katherine looks forward to their move to Thailand at the end of December. The twins have decided to remain in Hawaii with their new friends during Christmas vacation. She shops and mails their gifts along with Christmas cards to her friends. She admires the twins for their new-found independence. She takes some credit for having instilled it in them, and now she understands that she, also, has to learn to be independent. She packs up her winter clothes and mails them home, knowing they will be of no use in Thailand.

The film wraps in London a few days before Christmas. Bernardo is happy with what they have accomplished, and he is looking forward to the two weeks they will have off at Christmas time. They are booked into a fabulous hotel, on the beach in Thailand. After the cold and dampness of England, they happily anticipate the warmth of the sultry Thai climate. Filled with optimism and happiness they board the plane to Bangkok

During the long flight, Bernardo dozes a great deal. Not one to sleep on a plane, Katherine remains awake. She turns and watches him. She sees new lines in his face; lines that she has never noticed before. Her heart takes an extra beat. She is struck deeply. Time is taking a toll on him. She sits back and begins to think. She knows that his talent has not diminished with the years, but his ability to bounce back after pushing himself hard has diminished. Katherine realizes that somehow she had not noticed this before; she has only seen what she wants to see.

At that moment, she promises to herself that she will make his life as pleasant and easy as possible. She doesn't want to be a burden. Yet in her heart, she knows that he lives to make films. There is no way to slow him down and keep him happy at the same time.

When you are old and grey and full of sleep,
And nodding by the fire, take down this book,
And slowly read and dream of the soft look
Your eyes had once, and of their shadows
deep.

How many have loved your beauty with love
false or true,
But one man loved the pilgrim soul in you,
And the sorrows of your changing face,
And bending down beside the glowing bars,
Murmur, a little sadly, how Love fled
And paced upon the mountains overhead
And hid his face in a crowd of stars.

William Butler Yeats

KATHERINE'S DIARY

Bernardo is asleep beside me. He looks tired, worn out. Lines in his face have grown deeper. He is pale, but that could be the lack of sun in London. He seems so much older all of a sudden. Did it happen overnight, or haven't I really seen him? When we met, it didn't matter that he was older. At my twenty-five, his fifty-one didn't seem that much different. Now that I am fifty-one, I don't feel old. Bernardo was brilliant, so handsome, he still is. I was completely taken with him; nothing else mattered when we first met. All I wanted to do was to be with him for the rest of my life. When I fell in love with him, I never looked beyond that moment. Suddenly the years that separate us loom larger. I haven't taken a good look at myself either. I know I have some gray hairs, my laugh lines are deeper, but what else? I wonder if he sees changes in me too.

His presence still excites me, but sometimes I feel he works too hard to keep up his old image. Maintaining the vision he has always had of himself, capable of doing anything, must be hard on him. His prostate problems have upset him. That's nothing an Italian Stallion wants to deal with. His operation at a clinic in Texas, where they have great success with the treatments, seems to be a success. Yet it is difficult for him. Sometimes he feels like he is no longer the man he was. He worries that his lovemaking lacks something he used to have. I don't think he wants to face the results of aging.

I hope he understands that I'll always love him. He is still the wild and crazy man I met so long ago. He doesn't share his fears though. Sometimes he tries so hard to make me happy when we make love that I have the feeling he fears he might lose me. I can't imagine that happening to us. Never! Men have so many frailties, especially in the area of their sex lives. I love him deeply. It would be impossible for me to ever stop loving him.

He has given me an exciting lifestyle, a beautiful home, travels, no money worries, two fabulous children. Really, what more could I ask for? I hear women talking about becoming independent, doing everything for themselves. They sound so selfish, somehow. Most of them live the high life because their husbands work hard and earn a lot of money. They say that I should learn that I come first, to make myself happy. They say I can't make anyone else happy, unless I am happy myself. To be truthful, I am happy. I have no reason not to be.

My family has been the focus of my happiness. I never wanted anything else. Sure, my life has revolved around Bernardo's work... how it could be otherwise? I know things have changed now. The twins are gone, Bernardo is busy. I now see that he doesn't need my help, but this can be an opportunity. I would never have discovered how much I need to do for myself, if I hadn't come on this trip. It may be painful, but it will push me toward what is important for me to do.

I look over at him, sleeping, as a small snore escapes his lips.

I remember when we first met in Italy on the set of a film. I was young, and immediately attracted to him. He reminded me of Fellini, so full of life, enthusiasm, craziness and joy, alive in every moment, something I'd never been myself. I was hooked the moment he looked my way. I've often wondered if it was one of those preordained relationships. He carried me away. Literally! Little, old, ordinary me, never expected to live this life of excitement. There is no doubt that we were meant for each other. I've never questioned that. I've lived my life around Bernardo and it has been fuller for that. I know I have been able to provide a hub for him by taking care of our home and the children. That gives him so much freedom. I have to give myself credit for that. I have always been ready to go to him when he needed me.

Things have changed, though, now I feel like I am sitting backstage, waiting to be assigned my next part. Franko reminded me about that. I didn't want to acknowledge that he was right, but after my experiences in London, I can no longer avoid taking stock of my life. I'll have to toy with some ideas. Perhaps I'll find something to do in Thailand.

Who knows…? The Buddha is very big in Thailand. I see the Buddha everywhere, in all the travel folders. Maybe the Buddha will help me find my way.

THAILAND, AT LAST

Coated in exhaustion they are hot and sticky, as they struggle through the crowded Bangkok airport. The heavy, sultry air makes it difficult to breathe. People rush forward, wanting to get out of the airport as quickly as possible. First class passage makes no difference; everyone is an equal at Customs. Passengers are tired, and irritable. Nevertheless, it is a relief to finally be at journey's end.

As Katherine checks through Immigration, she thinks, 'Less and less do I enjoy long trips.' They display their passports and visas. They carry small bags. The rest of the luggage has been shipped ahead to the hotel. Travel with the director makes life easier. Bernardo's secretary Emily is very capable. All Bernardo needs to do is show up, and everything is already in order, as if by magic.

They walk toward the main entrance, and are immediately plunged into a crowd of people from all over the world. Everyone is searching for someone. Where is their driver?

MR. BERNARDO, the sign reads. Sam waves to them. He is a small Thai man, full of smiles and energy, happy to identify them easily. He clears the way; and people scatter as he hastens them to the car. They plan to spend the night in Bangkok and fly to Koh Samui two days later. Their reservations are at the elegant Shangri La Hotel in Bangkok.

Katherine's body and mind are confused with the time changes. They are hungry, so order room service. Bernardo drops his clothes on the floor and gets into a bathtub so he can soak out his aches and pains resulting from the long trip. Katherine takes a long hot shower, too tired to soak; she is afraid she will fall asleep in the tub. Two bathrooms in the suite make it very convenient. After her shower, she sits on the balcony wearing a soft terry-cloth robe provided by the hotel. She watches the boats and lights on the Chao Pharaya River that flows around Bangkok. Small boats paddle and putt up and down the river, it looks like a boat freeway. It is different from anyplace she has ever been. Ornamental rooftops of rich Oriental design are set among gargantuan hotel complexes that line the river.

After a quick meal, they fall into their welcoming beds, turned down with starched sheets. A sheet covers the blanket. Twelve hours later Katherine awakens, somewhat refreshed, and grateful to have an extra day to rest in Bangkok before they leave for the beach. She has no urge to get back onto a plane.

While she lay in bed, waking slowly, Katherine thinks about the twins. They are now adults, in some ways and she knows it is time to treat them as such. They are independent because they always have each other to count on. They are free-thinking and ready for new life adventures. Nonetheless, she misses them.

Bernardo, the ever-energetic being, admits that even he needs time to recover from the flight. They drag themselves down to the pool. The hot, humid air wraps around them and it feels good after all the dank, sodden weather they encountered in England. They sit in the Jacuzzi, letting the strong jets of hot water smooth out their stiffness. Trees surround the pool, and they relax in the lush green shade. The waiters, ever courteous, always smiling, are at their beck and call delivering drinks, sandwiches, and dry towels the moment they step out of the water.

Later in the afternoon, they walk out to the street and hail a small three-wheeled car called a tuk-tuk. They climbed into the back of the tiny car, noting the absence of seat belts. At each stop light, motorcycles idle, humming, piled high with families clinging to one another, taking off the moment the light turns green. Police officers wear masks to preserve their lungs. The pollution in the city is overwhelming. They see astonishing sights, but are too weary to enjoy much. They begin to cough and choke, and soon return to the air-conditioned hotel.

When they arrived the night before, there had been a message from the Thai location manager. He invited them to dinner at his favorite restaurant; Sweet Basil where the specialty is fabulous Vietnamese fare. Because the restaurant is far from the hotel, so the location manager has sent a car for them.

"My first meal in Thailand is Vietnamese, I can't believe it." Katherine laughs.

Ferns and flowers surround them in an elegant indoor garden. Her mouth waters as she looked over the menu. Katherine orders brochettes of beef, wrapped in a pungent leaf, and Bernardo has dumplings stuffed with shrimp and mushrooms. The succulent Vietnamese fare is worth the long ride. Katherine is delighted with her first real meal in Thailand, even if it isn't Thai food. She knows she will have plenty of Thai food during the next few months.

They depart in a small plane for Koh Samui. The craft lands on the northeast tip of the island, where a car awaits them. As soon as their luggage is loaded, they head to the fabulous Baan Taling Ngam Hotel. Neither of them can pronounce the name of the hotel, which means beautiful cliff, but it lives up to all the travel brochures they have seen before making their reservations. Their suite is situated on a cliff, down a long path, reached by a shuttle cart. Their view is open to the other end of the world, over the ocean. Everything that Bernardo requires for his work has been placed tastefully around the suite.

During their travels, Katherine has stayed at extraordinary hotels, but this is, by far the most incredible of all. Their suite is built into the cliff and their terrace faces out toward the sea.

Everything they could have wanted is there; huge vases of flowers, fruit, chocolates, robes, cosmetics, even magazines adorn their suite. The blues and greens of their room are reflected in nature outside their windows.

Katherine unpacks and gets them settled in, while Bernardo phones the studio. Katherine knows this will be a lengthy call so she decides to investigate the surroundings. Donning a flowered shift and barefoot sandals, she takes off up the path.

At the pool, water disappears over the edge of a cliff. She wonders if a swimmer might float over the edge, but none of them seems to be vanishing. Farther along the path, she finds herself at the main building. The lobby is filled with shops. She sits and watches the tourists come and go. Exotic jewelry, in all shades of jade is displayed in showcases. There are crystal carvings and beautiful fashions of Thai silk.

That evening, after dinner, they sit on the terrace, and watch a sunset of orange and pink turn to darkness over the horizon.

"This is perfect; I wish the kids could be here with us to enjoy the sunset" Katherine muses.

Bernardo is truthful. "My darling, I miss them too, but I love being alone with you for a change. The next months are going to be very busy, and I value the time we can be together now."

Katherine agrees, and decides to be happy in the moment.

During the next few days, they explore the Anthong Marine National Park where the multicolor coral and sea life fascinates them. Tiny fish drift by unafraid, looking them directly in the eye through the masks Katherine and Bernardo are wearing. It seems to Katherine that she is living in a fairy tale, as they sail past weird, extraordinary islands, rising from the sea. They snorkel and scuba dive. On other days, they sit on the beach, read and enjoy the quiet.

Christmas morning arrives and Bernardo presents Katherine with a bracelet of jade. Tiny elephants, their trunks intertwined parade around her wrist.

She throws her arms around him. "I love it!"

One evening they go out to eat at a restaurant on the beach where rough-hewn tables are set in the sand. The owner and chef describes how he goes out each morning to catch the menu for the evening meal. The fish of the day is juicy, the tastes and smells delectable and the menu offers platefuls of barbecued prawns, embellished with pepper and garlic. They overeat as usual. On another evening, they feast on fresh fish, served on a bed of vegetables, topped with a sauce sparked with fresh ginger and lemon grass. The food is fresh and healthier than they had eaten in London.

After Christmas, Katherine begins to sense that Bernardo is anxious to get back to his filmmaking. They planned their return to Bangkok on January 2. They could not check into the hotel in Ayutthaya where they would stay on location, because it had been fully booked for Christmas, a year in advance until after the New Year. Bernardo begins to spend more time on the phone and Katherine is grateful for the week of peace they have been able to spend together.

They fly back to Bangkok where Emily meets them, arms full of papers and information for Bernardo. Sam, the driver, pulls up with the car; Katherine climbs into the front seat. She wants to ask Sam about the sights, and she knows Bernardo will be engrossed with all the information Emily has brought him. She senses this day has come none too soon for Bernardo. His anxiety has disappeared, and now he is able to go forward on his project. She realizes that although he seemed older during the vacation, moving slower than usual, as soon as he steps into the limo, it is as if many years drop away from him.

KATHERINE'S DIARY

What a drive to Ayutthaya. My preconceived ideas went right out the window; there was hardly any countryside, only lots of big stores, manufacturing, and offices. There is barely any open space. The traffic is congested; I wonder how anyone gets anywhere. I've always been attracted to Thailand, beginning way back when it was called Siam. I like that name better. I remember when the movie <u>Anna and the King of Siam</u> came out, I wanted to dance with the king. "Shall We Dance?" Always the romantic, I pictured myself living in the palace, joining the harem, being a dancing girl.

Sadly, today's Bangkok bears little resemblance to that movie. It is a thriving metropolis.

Although there are temples everywhere, and spirit houses in front of homes and buildings, it is a huge city, full of high-rises, luxurious hotels and dreadfully polluted air. I wish it could return to the magical time like it appeared to be when I was young.

During Christmas, I wanted to enjoy my life with Bernardo without dissecting my thoughts. I knew once he got back to work, I wouldn't see much of him. His film family would take over and I would have lots of time to myself. I understand now, so it doesn't upset me. Emily, "Miss Perfect" (shame on me) met us at the airport. She is just… so…efficient. We were whisked off in a limo. The traffic was awful, stop and go for an hour or so before we could get on our way. Even the London traffic, known, as "the parking lot" seems tame compared to this.

I sat up front with Sam, so he could point out the sights along the way. As we drove along, it occurred to me that we might get where we were going, more quickly on foot. At first, Sam took a road that appeared to lead out of the city, and then all of a sudden he whipped the car around and began to drive in the opposite direction. I was totally confused. In the back seat, Emily laughed, she was used to this maneuver. It was the only way to get onto the road we have to take out of Bangkok going toward Ayutthaya. At that moment I made a vow that, I would never drive in this country.

To be truthful, I have been sort of worried about Bernardo but didn't want to say anything. He had a medical checkup before he started the movie. The usual one they require for insurance for the film. Maybe I am being silly he seems better now. In fact, it was apparent that as soon as he stepped into the car and started working on the film, his vitality instantly returned. He wants to remain strong and vital forever. If he can't do that, it will be difficult for us both. I'm in the middle. I mustn't keep quiet if he really needs help, and yet I mustn't nag him. Years ago, he told me about how, in his eighties, his father, had himself tested to see if he was capable of fathering a child. He was. Bernardo comes by this macho stuff naturally. He was devastated for a while by his operation, but our lovemaking is deeper and more sensual now. He is letting go of his urgent need to accomplish a goal. At times, he frets, because he wishes he were still the young stallion, and it worries him. I assure him I am happy, but I'm not sure he believes me, but I'm neither a man nor an Italian.

After we had been traveling for a while, I turned around and glanced at him. It was like he was in a different dimension. His weariness had miraculously disappeared. He was back to being his old enthusiastic self. I don't want him to ever feel old. Part of this is my being selfish, and the other part is for him. I don't think he could handle it. I knew when we married he would get older before I did. Duh! But truthfully, I was not willing to face that time before it was forced upon me.

I am fully aware at this moment, how important it is for him to be with people who love to do what he loves to do, and who vibrate on the same wavelength. When Bernardo is working, he is like an instrument in perfect tune. Directing is the perfect profession for him. He can ask for anything he wants, and everyone is at his beck and call. He has engineered his life to be what he loves, and for the most part, it is in balance. But sometimes when he finishes a project, and nothing new is immediately coming up, he gets depressed. It is how he operates.

I have to accept that I am no longer a" hands on" mother. It is time for me to find an interest, a passion for myself; something that inspires me like Bernardo's work inspires him. As Franko reminded me," Get a life." But for the time being, until something happens, I want to enjoy being here in this fantastic place. I may always be a person who has no passion except for my family. But on the other hand, who knows?

ARRIVAL IN AYUTTHAYA

The approach to Ayutthaya soon changes from four-lane highway into a dusty road. The countryside begins to live up to Katherine's expectations. Bougainvillea vines in multicolored shades of orange, purple and maroon creep up and over walls. Tiny homes and small stores are interspersed between greenery. Waterways are clogged with overgrown reeds, and polluted with trash. Katherine surmises that a hand dipped in that water might easily disintegrate.

The elegant Krungshri River Hotel comes into view as they cross a bridge. It looks like a palace compared to the rest of the town. Upon their arrival, they drive up to the elegant entrance. The doorman; a flawlessly groomed smiling young fellow, with black hair, dark brown eyes, greets them. He wears a starched white uniform.

The entire staff stands at attention in the lobby, awaiting the arrival of Bernardo and Katherine. As they enter each individual smiles, bows and holds out their hands to be shaken. All the while, the manager effusively offers any and all of his services. Never before has Katherine been greeted with such enthusiasm. The lobby is cool, the polished marble floor glows, exotic flower arrangements adorn the tables, and intricate oriental tapestries and paintings are placed artfully on the walls.

No worry about checking in; Emily has taken care of all that. A bellman takes their bags to their suite, which overlooks the Krungshri River. A balcony gives a feeling of openness through the glass doors. The air conditioning is welcome. The suite includes a bedroom for Bernardo, a bedroom and sitting room for Katherine, a screening room and a meeting room. It is tranquil and roomy. The setup gives Katherine privacy during the times Bernardo works late, and needs to sleep during the day.

Katherine's room is furnished with white wicker. Tiny purple orchid arrangements cascade from lovely little vases that sit upon the dressers. The color scheme with its shades of crème, mauve, and light sea green, make for a cool environment. Bernardo quickly looks over his rooms and pronounces them more than adequate. His mind is on other things. Immediately he heads for the production office. Work is an energy drug for him.

Katherine once again, puts the rooms in order, and then she too head for the office, which is a beehive of activity. People hasten everywhere, folders in hand, cell phones to their ears. Polite, they greet her as she enters and immediately return to their work. The beginnings of a film are always a total madhouse. There is always too much to do, too many people to contact, and to organize. Hopefully it will quiet down, once they began shooting. Even though this is a continuation of the same film, it is the same as starting a new film due to the move from another country.

That evening Bernardo returns to their suite. They order room service for dinner. The menu is translated into English. Gleefully choosing tasty delights, Katherine phones in their order. The woman who takes the orders appears to understand what she had ordered. When the food arrives, Katherine isn't sure if it is exactly what she ordered. Nevertheless, it is delicious. Glass noodles, small pieces of fish, vegetables sautéed in a lovely sauce, with teeny red peppers. They must avoid biting into the peppers or pay the consequences. It is just what Katherine wants for their last quiet evening. Shooting will not begin for a few days, but Katherine knows the following day Bernardo will be up early and off to see the new sets. He plans to begin to rehearse as soon as the actors arrive.

The next morning a strong coffee smell wafts into her room, Bernardo is performing his morning ritual. Two small cups of espresso begin his day. He offers Katherine a cup, but she declines. It is much too strong for her to drink that morning.

Instead, she asks him. "Have you the time? I want to tell you about my dream before I forget it."

His gray beard gives him an aristocratic look. He has shaved parts of his face and applied a sensuously scented, shaving lotion. She loves to snuggle into his neck and inhale his scent. He turns off the water and motions, "Come sit beside me and tell me all about your dream." He takes another sip of his coffee.

"I was looking for a place to live in my dream when I came upon a huge white house. It was really big, four stories, including the attic. As I remember, I began walking through the house. I can't remember much about it, except that when I came to the top story, the door was locked. I couldn't open it. I wanted to go through the door and see what was inside, but there was no key. There were many other rooms in the house and I could go into any of them, they seemed familiar, but not the attic."

"What a lovely dream, my love." Bernardo responds. "You know unopened doors long to be opened. This is a message from your subconscious." Bernardo loves to analyze dreams. "I wonder what would happen if you did indeed open the door. What would be in store for you?"

Katherine wonders too.

Later, she gathers her travel books and begins to read about Ayutthaya. Long ago it had been the former capital of Siam. In the seventeenth century the population had been a million people. Now, only historic ruins of the dynasty remain, along with picturesque views of life along the river's edge.

After a quick breakfast in the restaurant downstairs, Katherine is off to see the city on her own. The city has a reputation as a relatively safe place, and Katherine had no qualms about venturing out on her own. She greets the guard at the gatehouse. In his broken English, he asks. "Would you like me to signal a tuk-tuk for you?"

"Yes, thank you," she answers.

"Here comes one now." He signals and the driver pulls up at the gate. This tuk-tuk looks much different than the ones she had ridden in Bangkok. It is designed to look like a tiny pickup truck with two straight seats in the back. Katherine greets the driver.

He responds, smiling, "I am Pong." He helps her into the back and climbs into the driver's seat. With a big smile, he reaches into the glove compartment and hands her some postcards.

"You like, we go." He grins.

Looking through the postcards, she finds a place that appeals to her. She shows him which one and off they go after agreeing on the fare for the day. She has been warned to bargain with the drivers, but she isn't comfortable doing it and finally settles for $20 a day, 500 baht in Thai currency. She knows she may be paying too much. So what? She can afford it. She believes everyone can use some extra money. His car looks old, in need of a good paintjob. A lovely flower Mala hangs around his mirror and above that is a photo of the Buddha.

As the little tuk-tuk flies along its way, Katherine has to cling to handles in the back. They pull out into traffic, mingling with the ever-present families riding their motorcycles. They smile and wave at her. At home, she would have been frightened to death to ride in a vehicle like this, but here it seems right and she finds herself relaxing, laughing out loud, and having a wonderful time.

Pong pulls into a large asphalt parking lot lined with small markets. In the center is an enormous temple. Pong helps her out of the car, and leads her toward the temple. Scabby, malnourished dogs lie in the shade, by the entrance. Katherine loves animals and drawn toward the dogs, but she is afraid to touch them. One small, brown puppy with short fur and glazed eyes, stumbles along. She wonders if it will live out the rest of the day. She feels sad, but has learned an important thing thru her travels. She understands that she will never be able to cure the whole world of all its ills. She blesses the little dog silently and follows Pong into the temple.

"10 bhat please," Pong announces at the entrance; as he holds out his small pudgy hand. He purchases a candle, a flower, incense and some gilt to rub on the Buddha's belly. Pong points to the place where Katherine is to leave her shoes beside many others. Even though it is early January, the weather is sultry, the humidity high. Katherine is very warm, grateful for the coolness and peace inside the temple, Katherine follows the others who have come to pray. She imitates them, offering her flowers, lighting a candle, and setting it among others burning on the table. Last of all, she rubs the gilt on a small Buddha's belly. She is beginning to feel like a Buddhist devotee.

Katherine has never practiced a particular religion. As a child, she attended different churches with her friends; Methodist, Lutheran, Catholic and many others. Throughout her life she has dabbled in a few religions but never been truly drawn to any particular one. No minister has inspired her to feel God within his or her message. Her religion has been private and within herself. Thailand is very different. It feels right and she is attracted to the rituals. She walks into the inner temple and before her stands most colossal Buddha she has ever seen. It is golden and serene. She puts her hands together and bows imitating the others. She is deeply touched. She circumambulates the Buddha, fully penetrated by its power. Continuing to follow the crowd, she completes the circle and heads toward the door. In an instant, something has changed; something has opened inside of her. Perhaps it is her heart. There is a feeling of letting go of a contraction inside, a feeling of oneness with all mankind. It is as though she is in the perfect place, the perfect moment. She takes a deep breath is still.

She resists the return to earth as she approaches the bench where Pong awaits her. He feels like a good friend already. She wishes she could talk to him about her experience. Yet although he understands only a few basic words in English, she is sure he must know what she feels. She puts her hand over her heart and bows to him in thanks.

They continue their tour and drive to a less crowded area of town. They pass many ruins of deep red clay bricks. Pong turns into another parking lot. When Katherine steps from the car The Sleeping Buddha amazes her. It is gigantic; lying on its side, with a huge open hand. A single blossom lay in the center of the hand. Until her visit to Thailand, the only Buddha she has ever seen are the little, fat smiling ones in gift shops.

"Please, will you take a photo of me standing beside the Buddha?"

Pong nods and smiles his yes. She takes a close-up of the hand holding the flower.

The ruins are filled with narrow, crumbling bricks, piled one on top of another. In some places only the foundation remains. Tall pointed towers, called wats, are intact and stand as if reaching for the stars. It has been said that in ancient times they may have been antennas, reaching to the heavens.

Buddha energy pervades the entire city. It occurs to Katherine that she enjoys these ruins far more than the ruins she had explored in Greece years before. She begins to wonder if it was because the ruins in Greece were all about power, and these ruins are about God.

Everywhere she goes, people return her smile, it makes her feel very happy, so different from England, where people speak her language, but are so distant, so contracted. She feels more at home here.

Finally succumbing to the heat, she is ready to return to the hotel. Pong drives her back. As she thanks him, she notes that his Tuk-tuk is number 40. The air-conditioned lobby offers relief and it is a pleasure to enter. She walks to her room anxious, to shower.

LIFE IN AUYUTTHAYA

Katherine decides to rearrange the room where she will spend the next six weeks. At times, she sits in the lobby watching the maintenance men polish the floor to a gleaming finish, while the crew walks back and forth, wearing shorts, boots, and backpacks. She has no real desire to do much. She has grown indolent in the warm weather and needs something to perk her interest. The tropical weather saps her energy. She changes her diet, cutting out cheese, milk, bread, and wheat, eating mostly vegetables and fresh fruit. She becomes addicted to a watermelon drink called Tang Mo Pon, and orders it at every chance.

Pong takes her to the market where she finds a thermos that plugs in and keeps water hot all day. She buys a jar of Nescafe, so she can make a simple cup of coffee to replenish her energy. She begins to fear that if she does not some how get motivated; she will end up a complete couch potato, unable to move at all. She searches for something to keep herself interested and busy. She schedules a Thai massage. When the little Thai woman arrives at her door, she greets Katherine, and in her own way, indicates that she should keep her kimono on. She takes Katherine's hand and points to the bed. The small woman crawls all over her using her knees and elbows to push and knead her body. It is such a rugged workout that Katherine has to rest afterward. She shops for yogurt, fruit juice and flowers, and avoids sweets. She discovers that breakfast can be ordered the night before. From then on, the fridge is full of pineapple and watermelon.

Pong becomes her only tuk-tuk driver after she suffers a bad experience with another driver. Naive, she had believed that all the drivers are trustworthy and kind like Pong. One morning, impatient, she hails the first tuk-tuk that comes by. The driver is polite and takes her out of the city to an incredible temple surrounded with great tall wats and a museum. They see many unusual sites. At the last stop, he brings her to a temple with yet another large Golden Buddha. They walk into the entrance lobby, where he pauses for a moment.

"Leave your purse here with me, it is not allowed in the temple." The driver says convincingly.

She hesitates, for a moment thinking it is rather strange, but decides to trust him.

"One should go empty-handed to see the Buddha."

She puts her things down and walks inside the temple. A few moments later, she comes to her senses, and runs back to find the driver zipping up her purse. 'How I could be so stupid and gullible?' she wonders. Fortunately, her purse has many compartments and he only had time to look in one where he found a few dollars. She says nothing about the theft, but immediately instructs him to take her home. She makes sure to wait for Pong in Tuk-tuk #40, every morning after that.

Pong's vehicle is dented, rusty, and badly in need of a paint job. Katherine wishes she could take it for one evening and surprise him by having it painted. She knows that it would be meddlesome and so it remains her private fantasy. She and Pong establish a routine. When they return to the hotel each evening, they make plans for the next day. They schedule a weekly market day. When they enter the market, Pong asks what is on her list and he leads her to it each time. After she has loaded up her basket and paid, he takes her back to the hotel and unloads her bags at the front door. At that point, the bellhop takes over and brings them to her room. By now, she considers Pong a real friend and buys him a dictionary, hoping it will make it easier for him to communicate. It does not.

One morning after they have finished their shopping Pong takes her to a nearby park where he shows her a Buddha head carved into the roots of a tree. The Buddha smiles at her. Roots curl in all directions around it. "This is marvelous." Katherine exclaims. When she looks up the path, she recognizes some electrical cables used by moviemakers. There cannot be too many movie companies shooting in this town, she decides to investigate, she follows the cables.

"Come with me Pong." She holds out her hand and pulls him along. Pong is puzzled, but follows close behind her. When they turn the corner, she sees the production trucks for Bernardo's company. One of the truck drivers recognizes her and directs them toward the set. The company is filming on the side of a tall wat. They have built a platform. The art director has created artistic masonry that blends in with the ancient brickwork. In this way, they can film a dangerous fight scene on the side of the wat, without falling over the side. The new bricks are perfect and cannot be told from the old ones. The art director is extremely talented and Bernardo always prefers to work with him.

Bernardo spies Katherine, and waves. He makes his way down the side of the wat and gives her a welcoming hug. He is hot and sweaty, wearing a wet bandana around his forehead, and a wet towel around his neck. His outfit is simple, a light cotton shirt and trousers. Normally he dresses flamboyantly, but in this humid weather, that is impossible. Simplicity rules. A moment later an assistant director calls him back to work. Katherine sits in his directors' chair. Pong, fascinated, stands beside her. They watch for a little while, but soon the oppressive heat overcomes her, and they take off. Katherine wonders how the crew is able to work in the tropical heat. She has been on enough movie sets before, and has no desire to stay and suffer.

"Let's go back to the hotel," she tells Pong, knowing it is nice and cool in her room.

Katherine learns that the sightseeing books are wrong about Ayutthaya. They suggest that there is only one day of sightseeing in this city. It isn't true; each day there is another surprise. Pong takes her on a boat ride up the river. He shows her temples and large homes on the river shore that she would never have discovered from the street. She walks through the elephant corral where immense bronze replicas of elephants glare down upon her. The fence around the corral is constructed from logs as thick as telephone poles. Lion statues lie in ruins, but continue to look savage and still appear to guard the area.

At the Bronze Buddha, Katherine enters a small temple where she sees a monk lying on a mat at the Buddha's feet. He appears to be very devout until she realizes his eyes are glued to a television set in a corner cupboard. So much for serious worship, she thinks. Things are not always, what they appear to be.

Katherine hooks up to her email by way of Bangkok, hoping to stay in touch with her children and friends. It is far easier to communicate that way, the time difference is confusing; she never knows when to call without waking someone. Although she and Pong spend much time sightseeing, she speaks little English during the day. In the evenings, while she waits for Bernardo to return, she realizes she needs a diversion.

The showers tend to run luke-warm, but once in a great while there is hot water and she enjoyed the feel of it running over her body even though it is never as soothing as a bath. They were advised not to take a bath, because the water might be polluted. The hotel swimming pool is often deserted, except for a crew wife or two. She enjoys their company when she finds them there. At least she and the crew wives have something in common. She tries to swim a few laps each day, but with the humidity, she ignores exercise as often as possible.

Being a voracious reader, the stash of books Katherine brought with her is beginning to run out. The crew deposits their books in a box in the production office when they finish them, but Katherine has read them all. Finally, she has run out of things to read, so she plans a day in Bangkok. She has been pleasantly surprised to find that there are some good bookstores where she will be able to find books written in English. There is no way Pong can drive that far in the tuk-tuk, so she asks a company driver to take her. It is a long trip because of all the traffic, so she plans to leave early. Fortunately, the driver speaks English and understands exactly what she wants when she explains she is on a hunt for reading material.

They struggle through the traffic, commotion and noise, into the pollution of Bangkok. He drives up a side street and pulls up in front of two bookshops. It is better than she could have expected. She is delighted. He tells her he will park nearby and she is to call him when she has made her purchases. As soon as the car door opens, the heavy air and the acrid smells assaults her. The sweat begins to pour down her chest. Seldom does she sweat at home in Connecticut, but here it is not unusual. She knows how to dress correctly now, and wears only light cotton clothes. Although it is early in the year, the weather is extremely hot for someone used to spending her winters in snowy New England. Sometimes she misses the winter, the snow and the crisp air. On the other hand, she is thrilled to be here, enraptured by this country and the people. She has no complaints.

She dons her straw sun hat and walks toward the bookstore, pleased to know there is more than one store, just in case she cannot find everything at the first one. The latest best sellers, maps, and travel guides are on display in the window. She is amazed to see such a variety. She opens the door and steps inside. It is cool, a relief.

An old Thai man, standing behind the counter, speaks English. "May I help you? What are you looking for?"

"I'm not sure," she replies. "Some books written in English at this point, something I haven't read. I'd be grateful for anything, new or used."

"Aha.' He laughs. "There are many used books in boxes, in the back room, if you like. They have been there for quite a while, but so far, I haven't had enough energy to catalogue them. The newest books are on the shelf up front."

She is excited. "Great, I love old books."

He leads her to the back of the store to the dim room where old books are stored. The familiar musty smell makes her smile.

Although she plans to buy some of the newest titles, to take back to the hotel to share with the crew, she can hardly wait to look through the cardboard boxes. She feels as if she is in the presence of buried treasure. She finds a small wooden stool and sits down, closes her eyes, and basks in the wealth of books at her feet. Boxes of paperbacks, yellow and curling at the edges tempt her. She immediately finds some old favorites. Hemingway, Steinbeck, and Greene. She puts them aside, thinking that it might be fun to reread them.

A moment later she finds a real treasure. It is a box of books containing works by Anias Nin, Laurence Durrell, along with a set of Henry Miller paperbacks, Brautigan's Watermelon Sugar, and ee cummings poetry, even a novel about cumming's experience during the first world war. She does not need to go any farther before she decides to take the whole box. Next to it is another cardboard box filled with more glorious finds, including Emerson and Thoreau. Another box is filled with novels, Islandia, A Journey to Tibet, The House of Fulfillment, more Greene and authors she has not yet read.

What a bonanza! She wants to jump for joy. She has found enough books to last her for the rest of the trip. Like magic, she stumbled into the perfect place on her first try.

"I'll take these four cartons of books along with the other new ones. How much for the lot?"

Surprised by her enthusiasm, the clerk ponders for a moment, trying to come up with a fair price, unaware she will pay whatever he asks.

"These books all belonged to one gentleman. They came from his estate. "

His price is fair, and she pays happily.

The moment she finishes the transaction, the door opens and the driver walks in.

"Did you find what you wanted?" he asks.

She would have hugged and kissed him, but knew Thai people did not do that with relative strangers, so she refrains. "Yes, did I ever! Thank you so much for bringing me to the perfect place."

By now, they are hungry. "Let's find a place for lunch, before we head on home. I don't need anything else. I discovered a treasure."

She can hardly wait to share her find with Bernardo.

Back at the hotel, the bellhop carries the books to her room. "Just put them on the floor over there." she points. "I need to figure out where to put them all."

Full of excitement, she begins to unpack the books. They are dusty; she dampens a cloth and runs it over them. Lined up on the floor by the wall, they seem to have a life of their own and they beckon her to open them. She has to decide what to read first. Just like a child, she closes her eyes and stretches out her hands. She moves her fingers along the books, feeling them for some sign. A hard cover calls to her and she pulls it out. When she opens her eyes, she sees it is

<u>Forbidden Journey, The Life of Alexandra David-Neel</u>. The description on the jacket describes the story of a woman who traveled to Tibet in the nineteen twenties. She disguises herself as a man, illegally crossing borders, overcoming one monumental problem after another.

First, she brings the book to her face and inhales the scent. It smells like tobacco. She likes the scent. It is far more appealing than some odors old books have. Inside the cover, written in ink is an inscription: "Kerwyn McGuire Chiang Rai 1995."

They say the winter days
are short
but this one
as soon as it grows light
it grows dark.

The Ink Dark Moon

FIRST TRIP TO CHIANG MAI

By now Katherine has visited every possible site in Ayutthaya so Murphy's visit is timed perfectly. Another Buddha, another temple, another boat ride, more shopping, nothing keeps her interest any longer. There is just so much time she can spend reading.

The phone rings. "Hi! Are you ready for a trip to Chiang Mai?" Murphy has arrived in Thailand, and it seems she is able to read Katherine's mind.

"How did you know?" Katherine laughs in delight.

"Been there myself," says Murphy matter-of-factly.

Katherine has hoped she would be able to travel up north with Bernardo, but by now, she realizes there is little chance of that. He will never get enough time off from work. She is thrilled to have a fellow traveler, and rushes to meet Murphy in the production office, where they proceed to make their plans. One of the production drivers has a friend in Chiang Mai who takes tours. He gives them the friend's name. After a phone call to Mr. Tony, the trip is arranged. Following that, they make their plane reservations.

At dawn the following Tuesday, they fly to Chiang Mai. Mr. Tony will meet them there. The Bangkok airport is jammed with people from all over the world, heading north. It is winter in many parts of the world, and Thailand offers cheap warm weather vacations. Across from Katherine and Murphy sit a group of middle-aged Italian woman, waiting to board the plane. Obviously on a holiday, the dark-haired, olive skinned women laugh and joke with each other. Round, lusty and robust, Katherine imagines how they must fascinate and tantalize their husbands.

Thai Airlines flight takes off on time. Decorated in soft lavender, blue and green, the interior of the aircraft is serene. The snacks served far exceed the standard peanuts. They include a fruit drink. An hour later, the plane lands gently in Chiang Mai. They head toward the luggage pickup to locate their bags, all the while looking for Mr. Tony. They can see a short fellow with a big smile, dressed in black trousers and a starched white shirt holding a little boy by the hand. In his other hand he holds a sign that reads," Mrs. Katherine and Mrs. Murphy." They laugh and point to themselves and he comes directly over with a trolley for their belongings. Still sporting a big smile, he introduces himself. "I am Mr. Tony and this is my son Top." Tony and Top reach out to the women to shake hands. Mr. Tony leads them outside the terminal toward a vintage, bright red Mercedes Benz.

"Pretty classy," whispers Murphy raising her brows.

"First we go and get some vouchers for the hotels," announces Mr. Tony. The word vouchers sounds more like "washers." Katherine and Murphy make a motion with their shoulders, signaling each other not to question him.

Katherine has pictured Chiang Mai as a mountain village, but it is nothing of the sort. It is a large city. In her mind, she has imagined the people would be dressed in authentic Thai costumes. Not a costume is seen in the crowd.

Streets are lined with trees and bright colorful flowers, including potted bougainvillea plants of vivid purple, pink and orange; shades they have never seen before.

Mr. Tony pulls up in front of a travel office. "Let's go in and get the 'washers'," he says. Once they begin the transaction, they realize he means vouchers, which will save them money at the hotel. Pleased by his attitude, although it is not necessary to save money, they realize he is honest and can be trusted. He may get a kickback, from the hotel. Then, why not?

The hotel is similar to their hotel in Ayutthaya. Settled in, they go downstairs to meet with Mr. Tony. Their stay is going to be short and they want to see all they can.

"How did you get the name of Mr. Tony?" Murphy asks.

Tony laughs and explains. "The Thai names are too difficult to pronounce and most of us, who work with English-speaking people, therefore we take a simple name that can be remembered. You can just call me Tony. No need for the Mister."

When he tells them his real name, they fully understand.

"Where do we go today?" Tony asks. "It is still early."

"Show us whatever you think we should see. We don't know anything about the city, and there is so little time. Show us everything!"

Tony escorts them to the car. "First we head to the Temple Wat Prathat Doi Suthep. The Buddha in this temple is the largest in the north, the temple overlooks the whole city."

They drive through the university that covers many city blocks. Katherine is amazed. "This could be anywhere. It is nothing like Ayutthaya."

"The college is well known for its hospital and medical school," Tony informs them; reminding them this city is not a backward locale at all.

Up and up a winding road they drive; tourist buses circle around and down the mountain. When they reach the top, Tony pulls into a parking lot where there are many shops. "Let's head for the temple first," he suggests, while he leads them up the hill, toward a cable car that takes people to the top of the mountain where the temple is located.

"Years ago we had to walk up 290 steps to reach the top, but now they have installed the cable-car, and it is much easier to get to the top." He buys tickets and helps them into the cable car. Up the mountain they ascend.

The temple is magnificent, extremely ornate. The garden surrounding the magnificent building overlooks the whole city. There is a haze in the sky. Katherine hopes it is only morning fog, and not smog. Up more steps they go, and leave their shoes, alongside many others at the bottom of the steps. Following the crowd, they purchase the customary incense, flowers and candles.

Endless Buddha statues line the corridors and in spite of Buddha similarities, there is a slight difference in every one. Although Katherine has had enough Buddha sightings to last a lifetime, she is surprised at the subtle differences.

Deep inside the temple, they look up and see a towering Buddha, more enormous than either of them has ever seen. Following other pilgrims, they make their offerings at the feet of the Buddha. On the way out, they ring gigantic bells that line the walkway through the gardens. The deep sound of the bells echo down the walk and up into the heavens.

Stomachs rumble. It appears everyone is hungry.

"Does noodle soup appeal to you?" asks Tony. "We have the best noodle soup in Thailand. It is the specialty in the north." They hear his stomach grumbling too. Top, his son, looks ecstatic when he realizes there is a meal in his immediate future.

Tony drives up to a small open restaurant. Tables are covered with patterned oilcloth. Bowls of pickles, onions and various condiments sit in a circle in the center of the table. They inhale the pungent flavors while they place their orders. The soup is heavenly; accentuated with pickles, herbs, and spices. It slides silkily over their tongues. They slurp their soup as Tony brags, "This soup is so famous that people come from all over Thailand to enjoy it."

Murphy, her mouth filled with delicious tastes, mumbles. "I believe that."

"Here, have more of these pickles." Tony passes the bowl.

Their tour takes them to the Golden Mile; actually, a ten-mile stretch of road filled with emporia of every imaginable kind. Factory workshops line the boulevard. They drive slowly beholding shops laden with items for sale. There is practically anything one can imagine; including silverware, ceramics, cotton, silk, woodcarving, hand-made umbrellas, hillside crafts, and lacquer-ware factories. They are overwhelmed by the seemingly endless number of choices." Tony, please make a selection for us." They beg him.

Their first stop is the enamel and lacquer factory.

"I think you will like this." Tony grins as he pulls up to an attractive building. A fountain bubbles into a pond filled with huge carp swirling about. A tall, exotic woman, fully made-up, with long dark hair, greets them. Her tapered fingernails are decorated with intricate designs. "I'm Lula, please come with me." She gives them a detailed demonstration all the while explaining how enamelware is created. Watching closely, Katherine and Murphy follow the steps. First sanding, dipping, sanding, dipping again and more sanding. It is an intricate, time-consuming process. The finale is the painting of the tray. It gives them a real appreciation for the art.

As she watches Lula, Katherine is fascinated and puzzled by her manner. Lula is quite feminine and rather tall. Her voice is low and after a while she realizes Lula is actually a man. The sweet she/he woman is extremely anxious to please. After her demonstration, she takes them into the showroom where many lacquered items are for sale. It is the first time Katherine is able to appreciate lacquered art. Up until that moment, she had no idea how much work went into creating a small tray. Murphy is captivated and decides to buy a set of chairs with elephants carved into the base of the chair. At first, she hesitates, but Tony assures her that shipping is no problem. She bargains and makes a great deal, as far as she is concerned. Tony arranges for the shipping and soon she is handing Lula her credit card. Her packages are promised to arrive within two months. Katherine buys a few small articles.

The next stop is an umbrella factory. Displayed under a tent, are multitudes of huge paper fans, and paper umbrellas. Women, paintbrushes poised, sit nearby, ready to paint artistic scenes for them. "Whatever you like!" They chant, in high voices. "Come here; let us paint a picture on your purse, your slacks!" they call. "You like butterfly, rose, kitten?" Katherine chooses a butterfly to be painted on her purse. Murphy decides upon flowers to be daintily painted on the knees of her jeans.

Furniture is created in a large warehouse. The showroom is filled with lovely dining room sets, bars, beds, chairs. Ever anxious to please, the sales clerk informs them. "We make anything you like out of wood, and send it home for you." Murphy spies a fanciful wooden horse for her garden. Out comes her credit card again.

There are numerous shops and they walk through every one of them. At day's end, they arrive at a silk factory. Thai silk of brilliant shades of purple, jade green, and turquoise, the color of the Bahamian ocean, line the walls. Fabulous scarves, pillow covers and clothes tumble forth from the shelves as Katherine pulls them close to have a look. She wants everything, but knows she must make few choices. She buys yards of deep purple, jade green, a brilliant blue and black raw silk, astonishing textiles that will be made into shirts for Bernardo, who adores silk. Murphy is acquainted with his flamboyant tastes, and she assures Katherine that he will love it all.

The weary travelers set out for the hotel. Christmas shopping has been accomplished early this year. Tony drops them off at their hotel. His son is fast asleep on the seat beside him.

"If you like, there is a street fair each evening. Very close, take a Tuk-tuk, if you decide to go." They make plans to meet him the next morning.

Exhausted, they drop their packages on the floor in their room, and collapse onto their beds. Katherine opts for the first shower, while Murphy takes the second. They do not want to miss anything, so decide to go downstairs for dinner. The lobby is spacious, open with a shimmering marble floor. In the center a man and a young woman play large string instruments. Katherine is happy to see someone dressed in a traditional colorful Thai costume for the first time. The woman is beautiful and exotic.

Dinner is buffet style, similar to the restaurant in the hotel in Ayutthaya. After dinner, they bounce back to life and decide to go to the street market. It is a couple of blocks away from the hotel so they determine to walk. The night is warm, but nothing compared to the heat in the south. As they turn the corner, much to their delight, a vision extends out before them. Miles and miles of tiny stalls, lit up like a carnival, are revealed in the darkness. Traffic crawls at a snails pace, people are everywhere.

"What a blast!" exclaims Murphy. "I thought I'd seen everything at the Night Market in Hong Kong. This beats all."

They wander through stalls. Jewelry is displayed in small cases; tee shirts are displayed on the wall, hung high, right up to the ceiling, advertising just about everything. Food sizzles on small woks; people buy delectable viands and wander through the shops filling their mouths with delicious items. Household items are presented amidst everything else. There is something for everyone.

"Remember we only have two bags for the plane," Murphy reminds Katherine, who is making one purchase after another. She buys a dozen brightly colored, flowered cotton wraps. "Great to wear after my bath, while my body is still steaming," she confides.

Murphy, the wiser shopper, buys silver jewelry and small items. Exhaustion overtakes them. They are unable make it to the end of the market street. Finally admitting the day of travel and sightseeing finally has caught up with them, they hail a Tuk-tuk and ride back to the hotel. Totally fatigued, they collapse and fall into bed.

The next morning, true to his promise, Tony arrives early, while they are finishing their breakfast. He pulls up a chair, orders a cup of coffee, and begins to set out plans for their day.

"Top sends his regards; he was too tired to get up this morning." He sips his coffee. "Orchid and Butterfly farm first? Do you like snakes? No? I didn't think so! Okay, next... elephants at work, and if you like, an elephant ride after that."

They nod in agreement; their mouths full of food, then gulp down their coffee, and quickly take off. There is no time to waste; they don't want to miss a thing.

The countryside changes as they drive out of town, now lush, trees and bushes line the road. At times the foliage appears jungle like. The road climbs, and as the altitude changes, the foliage becomes sparse. An hour later, they arrive at the Orchid-Butterfly Farm. They see orchids hanging in the air as they peer through the wire fence. The orchids don't seem to be planted. There is no soil, just long rows of orchids, swaying slowly back and forth. "Is this how they grow?" they ask. "I've never seen anything like it."

At the front door a petite Thai woman pins a deep pink and white-spotted orchid onto each of their blouses.

"These people are so classy," says Murphy. "Thank you."

They stroll up and down row after row of brilliant multi colored orchids. Red, purple, pink, yellow, orange and fuchsia, orchids, hang like colorful birds, moving in the breeze.

Katherine wonders out loud, "Can we grow these at home?"

"Too cold, I believe." Murphy is doubtful.

"Butterflies, look at all of them, I've never seen anything like this!" Butterflies mounted behind glass are displayed on the walls of the gift shop. At least a hundred varieties are for sale. Murphy buys a few colorful ones for her grandchildren.

"ELEPHANTS AT WORK," the sign reads. Hundreds of cars are parked in a huge dirt lot, but Tony drives right up to the entrance and lets them out. "Please wait here. I will be right back."

He parks and soon is back to purchase their tickets, then leads them down a dirt path toward the elephants. They hear the crowd cheering ahead as they walk along. Little dusty children, dressed in local costumes, stand by the side of the path. Their noses run. They look very sad as they hold out their dirty hands. Katherine and Murphy cannot resist dropping bhats into their tiny palms.

Two Gibbon monkeys are perched on a tree branch above them. Slyly they eye the two women walking beneath them. A sign below says. BEWARE OF MONKEYS. Suddenly one of the monkeys' reaches over and snatches Murphy's orchid right off her blouse "Hey!" she shouts. It is too late. He immediately pops it into his mouth, takes it out again, and proceeds to happily dismantle it, all the while grinning at them.

They see elephants in the river below. Soon they arrive at a large arena surrounded by bleachers, and filled with people. Elephants are performing for the crowd. They stand on two legs and bow. A woman walks out and lies down in the center of the arena. On command, the elephant carefully places one huge foot on top of her stomach.

"Do you think you could do that?" asks Tony with a laugh.

The show finishes with the elephants playing soccer, kicking the ball back and forth. The two women had no idea it would be possible for an elephant to be so graceful. Katherine reminds Murphy. "Do you remember the songs, from Dumbo, about never seeing an elephant fly?"

Tony explains. "This is a way for the elephants to survive, now that they are seldom needed to build or farm. The man who works with the elephant is the mahout. He has a lifetime job and is close to his charge. The elephants live so long, and the mahout ages, so a younger man is brought in to learn and train to take care of the elephant. When the older mahout can no longer work the elephant, it still has a familiar caretaker."

Katherine is touched. She knows elephants often lived longer than people and had often wondered what happened to them. She holds out a dollar, and tries not to be nervous as the elephant gently removes it from her hand with his trunk.

Hungry again, they opt for another noodle shop. While they eat, Tony crosses the street and buys a large box of Jell-O-like suckers for their next stop.

"What's next?" Katherine asks. Tony hands her a brochure. "Long Necks." It shows women wearing golden bracelets that encircled their extraordinarily long necks.

"How do they do that?" wonders Murphy.

Tony explains. They begin putting the rings on their necks when they are very young. Eventually their necks stretch. The truth is, once they begin they can never take the rings off, because the neck becomes so weak, they can no longer hold their necks up on their own. The positive thing is that it is curious enough for people to come to see them.

Therefore they are able to earn quite a bit of money from the tourists."

Murphy moans. "How awful!"

"Awful as it appears, it allows the women to make a good living and support their families. It is very difficult for a woman to do that in our country." Tony recounts.

"I understand, in a way," Murphy says.

They approach the Long Neck Village from a dirt road. The price to enter is twenty dollars per person. Very expensive for Thailand, but they are happy to pay that amount, knowing that it is the only way these women can make a living. As they walk down the path toward their homes, they notice that all the men look normal and are dressed in tee shirts.

The children are very polite and when Tony hands out the suckers, there is no crowding or pushing. They smile when he gives them the suckers. The women have beautiful serene faces. In addition to the rings on their necks, they wear rings below their knees. They smile at the two women.

A rope, hung with brightly hand woven scarves, is tied between two trees. Tony indicates that they are for sale so they purchase a few scarves. They sit and play with the children. Later on the women and young girls began to gather in two rows and commence to do a beautiful leisurely dance, swaying carefully back and forth. It goes on and on. They must be very careful how they moved their necks. Tony appears to be bored, having seen the dance many times before. When the dance finished they say their goodbyes and head back up the path.

"Where do the women go when they get old?" Asks Katherine. "Everyone here seems to be very young."

"They go back to the hills where most of the families live." Katherine finds it difficult to imagine existing like that.

On their trip back to Chiang Mai, they stop to barter with mountain people who have set up a market beside the road. Katherine finally gets her wish to see people dressed in authentic costumes. They are also the first aggressive people she has met. There are no city manners here. The dark skinned women gather around them and exhibit their wares, pushing each other away as they shove their wares into the two women's faces. Katherine picks out a decorated metal hat she admires. The hat is tall, with designs pounded into the tin and yarn of bright colors. It is like nothing she had ever seen before. "Six dollars," announces the woman. A moment later Katherine turns and sees another hat she likes better. Even though she has not yet made an offer on either hat, an argument breaks out between the two vendors. They began to pull at her and yell. Their voices grow louder and louder. She is unable to understand them but soon she recognizes the solution. "I'll take both hats," The women immediately drop their price to five dollars, and they both go happily back to their stalls, counting their money. They all enjoy the bartering process. Everyone is pleased. The brilliant colors of the crafts, created by the mountain people, are glorious with the stitching and tinwork.

They are sorry they have no more time. They must leave for Bangkok on the last evening flight. They tell Tony goodbye. Their driver meets them in Bangkok. He laughs at all the bundles as they load them into the car.

That night, Katherine is both excited and exhausted. Bernardo tries to take in all she describes but he is overwhelmed. He has too much on his own mind. Fortunately, for him, Katherine falls into bed soon after dinner. In the middle of the night, after deep sleep, she wakes. She is unable to go back to sleep. After a few moments, a plan comes to her. It is only an idea at first, but she cannot quit thinking. She keeps running her mind. She begins to understand and sense how happy she had felt in Chiang Mai. Something felt very different to her up there. It beckons to her. She knows she wants to return as soon as possible. She takes her Tarot Reading tape out, and listens to it. The reading makes sense now. It reaffirms that this is the time to follow her muse and discover her own destiny. She reminds herself that she can never be of service to anyone else if she doesn't take care of herself first. What is it about this country that reaches so deeply into her heart?

TIME FOR KATHERINE

Murphy and Katherine meet for breakfast the next morning. In the busy coffee shop, they sip the strong coffee, while Katherine places her order for watermelon and pineapple slices. She takes a bite and sucks the juice out of the watermelon, mumbling, "Umm, this is the best watermelon I've ever had in my life." Juice runs down her chin. "Do you think I'm turning native?"

Murphy laughs and gets up to go through the breakfast buffet. They are good friends by this time.

"Murphy, will you tell me how you managed to stay happy and content during your married life? Your husband is as crazy as mine!" Katherine is sure Murphy must have all the answers, yet she doesn't give her a chance to respond, rattling on. "I thought I'd be a great help to Bernardo, but instead I feel like a burden. I know he wants to make me happy, but he hasn't any time, or the extra energy to do it. I didn't mean for this to happen."

"It takes time to learn what works for the two of you." Murphy says. "I've learned through years of living with my busy producer that I must be responsible for my own happiness. I don't wait for him any more. I take these trips when they come up, only if it fits into my life. Visitors on location, end up being outsiders because everyone else is so wrapped up in their project and they are the film family. In a way, it's sort of like bigamy."

Katherine, still sucking on her fruit, again, continues to mumble. "I'm beginning to understand that now."

Murphy continues. "Over the years, I've learned to be responsible for myself, to grow my own talents and strengths. It is the best of both worlds. I have independence, yet there are some remarkable reunions. It works for me."

Murphy is an open and sharing teacher, and Katherine appreciates the fact that she shares her experiences.

"When I was young, we believed our husbands were responsible for our happiness. You know, they were there to make us happy. What a joke that was. It took a bit of unlearning. Can you imagine what a big responsibility it must have been for those poor men? They had to support us, keep us safe and happy. It wasn't fair."

"Thanks so much for sharing your experiences. It helps me so much."

"Katherine, it took me a long time to learn. I went through years of heartbreak and disappointment before I learned I could not become someone I was not. I'm not a good camp follower."

Katherine nods in agreement. "It always sounds like such fun to go on location, but after a while, you find yourself just trying to fill the hours. I want to do something important. I need to find out what that is."

Much too soon, it is time for Murphy to return home.

The morning she leaves, Katherine hugs and kisses her goodbye. "Thanks so much, Murphy; I hope we can do this again, somewhere in the world. I wish we both lived on the same coast, but we can still e-mail and phone."

"Feel free to call me anytime you can catch me at home. I'll be sure to e-mail you too." Murphy was off with a cheery wave.

Katherine spends long time thinking about all that Murphy has said.

KATHERINE'S DIARY

Murphy is gone and. I am already missing her. Once again I feel lonely, rather useless, sitting here by the pool, so involved in myself. I wish she were still here so we could talk. I have to ask myself some important questions. Until now, I believed my life was all laid out for me. It never occurred to me that I would have to think, to make decisions about all the things that are happening now. I have everything most people only dream about. Yet, for some reason, it doesn't appear to be enough. Why?????

It feels nice and cool dangling my feet in the water.

I can see why I have avoided this. It's so much work, and basically, I am a lazy woman. For years, I tried to teach the twins to be independent. I think I succeeded with them. Why, now, am I am reluctant to take my own advice?

Let's go at it a different way. What if things were different?

What if I had nobody else to consider in my life? What would I do?

Come on Katherine, be truthful. Take a moment to consider.

1) Travel around Thailand.

2) Maybe do a book of photos based on my experiences here.

3) Learn Thai Massage

4) Learn to cook Thai food.

It sounds simple when I put it down on paper. The most likely thing to do is create a book. When I published my book of photos years ago, I felt wonderful, I was proud of myself; it was fun and fulfilling.

Maybe that is it. I could do a book. How do I begin? How will I frame it? What way do I verbalize what I want to do? Maybe a middle age woman alone in Thailand discovers herself. There must be many women going through this thing that is happening to me. Most of us are not so different. The funny thing is I never imagined it would happen to me. Fate has brought me here and given me the means to do what ever I need to do. On the other hand, I know many young people come here to have adventures before they settle down to "real" life. What about flowers, trees, temples? I am sure that has been done a thousand times. No, this has to be different. Can I do this with my photos? Maybe I can show a feeling of confusion, loneliness, and discovery. Nature usually offers answers. Like the fog lifting. Hey, this is getting exciting. There are many directions. Where do I want to go to do this?

I am drawn to the mountains. I love Chiang Mai. I could go back and see what happens. We did not spend enough time there. That experience only whetted my appetite. I will talk to Bernardo about this tomorrow. I can give Tony a call. Maybe he can find me a place to rent for two or three months. By that time, Bernardo will be finished with the movie. For me it can be a sabbatical, a retreat, a time of getting to know what I want for myself, without depending on anyone else. Nobody will have to worry about me. People take sabbaticals all the time.

What a relief. It feels good to have a project of my own. I am impatient and want to make plans.

When I met Bernardo, I was independent, working on films, ready to go at a moment's notice to places where I had never been. I could be anyone I wanted to be. Nobody knew me, and therefore had no expectations. Once I fell in love with Bernardo, I changed somehow. He did not ask me, but I wanted to please him. I guess that is natural. Now, looking back, I understand that I gave away my strengths. That woman must still be alive, somewhere inside of me. I will have to get reacquainted.

This may be a little frightening, but it could be fun. I have heard about "roads not taken" and how they come back to haunt you. Maybe this really is the important one I missed. I can take it now.

As I dig for wild orchids
In the autumn fields,
It is the deeply-bedded root
that I desire
not the flower.

<u>The Ink Dark Moon</u>

RETURN TO CHIANG MAI

Fortunately, Bernardo has a few minutes to spare, before he goes to see the rushes, which are delivered daily from the lab in Hollywood. The daily rushes are always a few days behind because they have to send them all the way to Los Angeles, and then wait for them to return a few days later.

Once Bernardo walks through the door, Katherine is unable to wait.

"I need to talk to you. It is very important." Katherine is excited.

Bernardo is taken aback. This is unlike his gentle wife. He puts up his hand as though to protect himself. She laughs.

"Katherine my dear, can this wait until we have dinner? You will have my undivided attention."

Bernardo is patient, but Katherine can barely contain her excitement.

"Okay, go ahead and shower, sorry I'm so pushy. I'll try to endure."

There is an excellent Chinese restaurant in the hotel; the food is exquisite. As soon as the waiter has seated them, Katherine begins to talk excitedly. "I think I have a solution for us." She blurts out. "If you agree, it will be perfect."

Bernardo brightens at each suggestion Katherine makes. "Katherine, that sounds like a wonderful idea, my love. No matter how much I love having you here, I worry because I don't have enough time to spend with you. I don't want you feeling lonesome or left out."

"Bernardo, I'm a big girl, and I'm not lonesome. Well, maybe just a little. I am just at loose ends! I have never felt like this before. I have never experienced this kind of emptiness. My life was always so full." She looks deep into his eyes searching for answers.

In his natural style Bernardo begins to direct. He is in his element. "I understand. I know when I work on a project, I get excited, wrapped up, totally focused on it to the exclusion of everything else. I know you loved being a mother. There was never a better mother. Do you remember when you worked on your book? You were totally focused. At the same time, you were there for us. You looked after us. I know you can do it. It is your time now."

Katherine nods.

Bernardo wants to make it easier for her.

"I think this idea of yours is perfect."

He leans across the table and kisses her. "Go for it, my darling."

The next morning Katherine is up early. She dials Tony's number in Chiang Mai.

"Tony, I need a place to stay up there. I would like to be out of the city. I had such a good time when we were there. How long? Let's say…three months or so."

"Amazing!" Tony replies, surprised to hear from her so soon. "What great timing. A friend of mine just called and asked me to look for someone to rent his guesthouse in Chiang Rai. It sounds like it might be perfect for you."

"This is fascinating," Katherine thinks aloud

"I'll check with my friend and then call you right back. When do you plan to come?"

"I can't wait, Tony! Is next Tuesday too soon?" They both laugh.

Katherine begins to pack. She makes piles of everything she has bought since she arrived in Thailand. One pile will go home with Bernardo's baggage. Cotton clothes stay with her; the weather will be getting hotter by the day. She loves wearing the simple clothes she had made in Ayutthaya; the colors are luscious. She packs a light jacket for the mountains where it definitely is cooler.

Books! Oh, yes, lots of books! She packs up the boxes of the books she bought in Bangkok. There will be lots of time to read, and when she finishes she can give them to Tony. She will send her computer home with Bernardo's things. There is always a cyber café nearby in Thailand where she can check her e-mail if necessary. This way she is going to be disconnected from everyone unless she wants to make contact. It will be a true retreat.

In the coffee shop, Katherine hears her name being called. Because of the Thai accent, at first she doesn't recognize her name, but when she realizes the call is for her she runs to the phone.

Tony is very excited. "My friend says he will be very happy to have you as his renting house guest, or whatever one calls it. He is very generous and kind. I think you will be very happy. The rent is three hundred dollars a month. You can use the pool, the kitchen, whatever you need. The guest house is separate, so you will have privacy."

"Tony," she exclaims. "It couldn't be better; I'll book my tickets right now. Will you be able to meet me?"

"Sure, just call with the time and flight number, and I'll be there."

The next Tuesday she boards the plane, full of excitement and a little bit nervous.

The procedure in Chiang Mai is familiar. Tony is waiting for her with a big smile, but this time he does not need a sign with her name on it. She spots him and runs toward him, throwing her arms around him, ignoring custom. He seems stunned for a moment but doesn't appear to mind.

"My friend didn't have much time to talk about arrangements before he left," Tony explains as he loads her luggage and the boxes of books into the trunk of the car. "He said not to worry; he will take care of the details when he returns."

"He must be quite a character, to be so trusting," Katherine says happily. "It has to be one of those things that are meant to be, the arrangements have all been so simple."

"Are you hungry, Miss Katherine?"

"Always hungry, you know me. Let us get some noodles before we begin our trip. How far is it anyway?"

Tony describes the trip while they enjoy their tasty lunch, and soon they are on their way up the highway, heading north. Katherine relaxes while they drive along and she proudly points out the places she remembers from their last trip.

"Tony, how did you meet my new landlord?"

"I met Mr. Barnett when he first arrived in Chiang Mai, just like I met you. He hired me immediately He had just moved to Thailand and he wanted to learn everything he could as quickly as possible."

"How did he end up here?"

"He said when he inherited a house from his father, he decided to move here. He plans to write a book. We have become friends over the months. When I take clients to Chiang Rai, I sometimes spend the night in the guest house where you will be staying. It is a wonderful place. I know you will be very happy. You'll see."

Three hours later, they arrive at the house. Nobody would be aware that the house existed were they to look from the road. The entrance is covered in bougainvillea vines, mixing with tropical foliage that climbs over the walls lining the driveway, giving a mysterious aura to the house entrance. As they turn a curve, the house is revealed. It sits below the road. An inviting screened in veranda runs all the way across the front of the house, complete with white wicker chairs. Ceiling fans turn lazily; the houseplants flutter in the soft breeze.

A peaked red tile roof presides over everything. The house sprawls out in many directions. The teak exterior is exquisite, hand rubbed with oil, which gives it a rich sheen and preserves the wood.

Katherine can hardly believe her eyes. Well traveled, she has been to many estates, even castles, while visiting Bernardo on location. Somehow, this is the most perfect place she can imagine; exactly what she wants. At this moment she is sure there is no mistake. Is this a dream? She hopes not. Could she have created this? She decides to let her busy mind quiet down and enjoy the experience.

A young Thai woman answers the door. "Hello." She greets Katherine with a smile and a handshake, and gives Tony a kiss on the cheek.

"Miss Katherine, this is Kai. She is Jonathan's house-keeper and she will take good care of you."

Kai steps forward and takes one of Katherine's bags. "Come this way."

She follows Kai through the house toward the cottage. She glances here and there as they walk through the house and out to the back patio. A large swimming pool, gracefully landscaped, curves in and out of the foliage. To the left of the pool stands a tiny cottage, complete with a small spirit house. "Is that my own spirit house?" Katherine asks.

"Yes, it is," answers Kai. "Here you are. I know you will be comfortable. Ask for anything you need, please. "Kai smiles happily. "It will be so nice to have someone else here."

Soon Tony arrives lugging more bags, and then goes back for the boxes of books, and the cameras. "See, didn't I tell you it was perfect?"

Tony stays for lunch and then prepares to leave. Katherine thanks him. "I don't know how to thank you. You brought me to paradise, a virtual Garden of Eden. Thank you so much."

After Tony leaves, Katherine returns to her room to settle in. It is delightful inside the cottage. Walls are soft white, the ceiling an off-white with blue-green trim, even an insert of a deep green color. She is amazed at the detail. A large ceiling fan moves slowly; the drapes billow lazily in the breeze. A cotton spread of soft pastel colors covers the inviting bed. She expected a tropical décor, but this room has an English feeling. Lamps are placed carefully anywhere one might read. It is as though someone had known she was coming. A large dresser, a generous desk and an empty bookcase complete the furniture. It cannot be better.

The bathroom is modern, including a huge shower of deep blue tile. She remembers the advice not to take a bath. Katherine longs for a soak in a big tub, but she knows she will have to wait until she is home again. A shower will have to do. Huge, fluffy towels of deep purple and turquoise hang on the racks. A fresh bottle of water sits on the sink. There are bottles of water everywhere; nobody drinks water from the tap. A large closet is a welcome surprise. A small refrigerator hums quietly in the corner, and an electric kettle sits on the table. She can fix her own tea or coffee in the mornings. A bowl of fresh fruit sits on the table overlooking the pool, completing the perfection.

After she finishes unpacking, she walks outside and looks closer at her own tiny spirit house. It stands on a tall wooden pole. Upon her arrival in Thailand she had discovered the tiny houses. They were very attractive. She learned that people keep them so the spirits would have a place to stay. When spirits have their own place, they do not come into the house. Every day offerings are made to keep the spirits happy. It looks like a tiny pagoda; a replica of a temple. Ever since she learned about these houses, she longed for one of her own. She picks a pink blossom and places it inside the house. In Katherine's life, there have been few rituals. She has grown up in an atmosphere devoid of the rich rituals of the East. She finds herself very much attracted to this way of life.

She wanders back into the house. Kai greets her and shows her around. "Dinner will be ready in half an hour." Katherine ambles around and investigates. The many empty bookcases puzzle her. The furnishings are typically English. Strange, she thinks. Is Jonathan English? She assumes he speaks English from what Tony has told her, but that is as far as his description goes. She will wait to meet her landlord in a few days. Undoubtly he will explain everything.

"Dinner ready," calls Kai.

A lovely table set with flowered china and candles awaits her. Fresh vegetables, glass noodles, bits of chicken, lemon grass and other delectable foods she is unable to identify fill her plate. This is her first homemade Thai meal and it is most tasty. She is aware that she has no desire to be anywhere else in the world, and thrilled she has taken this retreat for herself.

Happy as can be she returns to her room, showers, and slips into a cotton nightgown. The sheets are smooth and soft. She rolls over and reaches for her book. A few moments she realizes that she cannot concentrate, so she crawls under the cover and falls asleep.

KATHERINE'S DIARY

I feel right at home, and yet I have only been here for three days. I love sitting beside this lovely pool. It is hot and humid today. The sweat is running down my back, even while I'm sitting still. I feel like skinny-dipping. Dare I? I have to get into the pool. The pool looks like a lagoon the way it curves gracefully in and out. Large ferns and huge artfully placed boulders surround it. You cannot see the whole pool at one time; there are so many hidden crannies. I think I will risk it; nobody is here, Kai is gone, I have the place to myself. My landlord won't be back for a couple more days; I may never get the chance again. Why not be naked, I haven't been skinny dipping for a long time. Too long.

"What do you mean?" she asks, totally puzzled.

"You see, I prayed for you, I needed you so I could write. I needed you to show up and inspire me. I have had writer's block. You see, I never imagined you would actually show up. I only hoped you would come back into my mind. I had no idea that prayer could be so powerful." He is very happy and very amazed.

She is still confused. "What do you mean?"

"Of course, you wouldn't have any way to know what happened after I left the train in Wales. All I could think of was you. You were imprinted on my brain. I'd found the hero of my book. You were perfect. I could not wait to jot down my impressions of you that night. I did not want to forget anything about you, and how you made me feel. You awakened something inside of me. Something I never knew existed. It was as if lightning had struck in an instant. Sadly, after I got settled here, and had time to write, you began to slip away. I began to have writer's block."

Katherine listens intently.

"A few weeks ago, I went to pray at the biggest Buddha in Thailand. I threw myself down at the Buddha's feet and prayed for "my woman, my muse" to return, to show up, so I could keep on writing. I have never done anything like that before but here you are! Praise Buddha, my offerings will increase. I will never doubt the power of prayer again."

Katherine is stunned.

"I never believed you would arrive in person."

She begins to stiffen, and wonders just what it is that he expects from her.

Sensing her concern, he begins to clarify what he has said. "Don't worry; I need to use you as inspiration. I do not expect any response from you. Please relax. I know it must sound strange, a man you do not know, telling you this. Actually, I am quite harmless."

105

Katherine sits back and begins to relax. She realizes that he is actually very sweet. She studies the tall lanky man; his dark hair is turning to gray. His nose is prominent; the lines of his mouth stern, but his lips are generous. The decisive factor is his green eyes. His eyes penetrated her the first time they met; they are beginning to do so again. She pulls herself together and sips her drink.

Once they straighten things out, they are able to relax and act like normal people.

"Tell me what brought you here?" He asks. "What happened to you since we met on that train ride last year?"

Katherine recalls their conversation on the train and she gives him a short update of her adventures. She explains how this retreat has come about. "It is a miracle that brought me here for sure." She confesses. It feels right to share her feelings with him.

The truth is, this is a new world for both of them. They are embarking on a new chapter in their lives.

They make plans to have dinner together. Jonathan yawns; he is weary from his trip and needs to take a nap. Katherine wants to go to her cottage to relax and digest all that has happened. She floats back to her room, throws herself on the bed, laughing at the serendipity of it all.

KATHERINE'S DIARY

As my kids would say, this blows my mind. How could this have happened? After we parted in Wales last year, I never thought I would see this man again. My mind was focused on Bernardo; I was so excited about seeing him again. Jonathan, whose name I never knew, was only a momentary diversion, only a passenger on a train. I've often had conversations with people on trains, but nothing like this has ever happened before.

He looks very different now. On the train, he was dressed conservatively, in tweeds, sporting a cap. His skin was been pale and he had a beard. He is far more attractive now. He wears loose cotton clothes, his hair is longer and his beard is gone. He is tan and he stands straight. He looks so much happier than he did that day on the train. He appears to be stern, but that is not how he expresses himself. Especially when he is as surprised as he was... we both were!

Actually, he is very attractive. Naughty, naughty, I must remember I am married and on my way to discover myself. That is why I came here. It is important to remember that.

GETTING ACQUAINTED

While she dresses for dinner, Katherine is reminded of her daughter. After all, this is sort of a first date. She chooses a long, deep green silk dress; she had made in Bangkok. When she packed it, she had never suspected she would actually wear it before she went home. She adds a little extra makeup but not too much. It is a warm night, and she doesn't want the makeup to roll off if she gets too warm. She dabs on Rain, her favorite scent as she glances in the mirror. 'Not too bad for a fifty-year old.'

When she walks into the room, Jonathan looks straight into her eyes. She hears his breath catch for a moment. He smiles and then drops his eyes giving her time to feel his appreciation. The room appears to shrink, as they stand next to each other. The nap has done him good. He has regained his energy, and is obviously full of himself.

The sun sets as they drive through the countryside, past rice farms and large beautiful homes, interspersed with small shacks. Night falls; fog rolls in, covering the ground, making it difficult to see in some places. The road leads them to a restaurant where mist rises from a brook flowing down a small hill beside the restaurant. When they step from the car, the fog embraces them, so Jonathan places his hand on Katherine's back, guiding her up the paths leading to the restaurant.

"How on earth did you discover such a place?" she asks, as they walk over a small bridge. "It's so far out of the way."

"Soon after I arrived, I met the owner and we became friends." Jonathan explains, leading her to an outdoor table where he seats her. A moment later, the manager comes over and greets Jonathan with a big smile and a handshake. Jonathan introduces him to Katherine. She can tell they are good friends by the way they address each other.

"Who is this lovely lady?" the manager asks approvingly.

"An answer to my prayers," Jonathan replies with great sincerity.

The man laughs, "I wish we could all be so fortunate."

When he leaves, Katherine questions Jonathan.

"What did you mean by that?"

He hesitates for a moment. "I guess I'd better come clean. When I went to my room, I could not stop thinking about you, and the way I had prayed that you would show up. I thought you would appear in my mind; I never expected you to show up in person. I cannot stop thinking about this. I don't want to spoil it either. You are very beautiful and to be truthful, I could get lost in my attraction to you. I could forget all about my writing. This whole situation terrifies me in a way. All my life I have been too cautious, too doubtful. If heaven opened up, I would be the one to walk the other way, not believing it was for me. Sadly for me but perhaps safely for you, you are married."

The man does have a way with words. Katherine is charmed and admits to herself that she has begun to feel an attraction to him even if it frightens her a little. She has been in a fantasy of her own for the past few days. Realistically, it might make sense if she could actually face the reality of what she is doing alone, in the mountains of Northern Thailand, with a man she has just met. She needed to find a life for herself, not find herself in a relationship. Will it be possible to remain friends and leave it at that? It might take some work, but this may be the perfect situation.

Aloud, she says, "Yes. You are right. We don't have to worry. I'm a married woman. We can become friends, good friends, but still friends."

Visibly relieved, Jonathan replies, "Maybe we have been sent to support each other in our dreams. What is it you plan to do with your life?"

"Long ago, I had a career in photography, but now I'm not sure. I am considering a book of poetry, along with photographs. You know the Lonely Planet Tour Books? Maybe I can do a Lonely Tourist Book. Who knows?"

The waiter arrives with dishes of succulent food, placing them in front of Katherine.

"Great. For the moment, why don't we start with dinner? Here, try a bite of each." Jonathan passes a plate to her.

"Whew! This is strong. What is it?" Katherine waves her hand in front of her mouth.

"Raw garlic and raw ginger. Isn't it wonderful? I'll bet you've never eaten it like this." He laughs.

Her eyes begin to water. "This will certainly keep us out of trouble." She blushes as soon as the words are out of her mouth, realizing what she has suggested. She has never flirted like this.

More courses follow, with a variety of vegetables, glass noodles, little hot, red peppers, seasoned with unusual spices, and tiny pieces of fish and chicken.

"I'm full." Katherine pats her belly.

"Me too." Jonathan wipes his mouth with his napkin. "During dinner, I've been thinking. See if you like my idea."

She perks up.

"I'd love to be able to show you unusual places to photograph, some you'd never find on your own. I can be your guide."

"That sounds fantastic. But what can I do in return?"

"Ha! There is a lot I'd love for you to do, but to keep ourselves out of trouble and stick to our chosen paths, just being you is enough. You will be my muse, my inspiration. While I write, I may need to ask you a question, like how you would go about doing things, or what you think, that sort of thing. We can call it research. How does that sound? Would that be agreeable to you?"

"It sounds perfect." She sighs with relief.

The waiter brings them a complimentary after-dinner drink. While they enjoy their drinks, they are quiet, immersed in their own thoughts. They have discovered that they are remarkably similar in many ways, and together they are quite comfortable with each other. It is a relief to have established boundaries. Katherine wonders if they have known each other in a past life.

"Do you believe in reincarnation?"

He shrugs his shoulders. "I'm not sure. To tell you the truth, before I came here, I had few beliefs. I was always waiting for something to happen, waiting for something to change my life, something that made sense. I wanted to believe in.........you know." He stops for a moment; he appears to be gathering his thoughts.

"I'm not sure what has happened to me during these last months, living here among the Buddhists. They are very involved in their religion and it seems to have had an influence on me. I believe I am changing. I see the way they treat each other, the kindness and the life I experience here. I suppose I am beginning to believe in reincarnation. So in answer to your question, I must say yes. I could almost believe we could have known each other in another life."

Katherine smiles. "Do you think we are meeting for a second time, or have we been close in many lives?"

He grins. "Who knows? Let us see what we are able to create between the two of us in this lifetime, now that we don't have to go through all that getting acquainted stuff. How long are you planning to stay?"

"I have three months in mind. Will it be all right for me to rent your little house for that long? "She pauses. "Tony never did tell me if you had accepted my time slot."

"Believe me, Katherine you can stay for a lifetime, as far as I am concerned, but if you do, I will never finish my book. Stay the three months that you have planned, and then we can see what happens from there. Who knows, at the end of the three months, we may never want to see each other again. I am an ogre when I write. "

They gently touch their glasses. "To who knows?"

KATHERINES DIARY

I can't sleep. Over and over again, I think about my good luck, my good fortune. I truly love Bernardo. On the other hand, it is painfully clear that I want a friend who can accept me as I am, and support the changes that may occur. Until now Franko has been that best friend in many ways.

When I was growing up, we moved so often that I never had time to develop a deep friendship. Bernardo has been my lover and a friend too, but in some ways, he had kept me on a pedestal that makes it difficult at times. I have been afraid to disappoint him. Bernardo has always been the wild one and I have been the settled one. Lately, I have begun to feel the need for someone who will try to understand me. Murphy came at just the right time and inspired me. She might be the one if we lived closer. I wonder what she would do in this situation.

I always tried to be the "perfect" wife for Bernardo. It was what I wanted to do. Now, things have changed, and I dearly need someone I can trust, somebody who doesn't require me to play a role; someone for whom the outcome will be neutral. Bernardo never tells me to be what I've been; I just accepted my roles and actually enjoyed myself most of the time. Franko is right. It is time for changes. Bernardo is so busy; he doesn't have time for my problems at this point. Could Jonathan be the person I needed without realizing it? I won't allow myself to fall in love with him. Being a friend is one thing; a mate is different. I'm so sleepy now, that I can't t hold up this diary.

SETTLING IN

Katherine is up early. She considers taking a short walk before breakfast. Taken by surprise, she discovers Jonathan is already up enjoying his coffee by the pool.

"Good morning Katherine. It's a delight to see you first thing in the morning."

"I feel the same." She smiles.

"Can I pour you a cup of coffee? Join me for breakfast?"

Kai arrives with a large bowl of sliced fruit and a covered basket of toast.

Katherine beams, delighted. "Thanks, I like to start with a couple of cups of coffee first."

Over breakfast, they resume their on-going conversation. There is so much to say to each other. Jonathan has business to attend to in Chiang Rai. He invites her to accompany him.

"You can get acquainted with a local craft center where there is a lot to see and buy while I run my errands."

"Sure, that will be great." She has to remind herself that there is no hurry, no hurry at all, nothing to accomplish. This is time for her to figure out who the real Katherine is to become.

"We'll be back by dinner time." Jonathan calls to Kai as they are leaving.

He turns to Katherine. "If you don't mind, we might as well eat our meals together. Kai is a wonderful cook, and she would love to cook for two. Even if you like to cook, it would be hard for you to know what to buy at the market. I take it for granted you like Thai food."

"You're right. I am happy to eat it every day."

Jonathan pulls up to a large building. "Crafts, all made by local people are for sale here. Artisans from all over the North Country sell their goods. I think you will enjoy this place. I will be busy for a couple of hours, and then I will pick you up."

Katherine is pleased to be here.

"See you around lunch time." Jonathan drives away.

Katherine walks into the cool building. There is a counter at the entrance, where they sell cool fruit drinks. She buys watermelon juice, and sips it as she strolls up and down the aisles. There are elephant statues of every kind. She prefers the ones with the trunk pointing up. It is supposed to be a sign of good luck. She buys small elephants to send to the twins. She discovers many gifts she desires to buy. Shipping is reasonable, so she fills a basket. Cotton pants in bright colors for her, a couple of woven tablecloths, a necklace and lovely apron for Kai. She wants to repay Kai for her thoughtfulness. She had never seen these particular items during her many days of shopping in Ayutthaya.

The morning passes quickly, and soon Jonathan returns. They head for the local noodle shop. The restaurant is a simple place; the whole front opens to the street. Familiar jars of chili peppers; sour pickles and other condiments sit in the center of the oilcloth-covered tables. After checking with Katherine, Jonathan walks up to the counter and puts in their order. She has already told him about her addiction to the soup. The waiter delivers the hot and spicy soup with fried noodles on top, along with chicken and other tasty surprises. Katherine dives right in, finishes her bowl in no time, immediately orders another, and finally states, "I'm quite a connoisseur of your northern noodle soup, and this is the best I have tasted. Let's come here often."

Jonathan is awed by her enthusiasm. He gazes at her with pleasure. "What are you thinking?"

She glances up. She is thinking of the night before; and how much she has begun to appreciate the man who appears to be the friend she needs at this time. She does not want to make that confession yet. It is beyond her understanding and she worries that if she tells him the truth, it might make it all disappear.

"I was thinking about how easy it is to be with you...so relaxing. I am very comfortable."

"You're not alone." Jonathan begins. "I went to bed last night and couldn't stop thinking about how amazing it is that you showed up. Because you are here, I will be able to get my book written. Like magic, since you arrived the doors to my creativity have swung open. I could not sleep, I kept waking up, and each time I awoke, I began to write in my mind. I got up and began taking notes I am finally back on track. I can't thank you enough."

"You are so lucky; you know exactly what you want to do. I am still not sure. I published a book once, and that was lots of fun, but I don't have a burning desire inside of me."

"I think I understand," Jonathan says softly. "First of all, you've probably never had to think about it. I never imagined I would actually have a chance to do this. I do know now that when I let it all go, the control, I mean, everything seems to fall into place."

Katherine shrugs her shoulders. "Maybe, with your help, I'll figure out what's right for me."

"I hope so, because it's such a relief when you figure that out. At least you think you have; then things change again." Jonathan put his arm through hers. "Let's wander around; I'll show you the sights. "

They tour the town. Thoughtfully he stops at the drug-store and points out items she might need in the future:

toothpaste, shampoo, and lotions. They stroll through vegetable stands in markets where fruits of all sorts' mangos, pineapple, watermelon and more are artfully displayed. Jonathan buys her a bouquet of tiny purple orchids for the cottage.

"Kai writes out a list in Thai; I give it to the vendors. They know me now and she seems pleased with what I bring home. They must understand how little I know." He shows her an unreadable list in Thai language.

They continue to walk through streets lined with jewelry shops, kitchenwares, cloth, appliances, clothes and everything else she might want.

"Jonathan, I thought this was just a little mountain town. I had no idea."

"If you are so easily pleased, my dear, I promise we will have a wonderful time during the next three months, if nothing else."

"I wonder how you will get any work done, if you spend all your time showing me around."

They return to the house and part ways, both in need of a nap. Katherine is amazed at how indolent she has become. Thailand appears to have affected Jonathan in the same way. At dinner they talk some more. "I have it all figured out, I shall take my laptop with me and while you are stalking the perfect photo, I shall sit and write. It's as simple as that."

By the time dinner is finished and they say goodnight, they are quite comfortable in their relationship. Katherine feels she believes she can trust him. She gives him a big hug. "Thanks for being here for me, my friend. I need someone like you in my life right now."

He smiles turns away and waves a hand over his shoulder.

SURPRISES

Many questions run through Katherine's mind. How did a Welshman end up in Thailand? She wants to know all about him, but feels she must restrain herself and not be too nosey. She is amazed by the fact that she is actually here on her own, but what brought Jonathan here? What happened to make this situation possible?

That next morning, over breakfast, as though he had read her mind, Jonathan remarks, "You must wonder how I ended up here."

She laughs, "We must be on the same wavelength. I admit I'm curious. Tell me."

Jonathan sits back. "Make sure you are comfortable. I'm a storyteller, you know. This may take some time. "

She settles more comfortably in her chair. "What else do I have but time? Go on."

"My story begins at the end of the Second World War. It's rather romantic. After the war ended, an Irishman came to work in the village where my mother lived. She was young, and pretty, a healthy Welsh girl. The soldier and the girl fell in love, or maybe it was lust. The war had a profound influence on women; they were no longer as proper as before the war. Once my father and mother discovered each other, they were together all the time. Having survived the war, young people seldom thought about the future. They grabbed at any thing that might bring them instant happiness. In more ordinary times, their relationship might have led to marriage, but fate intervened.

"My father was a naturalist. He had been offered a job with a company in Thailand. It was called Siam at the time. The problem was that he had to leave for Asia immediately. My mother urged him to pursue his career. She never told him she was pregnant. I wonder why, but I wasn't ever was able to ask her. Perhaps it was because that was the only home she had ever known. Maybe she was afraid to leave and go to the other side of the world. It might have been as simple as she had always planned to marry her old beau but wanted a fling before she settled down in the village."

"Whatever her reason, once my father was gone, she accepted her beau's proposal. She confessed that she was pregnant. I guess he didn't care. He loved her so much that he looked upon me as his own son. I always believed he was my father."

"That's so romantic. How did you find out that he wasn't your father? How did you find your real father if you didn't even know he existed?"

"It took a long time; in fact he was no longer alive when I found out. I never got to know him."

"How sad that must have been for you." Tears fill her eyes.

"In some ways, it was. The truth is, I never knew him. I hadn't missed him. It wasn't as devastating as if I had known him all my life and then lost him. I only found out that he was my father when he mentioned me in his will."

"His will? What about your parents? Why didn't your mother ever tell you?"

"I'm not sure. After he left for Asia, he wrote to my mother, but she never answered his letters. She didn't connect with him again. After he died I received a letter from his lawyer that explained the situation to me, along with his will."

"He worked in Siam for a while, and eventually, he came back to our village on a vacation. One day he saw me walking in the village and realized that I might have been his son. Confused he worried that if he did speak to me and make himself known, it would upset the whole family. So many years had passed. He spent time in the pub, and asked about my mother. He felt it was best that he leave without making contact. I never heard from him never knew of his existence, until his will had been read."

"Both my parents had died years before. There was no one left to answer my questions. My father's lawyer sent a letter, and notified me that I had been left this house, along with a large sum of money. My father left me a real gift... the chance to be a writer... even if he didn't realize it."

Katherine has a hundred questions to ask. "He did leave you a letter! What did he say?"

"He declared me his only son, and explained why he had never revealed himself to me. He wished me luck. He said he hoped that what he had left me would help me achieve whatever dreams I had. He had found his own happiness in Thailand. I have a hunch that he wanted me to know about and also enjoy my Irish heritage. The Welsh are so much more practical people than the Irish."

"You don't seem too practical, for all I have seen of you, in the sense that most people are practical," Katherine exclaims! "Your Irish heritage is apparent when I listen to your story. I've always heard that following our dreams is the most important thing we can do. Bernardo has always followed his dreams. He has created them in films, and his life has been fabulous. I don't think I've really had any big dreams. I've had plans, great kids, a healthy family, all that sort of thing. Maybe that is all there is for me to do."

"Katherine, don't be so hard on yourself. It took me years to get to this place. I used to brood most of the time. I never looked inside; I went along thinking that what I had at the time was all life held for me. I was married, with two children, and what was considered by most, a perfect life. I didn't think I had any right to complain, so I kept my feelings and thoughts to myself. To be truthful, I was afraid to explore. I thought I might find nothing more glamorous than a dead end."

"What changed?" Katherine begins to feel that his former life story sounds very much like her own life at this moment.

"My wife and I were happy when the children were young. As the years passed we changed and grew apart. I assumed that we would be together for the rest of our lives, but we were divorced a few years ago."

"What kind of work did you do?"

"My wife inherited her parents' bookshop in London. It was the perfect place for me. When I first came to London, her father hired me. I have always loved books. To be able to spend all day in that store was beyond my dreams. I helped to make it into a thriving business. My son inherited my love for books, and when I left he took over the store."

"I've always loved books too. It would have been a perfect place for me as well. Do you ever miss it now?"

He laughs. "No, not at all. My father's letter arrived at the time I was getting anxious to write my book. I knew it was time for a change and suddenly opportunity knocked. I took it without looking back. I had no doubts; it was an offer I couldn't refuse."

There is more magic in his story than Katherine could have imagined. "How did you feel when you found out about the will?"

"I was stunned. First of all, I found out that I had a father I never knew existed. I could hardly believe that he had left me such a gift." Jonathan shakes his head in disbelief, as if remembering the moment he was told. "It took some time for it to sink in. My divorce was final; it had been a long time coming. After it was all settled, I didn't want to remain at the bookstore any longer. In an instant, there was a way out of it all. Funny, it was something I'd dreamed about, in a way."

"I'm touched and amazed. Thank you so much for sharing that with me."

"I love to share this. I've thanked my father over and over again. I wish I could have known him. Yes, Kerwin McGuire, the father I never knew."

"What did you say? What was his name? "

"Kerwin McGuire. Why do you ask?"

All of a sudden, something occurs to Katherine. "Tell me his name again."

She jumps up. "I'll be right back."

She runs from the house and into the cottage. One of the books she bought in Bangkok lies open on her bed. She turns to the fly page and immediately picks up two other books she had bought in Bangkok. Totally excited, she moves swiftly back into the house.

"Look at this! Look at this! What does it say?" She shows him the book.

Jonathan takes the book from her and looks at the name written on the flyleaf. Stunned, he shakes his head in disbelief. "Where did you find these? Oh my God, these must have been his books!"

She takes his hand. "Come to my room, Jonathan. It's even better than you can imagine. I found boxes of his books in Bangkok, and I bought them all."

"Boxes, you say?"

She pulls him to his feet and drags him to the cottage. He sits on the bed, and one by one she hands him all the books, piling them high for him to see. His hands are shaking.

"There are comments and notes written in the margins. I hope you will be able to get acquainted with him, through his books. They reflect a lot about their owners."

She explains, "I was drawn to buy the whole lot when the salesman told me they were all from one estate."

Jonathan, still in a state of shock, can hardly believe his good fortune. "I believe he kept an apartment in Bangkok. This is a miracle. Just think! His hands and eyes have touched these books. Now I will be able to understand more about him, who he was, and what interested him. Look at these." He opens one book after another.

Later, Katherine tells him to take the books to his house so he can look through them in privacy.

"What can I do to repay you?" He hugs her. There are tears in his eyes.

"Nothing, nothing at all. I don't know how this happened, but it might fill in some blank spots in your life."

When Katherine tells him good night, she feels very good, better than she can remember feeling for a long time.

KATHERINE'S DIARY

This is so crazy. I am being invisibly led to all that is taking place in my life and Jonathan's too. Jonathan was stunned when he realized I had bought his father's books. He gave me the biggest hug and then took the boxes to the house. I sat quivering after he left. I don't think he had any such reaction; he was so carried away and touched by the books. As for me, I think I had an overreaction to his hug. I mustn't do this. Do what? Well, let myself go on like this, giving into this whole crazy thing.

Only here in my diary can I acknowledge the feelings and attraction that are growing in spite of all we proposed about our relationship. I must use some self-control. Yeah! Sure! On the other hand, I've always had this fear of falling; even as a child. I was frightened that I would fall into an abyss from which I would be unable to return. Am I willing to take a chance? What will happen if I do give in to my desire?

I'm beginning to understand more about Bernardo. Once in a while I sensed he was having an affair with an actress. He never said so, and I didn't ask, but I knew how he gets carried away with his directing. He is so passionate. At this moment, I can truly understand how he may have been unfaithful, in spite of himself. To be honest, I have a hunch that he would do anything to get a great performance out of someone... or nearly anything. I never confronted him with my feelings. I didn't want to. It would be pointless, because truthfully I always understood that it wasn't anything about the relationship between us.

However, if it was true, does that give me permission to indulge in my own desires? Is it right for me to do as he does? Is it right or wrong? I am delightfully confused.

I am under a magical spell. Seductive, spellbinding. I love the feeling and yet in a way I could begin to question my sanity. There is a part of me, hidden away; a place with which I have never become acquainted. I've never allowed myself to be in a situation like this, not mentally or physically. At this moment, I am on the other side of the world, far away from everyone I know. Nobody here knows me. It is freedom somehow. There are no walls for me to keep up, no facades to hide behind, and no expectations from anyone. I'm on my own; only my conscience to guide me. I have to take responsibility for myself.

Bernardo would delight in this. He loves unusual, uncomfortable situations; he'd write it into a script. He wouldn't be happy that it is his wife, having these thoughts this time. Anyone else and he'd love it. He'd write a movie about it. He'd get a kick out of unadventurous me, diving into such an adventure. He would be jealous, too; he is just that way. It's time for me to get rid of the feeling that he's always looking over my shoulder.

I hardly know Jonathan. I don't really know him at all, yet I feel I do. He seems familiar. Has he put a spell on me, or have I done it all myself? The Tarot cards warned me, but do they give me permission to experience my feelings? Maybe. But to act on them? Should I go for it? I am in charge, even if I feel like I am caught up in a whirlwind.

I can't sleep, so I'll just keep writing.

Franko has been urging me for years to bring something different into my life. I wonder if this is what he meant. Maybe he just wants me to find my strengths. That may be difficult. I'm strong, but I am also used to being a "good" person, doing what is "right." Then again, I am beginning to feel this is the right place for me at this time.

Truthfully, I have never allowed myself to be totally myself with Bernardo somehow. In the beginning, I longed to break open his heart and crawl right up inside and to know him completely. I wanted him to feel the same way about me. Scorpios never let you know all about themselves, so it never happened. I tried as hard as possible, in the beginning, but eventually, as all couples must, we came to a place where we were mostly satisfied. Nothing is ever perfect, no matter how much we wish it could be. Bernardo is a wonderful lover, patient and often our loving is magnificent, but there is always a little place inside of him that he keeps hidden. I've learned to be satisfied with what he can give. I always feel he has given me everything he is capable of giving, and I have no right to ask for more.

My needs are not sexual; I'm satisfied in that department. What I am feeling now is deeper, more dangerous to feel, too deep, unless I am ready to pay the price. An author, I once read said, "We never open completely, to another. Because if we do, and if we give all we have to give, and it isn't accepted, we have nothing left to give." When I read that, I understood the reason most people only want parts of each other, not the whole package. Sometimes when I have gone beyond a certain point, been too passionate about my feelings, I feel people shut down, they walk away or give some sort of signal that I have gone too far.

I don't believe that will happen with Jonathan. He is a Gemini and more cerebral. At least I hope so. Oh God, please give me the courage to accept this gift.

It is late, and still I cannot sleep.

It is as though a magnet has reached deep inside of me, drawing me beyond myself. I feel a wildness I have never expressed before. Will I go unchecked, go berserk, become deranged, disheveled, madcap, outrageous, exceeding the bounds of reason? Am I morally loose, wanton, and promiscuous? Will I become indecent, immoral, unconstrained? After all I am fifty. I don't know. Something new is rearing its head. Will I want to live native and remain here in the jungle? Will I ever be able to return to everyday civilization?

My! So dramatic! This is so much fun. I don't need to be so serious. It is liberating to indulge, to go overboard. I wonder how free I really can be. It would be fun to run riot if nobody gets hurt. I can't quite imagine Jonathan letting go like that. He did live in London for so long and they are very proper. This county changes us. People do whatever they must to live and nobody looks down on them for that. Anything goes.

Maybe it is time to learn to meditate and calm myself down. I must admit that letting my imagination run wild is great fun.

You that comes to birth
and brings the mysteries

Your voice-thunder
makes us very happy

Roar, lion of the heart
and tear me open.

<u>Illuminated Rumi</u>

TOURING

Jonathan is ready to help Katherine get acquainted with the countryside. He plans touristy sightseeing trips and asks Katherine for her opinions. Following the first trips, they plan to go exploring deep into the jungle and the mountains. Wisely, he suggests they go slowly at first; so that by the time they go camping they will be comfortable with each other. Katherine appreciates that. Camping tends to be an intimate experience and she will be alone with a stranger, far from the rest of the world. They need to get to know each other a little better.

Their first trip is a boat ride, up-river. Their destination is a settlement where elephant rides are offered. The sun rises in a sky of pale orange streaks above them, as they head down a path through colorful gardens, past a pool where mist rises. There is a tiny pier where colorful, narrow boats are lined up, awaiting customers. They step into the first boat. The boatman greets them, and takes Katherine's hand helping her to get settled. He gives each of them a vinyl pillow to sit on. Once they are seated, the boat suddenly jerks and quickly takes off, making room for the next boat in line.

Jonathan reaches into his backpack and hands Katherine a windbreaker. "Here, take this, it's chilly on the river."

They sit back; a spray of water washes over their faces. Jonathan is seated opposite Katherine, his long legs stretched out before him. She feels his gaze upon her. It makes her a little uncomfortable, but she knows she must to get used to it. He seems to take pleasure in all she does. She understands he is studying her. After all she is the muse. She begins to admit to herself that she is enjoying her role.

The boatman pilots the boat slowly up the softly rolling river as it sways lazily back and forth. Rugged rock formations rise from the beaches. The motor is very loud, and if they wish to speak they must shout, so they are quiet. The trip takes an hour.

Thatched huts line the shoreline. When they round the last curve in the river, the compound is revealed. Elephants bathe happily in the river. Katherine had hoped to take an elephant ride when she had come with Murphy, but they didn't have enough time. Now her wish is going to be granted.

The boat driver tells them that he will wait and take them back when they are finished. He walks over to join some friends. Jonathan buys tickets for the ride while Katherine purchases a bunch of bananas for the elephant who will give them the ride. A moment later, she is surprised when the bananas are suddenly scooped out of her hands. She looks up to see a mischievous elephant crunching her bananas, skin and all. The big gray pachyderm appears to be laughing at her. She isn't about to argue with him. He is aware of that.

Jonathan returns with the tickets and leads her to a small platform. She climbs up and hoists herself onto a wooden saddle, built for two. It is tied onto the elephant's back; ropes knotted behind his front legs.

"Is it safe?" she asks Jonathan, as he climbs on.

"Of course. People do this all the time." Jonathan assures her. They begin to rock back and forth, as the elephant moves slowly down the path.

The movement of the elephant, while not as regular as a horse, is comfortable. They travel up the river and Katherine began to imagine herself living in a previous century, when elephants were actually used for travel. Too many movies, she thinks to herself.

Jonathan is clearly enjoying himself.

When the ride is finished, they stroll down the dusty street, through the little village. Souvenir shops line the road offering crafts made by the locals. Caged boa constrictors lie in circular heaps in a shop. Katherine moves toward the snakes and looks closer.

Jonathan winks at the owner of the snakes, and asks. "Katherine, would you like to hold one?"

Not sure, she questions warily, "What does it feel like?"

"Here, let me." Jonathan gives the owner the okay. He takes the largest snake out of the cage and hoists it onto Katherine's shoulders.

"It's not hungry, is it?"

"No. Of course not."

"It feels cool, really nice, actually." Katherine looks intensely at the snake, while she enjoys the coolness of his body wrapped around her. The reptile's skin is light brown and there are beautiful, dark brown markings on his back, outlined in black. His head is light brown and fortunately he appears content to have Katherine stroke him.

After a little while, Katherine expresses her pleasure with the experience, and the owner removes the huge snake from her shoulders. Jonathan is delighted. He is testing her to see what she will be able to deal with, once they go deeper into the countryside. He understands that although something is unfamiliar, she will be a good sport and take it in her stride.

The air is warmer on the return trip down the river. By the time they reach the hotel, they are hungry. A sign announces "BRUNCH NOW BEING SERVED" Two curving staircases grace the lobby. The ceiling is adorned with enormous lighting fixtures made from tissue-paper parasols surrounded by tiny clear lights. Large green windows overlook the front entrance, giving it a bright airy ambience.

The waiter seats them at a table near the window. Bright flowers growing in the garden beyond the open window, threaten to tumble in and join them during their meal. "Coffee first." A buffet composed of endless fruits, juices, breads and more beckon Jonathan immediately. Katherine relaxes over her coffee. They talk about their plans for the rest of the day.

"Shall we head for the Golden Triangle?" Jonathan asks.

"What's that?"

"Surely you've heard about all the intrigue, the drug traffickers. They often portray them in adventure films. Drug lords lurking in the shadows, and all that."

"Is that true? Will we be in any danger?"

"No, it's tame where we will be going."

"Damn! I was ready for some intrigue."

"The toughest people are the border guards. If you want to cross into Burma or Myanmar, as they now call it, it will cost you twenty dollars. Actually, this trip will be strictly tourist, but nevertheless, interesting. We can take a boat to Laos so you will be able to say you have visited another country."

Coffee finished, Katherine helps herself to the buffet and returns to the table.

Hunger satisfied, they head north, toward the border. On their way, they pass rural Thai villages, dotted with small houses covered by thatched roofs. A woman farmer plows the field walking slowly behind oxen. Rice paddies impinge on upscale homes of stucco. Most homes are surrounded by lovely gardens of bright flowers.

As they drive along, Jonathan explains, "I hope you don't mind my questions. I want to learn everything about you while you are here."

"I know the time will pass too quickly. It is precious and I may take advantage. I am greedy." Jonathan chuckles. He watches her with the eyes of a lover who takes in every gesture of the beloved. He sees her more completely than anyone ever has before.

"Sure, if you find me helpful, I'm fine with that," she states offhandedly.

"To be truthful, I find you so attractive, that I must work very hard to keep the line between my character and the feelings I have for the lovely woman who is my muse."

"I am touched; nobody has ever said anything quite like that to me before."

"You must understand that I have to allow myself to fall in love with my character to make her real and appealing."

Katherine quickly changes the subject. "Can we talk about something else?" She is uneasy.

Sensitive, Jonathan offers a way out. "Tell me about your family."

"Where should I begin? Let me think for a moment.

My childhood was unusual. I never had a permanent home. My father worked in the Foreign Service. We traveled all over the world; one year here, and another year there.

Actually, I loved it most of the time. It might have been difficult for some kids, and sometimes I longed for a sibling, but my wish in that department was never answered. To make up for that, my mother tried to spend as much time with me as possible. She had to plan her time carefully because she had the responsibility of entertaining people for my father at dinner, and cocktail parties in the embassy. Truthfully, she was a shy person and preferred to spend time with me.

"When I grew older, she encouraged my interest in photography. On my tenth birthday, she gave me a camera. I began taking pictures of the places we lived, my friends at the time, our pets, and our houses. I made scrapbooks. It gave me continuity in a life of little continuity. I must confess, I was actually prepared for our present world, where nothing remains the same for long. Truthfully at times, I longed to know how it would feel to live a settled life like most people do."

"Perfect." He says. "Go on."

"I think that is why I was so happy to be married, to have my children. I was able to live a life I never had as a child. I wanted my children to have security that I never had."

"What happened to your parents?"

"When my father retired, my parents settled down in an old stone house, in New Hampshire. My mother inherited it from her parents. We used to spend summer vacations there. It was a fantastic place and I loved to investigate all the nooks and crannies. My father was a collector of everything. During the years, wherever we were stationed, he would collect treasures and ship them home to that house. Each summer, when we returned to New Hampshire, there were dozens of large wooden boxes awaiting us. The postman would store them in the barn. When we arrived, my father would open the boxes. It was so exciting...... much better than Christmas! Often, he had forgotten what he had purchased and it was a surprise for him too."

"Things like what?" Jonathan is extremely curious.

"He collected pillars from broken down palaces, stones from ancient walkways. They are still stored leaning against the walls of the barn. I wondered where he was able to find all these things. He collected antique musical instruments, pianos, and harpsichords. He collected china dishes for my mother. There was no end to his purchases. He harbored a fantasy, a picture of the day when he would retire and put all those things to use, somewhere around the property.

"At least one of his dreams did come to fruition. His first love was books. He built an elegant library on the property. The walls were deep mahogany, shelves from floor to ceiling with a built-in heater and dehumidifier. The library smelled wonderful when you opened the door. You know how old books tend to get musty smelling. He bought a desk supposedly used by Hemingway. I always wondered how authentic it could be, after I learned that Hemingway wrote standing up. My father loved it; and that was all that mattered."

"I'm envious of your childhood." Jonathan confesses. "Please go on"

"My father planned to write a book about his life, but he never got it written. He didn't have the drive. His income was adequate for ordinary circumstances; still, the stone house took a lot of upkeep. He tried to do much of the work himself. After I married Bernardo, I was able to send them some money for repairs, but I don't know what they did with it. I tried to get them to put some of the collections up for sale, but my father never could bring himself to do it. He kept on dreaming and planning. He'd describe how he planned to use this or place that in the future. What could I do?

"In the end, there was hardly any room for either of them to walk through the house. Narrow paths led through their belongings, tiny paths to the desk, the bed and the couch."

"Katherine, this is amazing."

"The kitchen was the one room not crowded. My mother insisted on her own rights in there. But even there, they saved every little thing, every left-over. I'd find tiny bits of cheese wrapped in wax paper, secured by a rubber band in the refrigerator. I never remembered my mother being so prudent. We had servants when I was young so she didn't have to cook or care for the kitchen. Maybe it was because they were getting older.

"In the end the stone house was run down. A minimum of repairs had been made through the years. They still drove a car, but it wasn't safe. My mother was the eyes. She looked out the windshield carefully, giving instructions, while my father piloted the car. I always figured they would die together in an auto accident. I prayed they wouldn't hurt anyone else, but there was no way to convince them to give up their licenses."

"Did they?"

"No, they died under the oddest circumstances. Hard to believe, but they had a life of drama to the end. They were on a trip to Chicago, staying at a nice hotel. They had won a travel package. Fortunately there was a camera, in the hallway that recorded their demise. One afternoon they were on their way to their room when they passed a man in the hall. He was holding a package beneath his arm. He appeared very anxious. As he put his key in the door opposite their door, there was an explosion. It must have been a bomb in the package he was carrying. All three of them were killed. The bomb must have been meant to kill the man in the hall. It was amazing that they could figure it out. The surveillance camera caught the whole thing on film. They were at the wrong place at the wrong time for sure. I tried to convince myself it was for the best that they went together, but it was a terrible way for their lives to end"

"Oh! My God!" Jonathan is dumbfounded. "How did you deal with that?"

"After the initial shock, I looked for answers, but of course there were none. I don't believe they could have lived with out each other for long.

"And that is my story."

"Maybe you should write a book yourself," suggests, Jonathan. "Whatever happened to the house and all the books and things?"

"It's all there. Except for the books, most of it must be in tatters. I went up right after it happened, but I haven't been able to bring myself to clean it out. I don't know what keeps me from just getting it done. I was on location with Bernardo when they died, and after the funeral, I didn't have the time, or the strength, to face the task of clearing it out. I returned to the location after I hired a caretaker. He's been looking after the property ever since. I have no idea what condition it is in. I need to sell it, but there has been no hurry. Maybe when I go home, I will be ready to do that."

"My life has been very dull by comparison, at least until lately," explains Jonathan. "Do you mind if I use some of your history in my book?"

"No, of course. Go right ahead. I'd love to read your version of my life when you are done."

They arrive at the Golden Triangle area, eager to get out and stretch their legs. It is hot and dusty. The ornate gate before them reads "Golden Triangle," in both English and Thai. Carved birds atop the sign look backward in an awkward stance. Carved elephants sit grandly at the base of the gate.

"Do you want a photo of yourself in front of this sign?" Jonathan asks. Four young girls dressed in traditional, colorful costumes immediately descend upon Katherine. While he focuses, the children gather around her, giving her hugs. One places her hat on Katherine's head. They expect to be rewarded with bhats, but nevertheless seem so sweet and loving.

Afterward they walk through the park where the boat that will take them to Laos is tied at the river's edge. Jonathan holds Katherine's hand as he leads her down toward the river. They climb into a long boat similar to the one they had taken to see the elephants earlier in the day. Jonathan points out the stretch of land that is Thailand and shows her where Laos is located. They drag their hands in the water; the spray keeps them cool.

Their boat pulls up next to a houseboat. The boatman cuts off the motor, as they slowly drift toward a small pier, where he docks the boat. On her hands and knees, Katherine climbs up to the other boat, which isn't actually a boat, but a souvenir store. Three lovely Laotian women stand happily; ready to sell Gold Triangle tee shirts and other souvenirs. They offer the couple cold soda and speak short sentences in English. There are no other customers and the women appear happy to have visitors. Katherine buys tee shirts for the twins. Smiling, the women wave to them as they depart. Katherine has actually been in another country for a few minutes.

"Do you feel like going a little farther to the border of Burma?" Jonathan asks." I can't get used to calling it Myanmar."

"Sure. Burma always sounds like such a romantic, mysterious place. It brings to mind intrigue, tropical jungles and spies. Let's go."

Dust billows up in puffs as they drive along. It grows hotter as they approach the border. Quickly, Jonathan finds a parking spot on the main road, and they walk the rest of the way toward the border. Katherine sees the sign that says "Cross into Myanmar for 20 dollars," and at that moment she realizes she had no desire to leave Thailand, not even for a moment. She is happy in her newly adopted Thailand, and had no wish to set foot into what she considers a hostile country.

When she shares her thoughts, Jonathan concurs. "It's much nicer here. We will stay on this side." They approach another gate that proclaims it to be the northern most spot in Thailand. The gate is Pagoda style with a roof of rounded tiles surrounded by lacy carvings. As Katherine approaches, once again children rush up to have their picture taken with her. She happily puts her arms around them and hands them some bhats.

They walk through the dusty streets and look into windows for things they might need for future side trips. Mostly they just window-shop. During a tour of a jade factory, Katherine is fascinated by the workmanship of the jewelers, who hunch over their worktables behind the shop in small wooden booths. They watch them carve jade, into many shapes and she buys a small jade elephant for Bernardo. The sales lady puts it into a lovely small silk bag, and hands it to her with a big smile.

They head for home, hot and weary. Halfway home, Jonathan pulls off the road into the parking lot of a small restaurant announcing, "This is another favorite of mine." Dinner is served on the back deck, overlooking the river. The surrounding area is filled with beautiful flowers.

"They serve great Laotian food here," Jonathan explains. "You will enjoy it. You have become like a Thai native. They are always eating."

Seated beside the river, they watch the sun set. Light filters through the haze and clouds. The waiter delivers iced-cold Cokes. It is the perfect drink. The dusty day has left them dry. Jonathan orders for both of them. The food is similar to Thai, with subtle differences. They feast on spicy steamed chicken with chilies, lemon grass, kaffer lime leaves and coconut, prawns steamed in banana leaves, tasting of cilantro, lemon grass, chilies and sesame seeds that have seeped into the shrimp. They complete their meal with a dish of fresh pineapple and mint leaves.

Katherine has to confess. "You are a great traveling partner."

They are quiet the rest of the way home; the day had been full. Katherine tries to digest all she had taken in. The country is working its way into her heart, and affects her more deeply each day. Seeing it with Jonathan is perfect. For him it is equally also perfect.

Although I try
To hold a single thought
Of Buddha's teaching in my heart
I cannot help, but hear
the many crickets' voices calling as well.

<u>The Ink Dark Moon</u>

SURRENDER TO THE MOMENT

Katherine is amazed by the direction her life is taking. She has no explanation for what has happened. She no longer feels the need for one. She has surrendered and accepts her fate. All the questioning in the world will not explain why this is happening. She keeps reminding herself that she must stay on this new path, and not fall back into her old patterns of playing things safe, overanalyzing.

Early one morning Jonathan leaves for town to run some errands, while Katherine takes time to look through her photos. She needs to experiment with some different lenses before they set out on the longer trips. She hopes to develop an interesting photographic style for her book.

There is a knock at the front door. She opens the door and there before her stands a beautiful Eurasian woman, holding a child in her arms. She greets Katherine shyly. "Hello. My name is Rose."

Instantly Katherine feels a quick rush of jealousy. She is surprised at her reaction. What is going on? After all, she isn't in a romantic liaison with Jonathan.

The woman says, in perfect English. "I am here to see Mr. Jonathan." Her voice is soft and alluring.

Katherine struggles to regain her composure. "Oh sorry, please do come in. Is he expecting you? I'm his tenant, Katherine."

There is no question about it. This woman is drop dead gorgeous, stunning as only Thai women can be. Her long shining black hair frames her soft velvet skin and her slanted green eyes. She is slender and moves with grace. The baby is asleep in her arms. She walks through the house as if it is familiar to her, and heads toward the living room.

"Do you mind if I lay my baby on the couch?" she asks.

"Of course not, make yourself comfortable. Can I get you anything?" Now that she is able to gather her wits, Katherine begins to feel comfortable in the role of hostess.

A moment later, Kai walks into the room. She greets Rose and gives her a warm hug. Now, Katherine is even more curious.

Rose begins to explain. "I should have called, Jonathan wasn't expecting me. I wanted to surprise him. I know I should have come before, but I was too nervous."

Fortunately, for everyone, Jonathan chose that moment to walk through the door. Katherine watches his expression, and to her relief, he doesn't appear to recognize Rose. She is puzzled. "Jonathan, this is Rose; she is here to see you."

He reaches for her hand and smiles. "Happy to meet you Rose. Is this your child?"

"Yes," she replies. "Her name is Annie." Rose sits down next to the sleeping child.

Katherine is beyond curious. What is going on?

Rose begins to laugh nervously, as though she has an inner secret, a joke. She looks down, "Jonathan, please let me explain. This has to be confusing for you. I know you never met your father, you never knew about him until they read the will to you." She hesitated. "Oh dear, this may be a huge surprise, I fear. I am your half sister. Your father was married to my mother."

Katherine looks around quickly to see if anyone had heard her sigh of relief. No matter how lovely this woman is, she is his sister, after all. She immediately feels much better. Now that she is getting to know Jonathan, she is selfish; she doesen't want their relationship to disappear. If she is truthful, she doesn't want to share him. She doesn't want to lose what they have established between them. She is used to sharing Bernardo with his movie crews, but she knows most women would not be as generous or understanding as she has been.

Kai stands back, amused by the situation. Perhaps she is able to sense Katherine's feelings. "Can I get you all something to drink? Everyone go sit out by the pool? I'll keep my eyes on Annie."

Jonathan, relieved to have a moment to absorb the information, turns to Kai,"Yes, please, why don't we have some snacks too?"

Katherine wants to be polite. "I'll go over to my cottage and give you time to get acquainted."

Jonathan disagrees immediately. "No need, Katherine. I'd like for you to stay here and listen. I may need someone to lean on." Softly he said to her, "You are also one of my family now, and I want to share this with you. If you don't mind, I may be able to use some of your reactions in my writing."

They move to the patio. Trees and plants move lazily in the tropical breezes.

Rose begins. "My mother is no longer alive, and of course as you know, our father died recently. I am so sorry you never were able to be acquainted with him He was a wonderful man. You have his eyes. So do I." She hesitates. "I'm not sure where to start, there is so much to tell."

They sit there, listening to the story, questioning Rose. The baby awakens, and Rose nurses her while they continued to talk. Kai enters and leaves refreshing drinks, listening discreetly.

"When your father came to Thailand, he was a student, here to study the habits of big cats not long after the Second World War. He had been offered an apprenticeship from the

United Nations; It was an opportunity he couldn't refuse. He left Wales but continued to write to your mother asking her to join him. She never answered his letters. He learned a few years later, that she had married the Welshman whom you believed was your father. He respected her judgment, and never got in touch. Many years later he went on a trip home and he passed through your village. When he got a glimpse of you, he sensed you might have been his son, but he never knew for sure. He didn't want to upset your life; so he left without contacting you."

"Not too long before your mother died, she requested that your real father be contacted and told him about you. I have no idea how she found him. When he found out about you, he wasn't sure what to do. He was elated, surprised, yet somewhat saddened to have missed the relationship he might have had with you. Sadly, at the same time that he received the letter from your mother, he found that he didn't have long to live."

"He knew he would never get back to London to meet you, so he immediately rewrote his will, leaving his house to you, along with a large sum of money. He was very wealthy and provided for me generously too. There was plenty for both of us."

Jonathan is stunned and ecstatic at the same time. More pieces of the puzzle of his life begin to fit. He had lived his childhood as a single child. Now he finds that he has a sister, and a niece. In an instant, he has become an uncle.

"So our father was a grandfather. Did he get to meet Annie?"

"Yes, Annie was born a month before he died and he held her in his arms a few times. She made him very happy; he loved children."

"Rose, where do you live?"

"We live in Chiang Mai; my husband works at a large hotel. He is head chef. We don't get up this way very often."

Jonathan stood up. "May I give you a hug and a kiss?"

"I've been hoping you would." Rose's teary words come as he reaches for her and embraces Rose and the sleeping Annie all at once.

KATHERINES DIARY

What is happening to me? I'm caught in quicksand, in a vortex. I don't think I have the strength to resist this adventure. I feel my emotions bubbling to the surface, feelings I have seldom let myself feel. I had to laugh at my jealousy before I realized that Rose was actually Jonathan's sister. I could immediately let that go and like her. But for a moment the jealousy reared its head big and ugly. I always have felt that Bernardo belonged to the whole world and I had no right to be jealous. But with Jonathan, I am feeling things I never realized about myself. I wonder what he is learning.

I am happy that he has found his family, even if it is too late to know his father. I wonder if his father knew he would come here and meet them. This is so mysterious. The story that is unfolding is far more amazing than any movie I have ever seen. There is nobody here to do the editing inside my head any more. It is a great freedom. I hope I don't fall on my face and regret what is happening. But what the hell? If I don't do this now, I may never get the chance and I'll have more regrets when I am an old lady.

Playing it safe, doesn't get me anywhere. I always liked what an old friend use to do for herself. Each year she would do something she had never done before. I guess this may be what I must do now at this age. it seems a little more than I could ever have planned.

JONATHAN'S STORY

The next morning, Jonathan and Katherine sit at the breakfast table. Jonathan spreads out a map and begins to mark locations he thinks will interest Katherine. He highlights them. Then they talk about the pros and cons. They have to keep the weather in mind; seeing as it will become hotter and hotter in the days ahead.

A downpour is projected for the day, so they move the map into the living room and spread it out on the coffee table. Jonathan describes a place; Katherine considers it. When she expresses an interest, he marks it on the map. By lunchtime, they have the next two months mapped out. They plan to keep a flexible schedule, so that they will have as many options as possible for their adventures.

"Let's take it easy, now that we have done all the planning stages." Katherine said. "I don't want to take up all your time. I don't want to impose."

Jonathan smiles at her. "I'll give you some time to yourself if you need it, but please understand that you aren't taking up my time, you are giving me your time, inspiring me. That's what a muse does, my dear. It's the job you accepted, you know, to be a muse.

"My new career sounds pretty good to me. What does one really expect from a muse, what is my job description?"

"Only to inspire! After all, the muse was the goddess of the arts."

"Oh, if that's true, I must be a thought provoker, idea giver, help you to become a fantastic and poetic writer, to express yourself like a genius. And what else?"

Jonathan laughs out loud. "It sounds perfect to me."

The afternoon lies ahead of them, and Katherine still wants to know more about Jonathan and what his life had been like before they met.

"When did you move to London?"

He begins. "After university, I set out for London. I knew I'd never be able to find the work I wanted in Wales. The first job I applied for was a post in a bookshop. They were looking for a manager/ trainee. I hoped I might fill the position, as I'd always loved books. Now I realize I must have inherited that love from my father. My mother was not much of a reader.

"Things went well. I got the job and went to work immediately. At first all I could afford was a bed-sit, my meals, and a few clothes. In time I worked my way up to manager. Eventually I met Marjorie, the owner's daughter. She was attractive and funny. I fell in love. Soon after that, we were married and had two children. We bought a home and when her parents passed away, they left the store to her. I became the proprietor. Marjorie never had much interest in the store. She'd had enough of books in her life. Besides, she was busy with our family. She had chosen to stay home and raise the children, while I ran the store. It worked for both of us, and she seemed happy with the arrangement."

"What happened? It sounds perfect." She is puzzled.

"Oh, it was perfect. Books always excited and thrilled me. Each morning when I unlocked the door of the shop, there was the wonderful smell of new books. Sometimes I'd feel intoxicated, overtaken by dizziness when I stepped inside. I knew deep inside that the authors were inviting me to a celebration each one was offering me something extraordinary. When new books arrived, my level of excitement would rise, as I unpacked, catalogued and placed them in their rightful place on the shelves. I know I sound crazy, but it is how it affected me."

Katherine understands completely that he is telling his truth.

"I loved the challenge of locating hard-to-find books for customers. I read everything... fiction, history, non-fiction, poetry. It was an incredible experience to have all those books at my fingertips. "

"Inspired by the authors, I tried my hand at writing. On my time off, and during quiet periods, I wrote, I formed a writer's group that met one night each week at the bookshop. That helped me immensely. We wrote essays, then read and critiqued each other's work. When authors came to the store for book signings, I questioned them and inhaled their essence, hoping it would affect me in a positive way. I'd ask how they had become writers; actually been able to write. I wanted to know how it had been possible to give themselves permission to take the time, be a writer before they were successful. I didn't seem to be able to give myself permission.

"Truthfully, I wasn't truly ambitious; I had no burning urge inside me. I was where I wanted to be, and couldn't imagine doing anything else. I thought I was satisfied. I began, like so many Englishmen do, to stop at the pub on the way home from work. I'd have a few pints too many. It became a nightly habit. Eventually, my wife no longer waited dinner for me. Time passed, my children grew up. My son loved the bookshop and he began to come and help me when he had the time."

"My wife decided to go back to work. She entered the fashion world; it had always been one of her passions. She climbed the ladder of success quickly, and soon was off on buying trips. On one of these trips, she became romantically involved with her boss. We finally had to admit things were difficult between us. We had changed. She wasn't interested in the bookshop, nor was she interested in me. She confessed her infidelity and told me she was sorry."

"In a way, it was a relief. To be honest, we had changed and it seemed that we had finished whatever our relationship had demanded of us. Our children were off at college. There was no anger, because there was no passion left. We agreed to go our separate ways and remained friends."

Jonathan gets up and begins to walk around the room. He looks different now. It was as though during the time he has been telling his story, a huge weight had been lifted off his shoulders. Obviously, he had made the right decision. His life was brighter, and she can see the changes happen in him right in front of her eyes as he tells his story. Maybe he also needed a good friend as much as she had. In the end, he looks relaxed, his shoulders have dropped, and he seems quite happy.

He continues. "The urge to write grew within me, but I couldn't figure out how to find an income to keep me going, if I wanted to write full time. I couldn't quit work. Even though my son was willing to take over the bookshop, I was afraid to just up and quit."

Jonathan takes a deep breath and seemed to fill with joy. His face begins to glow. "And then the letter arrived. Everything changed in an instant. The letter informed me of a father I never knew existed, and told me of my inheritance. Right out of the blue, I was set free.

"My son took over the bookshop; my wife was free to go to her lover without guilt. I was thrilled to be able to come here to Thailand and follow my dreams."

Katherine can picture him opening the letter.

"It was a dream, far more magnificent than anything I could have imagined."

"I'm sure you were stunned and imagined you were dreaming. I would have."

Jonathan was remembering. "Last September, when I saw you on the train in Wales, I was on my way to say goodbye to some of my old friends. When I sat down beside you, it was like a breath of fresh air. I couldn't forget you. I think I told you I was off in a few days."

"Yes," she laughs. "I remember you saying you were off to Asia."

"Ahh, yes, I left England full of energy, hope and some apprehension. I wanted to follow my dreams; hoping I could really live up to them. I was hoping I wasn't just a phony. The thing was, it caught me by surprise. I just went for it all, not thinking; quite unlike myself."

He smiles again, remembering his arrival. "It was December and the weather was perfect. When Tony delivered me to this house, I was amazed. I had expected a small cement block house; instead I found a small estate."

"First I got settled in and became acquainted with the countryside. Only then, I sat down to write. In the beginning I seemed to be doing okay. I wrote a simple outline for the book; I had been thinking about it for years. My inspiration came from some poetry I had read. A woman, who lived in tenth century Japan, had written passionate poetry to her lover. I wanted to create a woman like the one I found in the poetry. I wanted to create the feelings she invoked in her readers, but when I began, something was missing. I couldn't make it happen." I had the dreaded writers block. I didn't know what to do. Tony suggested going to the temple.

"I said my prayers to the Buddha. The afternoon I found you in the pool, I knew my prayers had been answered. I had never forgotten you, after we met on the train. Something about you inspired me to be able to express what it was that I found in my Japanese heroine. I thought I would be able to remember you. I tried to impress you on my brain, but something happened and I lost you. But now you are here."

POETIC INSPIRATION

After dinner, they continue their discussion. Katherine is curious about the poetry that is Jonathan's inspiration.

"Come with me." Reaching for her hand he leads her into his bedroom.

The room looks as if a tornado had rushed through. A beautiful silken quilt has fallen off the side of the bed, and pillows are tossed everywhere.

Looking around as thought he had not noticed, Jonathan apologizes. "Please excuse the mess. Kai wanted to clean, but I didn't want anything disturbed. We made an agreement so she waits until I ask her to do it. As you can see, I haven't asked."

Katherine is excited to be able to glimpse into an intimate part of his life. It is Jonathan's private domain. The scent of yellow rose incense fills the air. Pungent and exotic, it stirs her feelings. The tabletops are piled with papers. Above the desk, he has tacked photos, quotes, and poems.

"Here are my favorites." He hands her a book. "Sit here on the bed, if you don't mind."

She opens the book.

"Remember, these poems were written over a thousand years ago. Utterly amazing. In my youth, I took poetry classes, but soon realized that poetry wasn't my calling. Still, I loved reading poetry. When I discovered these poems had been written by two Japanese women, I couldn't help but fall in love with them. My passion went to new heights. I wanted to take them into my arms, make love to them, and feel what they were feeling. I wanted to lie beside them. In those days, lovers wrote poetry to each other to express their deepest feelings. I wanted to create a woman like that, who could feel deeply and express herself so passionately. She haunted my dreams. In reality, where was I to find her? Only in my dreams.

Katherine is astounded; he has taken her breath away. She has no idea that Jonathan has such a deep romantic side, so passionate in spite of his serious British demeanor. She had expected his sense of humor and wit, but this new side of him surprises her. She begins to wonder if she is as safe as she thought she was. His passion begins to stir her.

"Life was very different a thousand years ago, but I believe we still have the same longings." He explains. "Perhaps our expectations have changed. Women are no longer so dependent on men, but I believe all of us long for that perfect love."

"Jonathan, you are such a romantic. Will you read for me?"

"I'd love to read to you."

He picks up a book and begins to read, his voice filled with emotion.

Katherine's mind goes back a thousand years.

> *Those nights when we slept,*
>
> *behind love's*
>
> *jeweled screen,*
>
> *were we even aware*
>
> *of the open dawn skies?*

Katherine inhales trying to catch her breath.

> *Remembering you....*

The fire flies of the marsh

Seem like sparks

That rise

From my body's longing.

Her eyes fill with tears. "Oh my God, those are so beautiful. It feels as though someone has looked deep inside the heart of me and revealed my longings."

Jonathan continues. "What I love about this poetry is that it shows nothing of what the lovers have actually done, only the effect on the poet. The poem comes alive, as though I have experienced it myself. This one is by Ono no Komachi."

When my desire grows too fierce

I wear my bedclothes

inside out,,

Dark as a night's rough husk.

"This is one of parting."

I thought those white clouds

Were gathered

Around some distant peak,

But already they have risen between us.

He hesitates as he sees tears fall from her eyes. "Please continue." she says.

It seems a time has come

when you have become like those horses

wild with spring

who long for distant fields,,

where light mists rise.

"Another."

> *The pine tree by the rock*
> *Must have its memories too.*
> *See how its branches*
> *Lean toward the ground.*

"And, finally one last one by Shikbu."

> *Lying alone,*
>
> *my black hair tangled*
>
> *uncombed,*
>
> *I long for the one who touched it first"*

Katherine is deeply touched. Jonathan hands the book to her. "It is called <u>In a Dark Wood.</u> It was translated by Jane Hirshfield. You are welcome to borrow it. I have another copy."

"I feel seduced. I'm so shallow. These women were so erotic, so talented. How were they able to reach so deeply into their hearts that they could convey all this in poetry. I feel everything they were feeling. I believe when a writer is capable of bringing a person to such understanding within themselves, they are perfection. You want to do that too. Jonathan, I admire you. It is difficult to free yourself of the fear of self-revelation."

Jonathan laughs. "It may seem that way; actually I have done so little. There is so much more to reveal and sometimes I wonder if I will ever be able to do it. Even though this will be fiction, there is always some of the author in their work. It terrifies me at times."

KATHERINE'S DIARY

How deeply the poetry affected me. It reminds me a little of how classical music never appealed to me when I was younger, but now reaches deep into my heart and emotions. I don't know how to explain it. This incredible poetry is way beyond that.

As a child, my mother used to read to me from <u>A Childs Garden of Verses.</u> My favorite poem was one about how I have a little shadow that goes in and out with me, or something like that. I wonder how I can recall that, when I can't even remember things I read last week.

Up until now Rumi has been my favorite poet; he always evokes deep feelings of connection.

I think it is fantastic that Jonathan is inspired to write about those women in his book. He wants to recreate the poet's emotions and feelings. As for being a muse, I can't understand, how little old me can ever be of help. My true love is Bernardo. I love my kids, but the way the poets express themselves seems much deeper. Would I ever be able lie in my bed and think these thoughts, let alone write them down? Not likely. I don't have the talent, or the brainpower to create visions such as these. It is an opening of one's soul; such a potent offering, nakedness. Does my soul have feelings like this, deep inside?

I am so ordinary. These women are in no way ordinary. After reading these poems, I fear I may let Jonathan down. He won't find that sort of muse in me. I may not be what he needs. On the other hand, I am surprised by my growing feelings for this man. I feel so very close and I trust him. I want to help him. I feel as if he is taking my hand and pulling me out of myself. Maybe it is a two-way street. I'm glad we made our agreement so we can both go as deeply within as we are able. It's one of those "jump off the cliff" kind of experiences. I hope I can fly.

JUNGLE TREK

"Food and water, all packed?" Jonathan mumbles to himself, as he takes stock. The car has been carefully tuned up and gassed for their first long trip.

Katherine observes Jonathan. *'He must be wondering how I am going to behave while we are camping. He seems a little nervous.'*

In reality, Jonathan has no need to be nervous about Katherine. She is ready, her backpack filled to capacity, an extra pair of shoes slung over her shoulders. A floppy hat, with a big brim is perched on her head and she is wearing a photographer's vest, covered in a multitude of pockets, each filled with an item for her camera work.

Jonathan stares at her vest.

"Like it? It's my camera case. I can carry everything I need in the pockets."

He laughs in relief. "I've got the tent in the car."

She knows he is nervous and decided to tease him a little. "You mean there won't be a grand hotel where we are going?"

"Doubtful," he relaxes, now that he understands that she is kidding.

The places they have chosen to photograph are far off the beaten path. She plans to take photos of sites few people have ever seen, places where the ordinary traveler would never go. It is going to be a very special trip.

"How do you know about all these places?" Katherine asks.

"When I first arrived in Chiang Rai, one of my father's friends took me on a trip to the place we are going today. It's a fantastic place. Hope I can remember the way."

She gives him a perplexed look. "You're kidding."

"Of course! You saw the map, when we were planning the trip."

They climb into the car and are off. "Our first expedition."

This is a ritual that will be repeated again and again during the next months they spend together. Katherine is quiet. She is both nervous and thrilled. For the first time in her life, she is doing what she wants to do, without anyone else to consider. She has to trust herself. Either she will learn to fly or she will crash. Jonathan will be her guide, and he is delighted to take her on this trip. She tries to breathe in the experience and let go of her expectations and concerns.

They drive farther and farther north, toward the mountains. The ground is no longer green and the foliage is withered in some areas. Katherine asks why.

"They don't have much rain at this time of year, so everything dries up. Soon, after spring, they will have a deluge, and some of the places we are going will be impossible to navigate at that time. Hopefully, it will remain dry while we are here."

He turns off the main highway and drives up a road that takes them to a deserted parking lot.

"We'll unload here and leave the car. It will be safe."

They set off for the jungle. Once they leave the main road, the dryness disappears. The jungle is full of growth, huge trees, and low bushes, vines that climb the trees. It seems as if the foliage might swallow them. It was obvious;

nobody has been here for a while. The path is barely visible, untraveled. It is as if they are the only people in the world. Loaded up with packs, large bottles of water and water purifying pills, they take off down the path. Jonathan carries the tent and leads the way. Both of them carry walking sticks; he also carries a machete in a holster. "We have to be prepared to cut down any growth that might be in our path."

The bushes are low, but Katherine can see into the distance where they are heading, the foliage grows taller and thicker. They can barely see the path beneath the weeds and shrubs growing up alongside it. The foliage soon turns tropical, and in no time they are beneath a canopy of tall trees.

The grass at their feet is tangled; the bamboo and palms are leggy, reaching up to get their share of rays from the occasional bits of sun they can find. Above them is a tunnel of trees but they cannot see the light at the end. The jungle is quiet at first but soon bird and animal sounds increase. Birds, insects and other animals, begin a chorus. Once in a while they stop and listened to the melodies. They can no longer see the sky the greenery is so thick. A bright color flashes by and catches their eyes. It screeches and flies up to the treetops.

"Is that a parrot?"

Moist and humid, the forest floor smells of rotting leaves and roots. Sultry, steamy vapors rise from the ground. There is no breeze. The path continues to lead upward. They come to a large tree that has fallen across the way, blocking the path.

"Guess my knife will be useless here," Jonathan laughs. "Let's just sit on the tree and have our lunch. It's time and we will find a way round after we eat.

Katherine is hungry and she immediately reaches for the lunch Kai has packed for them. It is a noodle dish, accompanied by chopsticks. Cold, it tastes perfect, along with a bottle of cool water. Sliced pineapple ends the meal, with a sweet taste.

While they eat they feel eyes upon them. A small monkey appears and moves close to them. It seems to want to be friendly, but plays hide and seek. Katherine throws a noodle to him. He dashes over, picks it up and runs off. He reappears a few moments later. When they throw him a piece of pineapple, he sits in place watching them, and gobbles it right up.

They hack an opening around the top of the enormous tree and continue on their way. The greenery began to lighten up when they come across a stand of wild bananas.

"We can always eat these if we run out of food," Jonathan jokes.

A moment later, a path is revealed. It opens up and leads them to the top of a mountain. "I think we are almost there. This looks familiar." Jonathan reassures her.

The trees change to pine and oak stands on the hill. They can look down and see the savannah in the valley below. They enter the woods and they hear the sound of rushing water.

"We are here."

Katherine looks and sees a deep lagoon, filled by a waterfall bubbling over a cliff above. It is paradise.

"This is it."

"Oh Jonathan, it's beautiful, absolutely perfect."

She strips down to her bathing suit. "Is it safe to dive in here?" Without waiting for an answer, she dives into the cool water. Jonathan follows her a moment later. She dives deeply and then rises to the surface, slicking her hair back from her face, relishing the cool water on her skin.

Jonathan is sitting on a rock by the time she comes out of the water. "I am enchanted by your beauty, your excitement and spontaneity. Thank you, my muse."

She doesn't know what to say.

"You know, in England, most of the women don't even know how to swim."

"Why?" she asks.

"The water is too cold at the beach, and there are few public pools. It doesn't seem to be a priority for the middle class. The rich learn when they go on their vacations in warm places."

She paddles around, floating on her back. "Have you ever gone behind the waterfall?"

"Yes! There is a little cave behind it. I'll take you after we set up camp. It is a mystical place."

Jonathan finishes setting up the tent. He puts their extra clothes, towels and other things they need to keep dry inside the tent. The cameras and notebooks are wrapped in plastic. He builds a small circle of stones where they will cook later. They search for broken branches and twigs for the fire.

"Do they have Boy Scouts in England?" she asks, as she observes him putting the camp in order.

"I was never a scout, but my son loved to camp. I had to learn to do it for him. I actually liked camping very much, once I experienced it. On holiday, we took a week's trip in one of those long boats that go into the canals. It had a little stove in it and I learned to make a fire and cook simple meals."

"Are those the ones I saw in the countryside?"

"Yes, you can rent one and navigate nearly the whole of England. At night you put into a pub and have dinner."

"That sounds like lots of fun."

"I would like to take you on one someday."

Camera in hand, Katherine began to wander around the area. She really wants to get the feel of the locale so she takes the camera with her. Sunlight filters through the treetops. It hits the water and it is spellbinding. While she investigates, Jonathan is content to sit and read, until the light began to fade. Soon it is time for dinner. Cross-legged on the ground; they cook dinner and eat with chopsticks.

Katherine is exhausted by the time they finish dinner. "Guess I'll postpone the swim. I'm very tired. I hope I don't snore." They exchange a brief hug, she bends down, and he reaches up.

She crawls into the tent, changes into her sleeping clothes, and lies back on the pillow, content. She drops off to sleep, awakening slightly for a moment when Jonathan comes in. He stops for a moment, sighs and then crawls into his sleeping bag and is still.

The next morning when Katherine awakens, Jonathan is still sleeping. Quietly, she sneaks off to the lagoon for a skinny dip, before he wakes up. She knows he had been tired and figures he will sleep for a while longer. She takes a towel with her. Slipping quietly into the pool, she swims around lazily, not realizing Jonathan is awake until she hears a stick crack. When he realizes she is naked he turns away quickly and returns to camp. By the time she gets back to camp, wrapped in a towel, he is brewing tea.

"Oh my dear, I'm sorry to have interrupted your swim. I didn't mean to interfere." He seems uneasy.

She assures him. "No problem, what's the matter?"

He confesses. "I have to be honest. I hope my honesty doesn't drive you away. I find you so attractive that sometimes I can hardly hide my feelings. I know I must not act on them, or it will ruin everything."

She turns away. If she admits the truth, she will have to confess that she is beginning to feel very much the same way. She walks to the tent and returns fully dressed in tee shirt and shorts.

The tea tastes good and she savors it. "What perfect jungle service. I give it five stars." They are relaxed again.

Jonathan makes some suggestions. "Maybe we can walk to a place I remember. There should be some spectacular views, and undoubtedly we will catch a glimpse of something unusual." It sounds great to her. They put the food away and head up the mountaintop.

Snap, snap, a branch crackles. A family of parrots screams before they take off in vivid flight. She captures their hurry on film.

Jonathan observes her. "You see things with your photographer's eye that I would never see. You see light and patterns where I see none. Your eyes catch movement so much more quickly than mine do. Thank you for sharing your skills with me. It makes me more aware."

She is flattered. She feels useful after all.

He continues. "Sometimes descriptions and details are difficult for me to write. Along with your helping me with description, you are teaching me about the woman I desire and how to create her... and much more, I assure you."

They are quiet as they walk along, peaceful and comfortable. At the end of the day, they take a swim before dinner. Jonathan leads the way to the cave behind the waterfall. There are stairs leading up to the small cave. As they enter the cave, they see primitive scratches on the stone wall apparently drawn by cave people. They try to imagine what the scratches meant to portray.

"Kang loves Jane," jokes Jonathan. They both giggle.

The sun sets, making patterns through the falling water before they turn to rainbows. They are enchanted.

Reluctantly, Jonathan gets up. "Come on, it's going to be too dark, if we don't head back now."

Katherine dives into the water and swims through the waterfall. Jonathan follows her. Dinner is simple, noodles, vegetables and tea. They are content. Life is easy and natural at this moment, so far from the rest of the world. Neither of them has any wish to be anywhere else.

Once again, totally exhausted, they fall to sleep. A loud crack of lightning, followed by deep booming thunder overhead, jerks them awake. The tent shudders with a sudden gust of wind as rain began to beat down heavily. Katherine, without thinking, rolls over toward Jonathan. He takes her in his arms, and holds her until the storm passes. Neither says a word. When the rain stops, they rolled back to their own side of the tent. Katherine is filled with confusion; along with deep physical longing. Her heart pounds wildly.

KATHERINE'S DIARY

Franko tells me he feels like he is growing younger as he grows older. Is that what's happening to me? Lately I feel more like a teenager with a crush, than a fifty-year old married woman. Before we took off, I hadn't thought about the sleeping arrangements. Well Really! Did I think we'd have separate tents? Dumb! Now that I think about it, I'm rather proud of myself at taking things in stride, and amazed at the same time. Wouldn't the twins be surprised at their mother? I never, ever imagined that I would be doing anything like this at my age.

I have to admit, I was frightened when the lightning struck. I felt so safe in Jonathan's arms. On the other hand, I am shocked at my feelings. I must be careful. I have to remember my promise to myself and to Jonathan too. It would be so easy to respond to him in the moment, but this is supposed to be all about my finding out about my strengths, not leaning on someone else. Besides, what about Bernardo? Who is this new person? Will I like the person I am discovering myself to be? I'm not sure. There are things that I have accepted as being "right" and I have tried to do what I thought was best for my family and myself. I have been happy up until now. Was I distracted by being a mother and a wife? Is there anything wrong with that picture? Who is this new Katherine?

I have to laugh at myself. The other night after my shower, I stood in front of the mirror and looked at my fifty-year-old-body. Actually I don't look too bad. I'm not model thin, but I'm not fat, either. Things sag a little, but still, I must admit I am rather attractive. I believe I would be attractive to someone my own age. Bernardo likes the way I look. That is fine. I think I might be a bit uncomfortable with a twenty-year-old fellow. But who knows? It might be lots of fun, but I fear I'd end up comparing myself to a younger women and I'd lose the contest for sure on that count!

I like the lines around my eyes and the white that's creeping in to my hair. I like being my age, and it seems Jonathan also appreciates whatever he sees in me.

What does he see? What is happening? Does his sharing of his feelings make me begin to accept that as truth? I've never paid much attention, because I've been with Bernardo for so long. I felt secure in his love; he knows who I am and accepts me. If anything happened to Bernardo, it would be difficult to try to date at this age. I don't think I could even do that. I must admit I love having this relationship with Jonathan, so far. I don't need a lover. It's easy and relaxing except for the moments when my physical desire rears its powerful head. I may have to stand back and watch myself while I learn. As the kids say, I gotta be cool.

MEDITATION RETREAT

"I've located a dark room, so you can do some work on your photos." Jonathan is proud of himself. He realizes that she would like to be able to print some of her work so that she can see how it looks before she continues on her photographic journey.

Jonathan writes each evening. "My writer's block has vanished." Not wanting to let the magic disappear again, he sits at his computer for hours. Katherine hears him laughing to himself. She imagines him frowning as his fingers move quickly over the keyboard, stopping only when he is called for a meal. Sometimes he forgets to stop and eat.

Long before Katherine rented the cottage, Jonathan had made plans for a ten day Buddhist meditation retreat in southern Thailand. Now, he offers Katherine an invitation to join him.

"I've always wanted to do something like that. It would be wonderful."

He explains. "I first became interested in the Buddhist way of life when I arrived in Thailand. Since I've been able to study my father's books, acknowledging his interest in Buddhism, my own interest has intensified. I want to know even more."

His sister Rose explained how his father disappeared from time to time. She believed he had gone on retreat at these times. He had been private about that.

They make travel reservations. A week later, they fly south to Bangkok, and plan to take a train the rest of the way. The description in the brochure gave instructions and described the retreat: Bring simple loose clothing, shoes that will slip off and on easily, no books, no writing in diaries. This was to be a silent retreat, a new experience for both of them.

Katherine is unable to remain quiet during the flight. She knows they will be silent for the next ten days, and she appears to be making up for that in advance. "I'm nervous. Do you think I'll be able to last the whole ten days in silence? What do they feed you?"

Jonathan laughs and laughs. "I'm not sure; I've never been on retreat either. I think it will be about facing yourself and what you most fear. Usually we stay busy, so we avoid feeling that." She senses that he is also nervous.

"In the west, we pooh-pooh the idea of a Teacher or Guru. There seems to be some sort of prohibition against learning from another human being. In truth only a higher soul can communicate what we need to know. There is so much indifference in our world. We have big egos and we are sure we can do it on our own. At least we think we can. I can't see where that has gotten us very far. We hire a teacher to climb Mount Everest, but not for learning about God and spiritual life. Unlike half the world, which live their religion full time, the Western ego is too powerful. It doesn't want us to be happy; it wants us to be discontent. We will do anything not to look inside ourselves. It's easier to go shopping, read an exciting book, have sex, work hard, drink; all of that. Seldom do we ever stay still enough to know ourselves. It is difficult to drop out and take the time for that."

Jonathan looks down at the book in his hands. The monk who teaches the retreats wrote it. "I think inside, we all have a yearning for something more. At this time many lives are turning into a nightmare. The sun is setting on the hopes of much of mankind. That's one of the reasons we need Teachers and retreats. We all need support. They say all wisdom is inside of us. We are born with it. It is already the case, the truth, but we need help to rediscover what we already know. Society seems hell bent on keeping us from knowing; nothing must change. Yet everything changes. Truth is freedom; and those in power fear our realizing the truth. I always felt that if we could learn those secrets, the "powers that be" would have no control over us. It doesn't matter what country we come from, it is basically the same."

Katherine nods in agreement. "You are right. At this time of my life, I'm just beginning to understand how Bernardo kept me busy, my kids kept me busy. It was always with my permission. I never had an urge or saw the need, to dedicate myself to a search for happiness. I thought I <u>was</u> happy. My friend Franko believes in reincarnation. He once told me that people with old souls have been in a spiritual life before. They tend to be more serious in this life. It's natural to them."

Jonathan agreed. "That makes sense to me. I wonder if my father believed that. Something brought him to this side of the world where spirituality and religion hit you in the face at every moment. People don't avoid it; they embrace it wholeheartedly and celebrate it at every opportunity. Yet, within most religions there are still people who want power."

Katherine enjoys the discussion. "I used to think religion was for people who were poor and had little to celebrate. Religion was just a crutch. I believed we needed to depend upon ourselves, be strong. Now I understand that actually has little to do with it. It does help some to carry on with adverse conditions, but I wouldn't call it a crutch. Better, I'd call it faith. With all the material things we have available in the western world, I seldom see the happiness in people's eyes that I do here. Isn't that strange?"

Jonathan looks into her eyes. "I've learned that my own worst enemy is me. My ego doesn't want me to be happy, but my heart tells me that I must search for the truth and live it when I do find it. The ego loves to tempt me, to distract me. Maybe that was what the writer's block was all about. I believe you came along to force me to understand. Since you've been here, I've been able to create again."

"That makes me feel so good. I'm glad to hear you say that. I have been used to having Bernardo be the one to voice ideas in my life. I believed he was the force behind everything. He's dynamic, well read, passionate and intelligent. I never questioned his authority. It makes me very happy to know I can inspire someone else besides my children. "

They are quiet for a while, lost in their thoughts. After the plane lands, they walk though the gate; no customs this time. There are crowds of people, and once the door to the airport opens, they are assaulted by the heat and noise. Their plans include taking the train from the Bangkok Noi Station in Thornburi. They are greeted by a mélange of cars piled up in traffic; drivers talk indifferently on their cell phones, always keeping an eye out for any movement on the road. The splendid display of BMWs, Mercedes and various sports cars does not move for ten minutes. Traffic is jammed like a parking lot; the air thick with fumes.

Seven men vying for their business immediately sur-round them. They choose the first man who comes up to them, and climb into the back seat of a tuk-tuk; the upholstery feels sticky from the humidity. It takes them over an hour to reach the railway station, as the driver moves gingerly through the immobile cars. Each traffic light looks like the starting line for a motorbike rally, with hundreds of motorbikes and tuk-tuks poised to take off as soon as the light turns green.

They reach their destination with plenty of time to have lunch. First they stow their belongings in a locker at the station, then they walk around the area. They luck out and find a delightful restaurant, hidden among the many markets that line the streets. They indulge themselves, sure that the meals for the next ten days will be bland and sparse.

"Five spice ribs with broccoli and noodles, and coconut soup."

"Don't forget the beer."

They walk back to the station, retrieve their belongings and immediately heard their train ride being announced. "Let's hurry." They rush to board the train.

The seats are wooden and old, but comfortable. Adopting a leisurely attitude, they gaze out at the countryside. Tropical flowers and palm trees grow abundantly; alongside the tracks it is a much different terrain than the pines groves that grow in the north. At the beginning of the trip, the train tracks take them near the ocean, and then veer back inland and later back again toward the ocean. A few hours later, they reach their destination and disembark at a beautiful old train station.

A monk in a bright orange outfit stands on the platform awaiting their arrival. He smiles brightly.

"Are you Katherine and Jonathan?" He speaks perfect English.

They nod yes. "Please call me Ballu, come with me."

They follow him to a car, where a driver awaits. He opens the trunk and puts their bags inside.

"We must stop by the market to pick up some food, if you don't mind. Something came up suddenly, this morning, and I was unable to shop before your arrival."

"No problem." They are delighted to accompany him. They will see what they were going to eat. They drive a short distance to an open market. Bins and baskets are filled with pineapple, watermelons, bananas, melons; many items Katherine has never seen before. In Chiang Rai, Kai had always given Jonathan a list when he went shopping. He just handed it to the sales people and they filled the order. Katherine had never paid much attention. They follow Ballu around the market, and carry his baskets. "What's this?

What's that? They ask him questions about the things he buys. It begins to dawn on them that the food they will be eating on retreat is not going to be dull after all.

The afternoon is nearly gone by the time they arrive at the retreat center. A feeling of peace surrounds the grounds and the building.

"It looks like a resort "Was this always a retreat center?" Jonathan asks.

"It was a hotel built by a wealthy man, at one time, many years ago. The government rerouted the road, and business fell off. A generous patron bought it and donated it to us for a retreat center."

Ballu shows them into the Center and calls the kitchen help to come and get the food. He leads them down a path to a small cottage. There are two single bedrooms in the cottage, small and simple, all white. Each room holds a single bed, a small closet, a shared bathroom with a shower, and a window that looks out to the ocean.

Upon parting, Ballu gives them instructions. "Now we begin the silent retreat. No more words. Dinner is at seven. We have a rule of lights out at ten. I hope you will sleep well." Neither of them had any doubt about sleeping well; the waves breaking outside beneath their windows, would lull them to sleep.

LEARNING TO BREATHE

They shower early the next morning, and are ready to begin their silent retreat at 5:00 AM. Quietly they walk down to the main hall. A monk silently directs them to the meditation room. They take their places on opposite sides of the room. Cushions have been placed for the meditaters. Katherine sits beside two older women, and a young blonde woman. Jonathan sits on the left of the room, alongside five men. Three men are similar in age to Jonathan, while two others appear quite young.

The room is dimly lit, the only decoration a vase filled with small purple orchids, spilling over the side. A moment later, more people enter the room. Katherine sits with her eyes closed, and relaxes into the silence.

Tinkle. Tinkle. The sound of a clear bell, tapped by an orange-garbed monk, catches their attention. He smiles sweetly and begins to instruct them about the Dharma, the practice.

"Although this is a silent retreat, I must first explain. You are all beginners and there will be questions. I will answer them after each meditation period. That will be the only time we speak."

He proceeds with his instructions.

"We surrender to the breathing, let the breath unfold naturally. By letting our breath unfold, without tampering with it, in time, we can do that with other aspects of our experience. We might learn to let the feelings be, the mind be. Normally we try to control the mind because of what we fear we might find there. Yet it is through letting the mind be, that we eventually learn to relax and go into the freedom that is our true nature."

"This practice is an invitation for everything inside you to come up. You will become acquainted with your wild mind. We all have that mind and it can be overwhelming at first. It has been there all the time, but we avoid getting acquainted with it."

"Our ultimate goal takes time to develop. It is not easy. We must allow everything to come up, with all its energy: anger, loneliness, disappointment and despair. We have to allow these things to arise and be transformed by the light of awareness. There is much energy in these states and most of the time we suppress them. Therefore, we lose all the energy that is in them and also expend a great deal of energy keeping them down. What we gradually learn is to let these things come up, and be transformed, to release their energy. You don't solve problems in this practice, you dissolve them."

"Be aware that the wild mind will try to discourage you. You will be aware of thoughts coming up. When the bell rings you will want to dash for the bathroom or dinner. We all want full and total enlightenment immediately, but it takes time and training. Your ego will resist. It is unavoidable. We want to get to a deep steadiness. There is no special way to breathe, so do what is most comfortable for you. You can count to ten if your thoughts interfere, and then begin at one again. It may be helpful at first, but later you will not need to do it. It is good to wean yourself from any aids as soon as possible."

"That is more than enough for now. Let's get started. The first meditation will be an hour, after which the bell will ring and we will gather in the dining room for breakfast and questions."

He rings the bell and leaves the room. Katherine sits with her eyes closed. She is grateful that she had done a few sittings in the past. She knows that she will not be comfortable for the whole hour. Soon someone begins to fidget a little, then another. By the end of the hour when the bell rings, they are all relieved to be able to move around.

In the dining room over breakfast, they sit, smile and nod to each other. Jonathan takes Katherine's hand and squeezes it as he smiles at her. They are served bichu tea, made from twigs. Fruit is served in large dishes, placed on the table in front of them. Beautiful small dishes with a blue pattern are passed around for each individual. Although Katherine expects to be hungry, she isn't hungry at all. She helps herself to a small variety of the fruit they had bought at the market the day before. All of a sudden, eating doesn't seem to be very important to her. She feels nourished by the meditation.

After breakfast, the monk leads them on a walking meditation through the gardens and along the ocean shore. It is the first time most of them had ever been silent for such a long period. Katherine hears the waves breaking, the gulls squawking, the leaves rustling as the wind blows gently up from the sea. She imagines she can even hear her own heart beating.

A subtle healing begins inside of Katherine. Her relationship with Jonathan has become increasingly intimate. Her feelings toward him have brought up things that she has never before allowed herself to feel. She has no experience to fall back on. She is changing, learning to be selfish because there is now more time for her. She is giving herself permission to go to the hidden places inside herself that she has never opened. She longs to talk to Jonathan, but knows that if she does, it will dilute her experience. For the first time in her life, she has a friend on the same wavelength. There will be time later for talk.

After the meditation walk, lunch is served; rice and vegetables. The next meditation is to be in the afternoon, now they are free to rest, take a nap, or do whatever they want to do. Jonathan and Katherine head to their cottage. Both are weary and want to rest. They fell into a deep sleep, only to be awakened by the sound of the little bell, announcing the next meditation at three.

As Katherine becomes familiar with the procedure, she begins to relax. She sits in the same place each time. The monk rings the bell, and they sit for an hour. That evening, once again all the retreatants have dinner together in silence. Everyone is in bed by ten.

Each day is a repeat of the day before, but no sitting feels the same. Some days the breathing is difficult, and some days, by the time the bell rang, Katherine realizes that the whole time she had been thinking about dinner, while the curry scent wafts in from the kitchen. When a mosquito began to buzz in front of her eyes, there was no way she can keep her eyes closed. But no way can she bring herself to swat it. It just wouldn't do in meditation. She goes back to breathing and being calm. She is relieved when the meditation comes to an end and she can escape the mighty mosquito.

Her back begins to itch. It is all she can do to keep from scratching. She gives in and scratches the itch, and having done that, returns to meditation. At that moment she understands attending to the matter at hand and letting it go, is the point.

Often when they finish a sitting, she begins to wonder what is happening to Jonathan. Is he having the same thoughts, the same problems? It is a private experience for each of them. Sometimes she feels a great sadness that cannot be explained. How is Bernardo? How are the kids doing? Are they okay? She left an emergency number if there is a real problem. Nobody has called.

Thoughts bombard her, one after another. Her mind feels like a wild animal. It is difficult not to be able to share and discuss what is coming up. During the sittings, Katherine watches her thoughts, and she tries to release them, but they keep returning over and over again. She attempts to keep her feelings neutral, but gets bored and begins to have fantasies of a different life for herself. She ponders questions. Would I want to remain in Thailand and become a full time Buddhist devotee? What will happen to the friendship with Jonathan when I leave for home? Can we continue to keep our relationship on a friendly basis when I leave? Do I really want that? What would it be like to walk into Jonathan's bedroom one night and crawl into his bed? What would I do if he came to me? She begins to let her mind roam free, to imagine things she would never have thought about before. Sometimes she realizes what she is doing, and begins to count from one to ten.

When pleasant thoughts intrude, it is fine, but when they are unpleasant, she resists and wants to push them away. Her back begins to ache toward the end of the hour. As the days go by, she feels she is becoming more mindful, more alert, and more sensitive. She learns to allow unpleasant feelings to arise, no longer wishing to avoid them.

She is sure Jonathan must be going through the same experiences, and wonders how he is able to deal without his computer at his fingertips. Normally he writes everything down, records everything. She misses her journal also. As for Jonathan, he always says he is unable to get anything straight in his mind, until he sees it written down on paper.

One evening the monk gives a talk about attachment. He explains that attachment is the fundamental basis for all suffering.

"It is attachment to things, being "me" or "mine", that is the supreme addiction. Letting be and letting go, is learned. In time, you will be able to tap into intensive happiness, a peace that arises when the mind grows calm. You want to remain in that state. You believe you can. But no! The ego gets frightened, because there is no room for the ego in that happiness. After a while, the anxiety diminishes and one finds oneself in a place that is wonderfully silent. When one comes out of that place, life seems easier." "The teacher looked at them and continued. "Your life won't move along in a tidy way, yet things won't be so overwhelming. Everything is impermanent. You will learn to practice with that."

The meals are simple and nourishing. The walks are a delightful experience after they had been sitting for so long. Each day feels more peaceful, and Katherine begins to notice changes in Jonathan that lead her to believe he is feeling the same way.

On the last night, the monk gives a talk about fear. "The normal thing we do when fear comes up is to do something else, to try to avoid it. We don't deal with our fear. We see it as a problem. You start to identify with fear. Through this way, you are leaning to give total attention, total mindfulness to the movement of energy known as fear, no longer identifying with it. You will find that risky and frightening. We are afraid to face our fear. After a while, you will get to a point where you can just be with the fear, no matter how terrible it seems."

"You begin to see that once it is observable you can work with it. You cannot escape, but you can learn to work with it skillfully. Yet, as you meet one fear, and get acquainted, you uncover others. Eventually the self falls away and you just breathe. While you identify with the body and yourself, you identify with the self, attached to the feelings. After a while, you no longer create self."

"Wisdom is the art of living happily. Much of being able to do that is to see how well we live unhappily. You look carefully at who you think you are, and what you think you are doing. Thereby you see who you really are."

He is silent for a moment. "The sitting tomorrow morning will be our last. Thank you all for coming. Please remember the silence until you leave, and even after that if it is possible."

The next morning, after their last sitting they walk back to the cottage to pack. They have made plans to spend the rest of the week on a beach farther south.

Sitting close together, as the train meanders along the shore, they are very aware of changes inside. They have truly opened to life…to its ten thousand joys and its ten thousand sorrows.

*How can I keep my soul in me so that it doesn't touch
your soul?*

How can I raise it high enough, past you to other things?

I would like to shelter it among remote, lost objects,

*In some dark and silent place that doesn't resonate when
your depths resound.*

Yet everything that touches, me and you,

takes us together like a violin's bow,

which draws one voice out of two separate strings.

Upon what instrument are we two spanned?

And what musician holds us in his hand?

Oh sweetest song

Rainer Maria Rilke

SOUTHERN BEACHES

They remain silent during the ride to the beach. To the onlooker, it might seem as though they are stunned, but that is not true. They have been silent for ten days, and have no wish to break the silence. The train is crowded. They sit close together, their bodies touching. Katherine had assumed they would be talking non-stop, but now she finds she does not want conversation. She enjoys the warmth of Jonathan's body, so close. In the past, they have seldom allowed themselves to touch, and it has been ten days since they have been close at all.

Something is different. Something has changed. Jonathan's cotton shirt and her thin cotton dress barely protect her from the exquisite sensations running through her body. Katherine's first reaction is to pull away, but then she remembers what the monk said about fear. She relaxes, and the part of her that she had held so tightly in control, begins to drift away. She is sure Jonathan senses the change in her, but he doesn't let her know. He doesn't want to scare her away. She knows he wants her; he has often indicated his desire. He is far more honest than Katherine, but he had made a promise in the beginning. She believes that he is honorable and won't try to satisfy his longings unless she feels the same.

As though Jonathan knows exactly what she is feeling, he speaks. "You are a delicate flower, coming into full bloom. I hope to be like the sun and nourish you, so you can build your strength. With good fortune, it may grow into wild abandon."

Her eyes open wide, as she looks directly into his.

"Don't worry about me, I will be patient and gentle with you."

His tenderness goes straight to her heart.

He lightens up. "Do you think I may have read too many romantic poems? I promised to keep our relationship strictly platonic, but, damn, you grow more beautiful and wonderful each day. I don't know if I will be able to keep my promise."

"Tell me what you feel."

"Like I have taken a long, long shower. So much has been washed away. I feel clear, clean, and empty of what has gone on in my life before this time. I feel as though I am starting at the beginning again."

Katherine agrees. "Me too. That's a good way to put it. I've never felt like this before. Being allowed to think, to feel anything at all and not have to back away, is such a gift. I must admit, I am a bit apprehensive about dealing with my wild mind. On the other hand, I realize it is a gift beyond comparison. Now I have to see if all this will continue."

Jonathan changes the subject while they eat their lunch. "One thing for sure, we must continue to meditate every day. The discipline will be good for us. You never saw the room upstairs at the house. My father must have done his sitting up there. When we get home, we can get it cleaned up and use it for what it is meant."

Katherine is thrilled. "That will be great. If we do this together, it will be easier. I know, when I'm alone, I tend to begin something and lose interest after a while. If we both meditate, we won't let each other down. I always wanted a partner in my learning. Bernardo never had the interest in mediation. He is totally involved in his own projects. "

A few hours later they arrive at a small fishing village. The cottage where they are to stay belongs to one of Jonathan's new Thai relatives. It is remote and relatively close to the beach. Jonathan has a key, and a map that shows the way to the house.

There is a small white building with a thatched roof at the end of a sandy path. The late afternoon sun gives the cottage a golden hue. Windblown plants surround the house, which faces the sea. A table and chairs are chained to a tree in a sand-covered patio. The wind has deposited a small pile of sand in front of the door.

The interior of the cottage is bright and clean; the sand has not crept through the crevices. It is small, only two rooms, a bedroom and a living room, dining and kitchen all in one. On the table is a note from the caretaker and also a map of the area, with suggestions about where to eat, to market and more. They put their things inside.

The sun is setting, so they run down to the beach. Brilliant red, orange and peach colors streak across the sky, while a long swipe of golden light flashes in flares. The sky rapidly changes as the sun sets. Entranced, they remain on the beach until dark. Shortly thereafter, they recover from their experience and without thinking they turn and wrap their arms around each other. It is the most natural thing to do. They stand silently in the dark; their hearts beat as one. Much later they release each other and head back to the cottage.

Katherine can hardly bring herself back to earth. She is unsure of what was is happening. She knows she and Bernardo have always been very affectionate, but never have they stood together for so long their hearts beating as one. Bernardo is always in a hurry, seldom in the moment, always on to his next project, his newest idea. This experience is new for her. Time has stopped for a few moments.

They are not yet hungry, having been nourished by the beauty of the sunset. Katherine feels as though she has gulped down many glasses of champagne. They walk back into the cottage where, upon investigation, they find a few snacks and some ice-cold beer in the fridge. They take their food outside to the table and sat quietly together. They have begun to communicate in a new way and neither of them wants to break the spell.

When they walk into the bedroom later, they realize there is only one large bed. They expected there might be twin beds.

"I'll take the couch if you like," Jonathan offers immediately.

Katherine looks at him with a little smile on her face. "I think we can handle this. It's a huge bed, and I don't want you to have to spend the rest of your vacation with your feet dangling off the end of the sofa. We can share it; after all it is bigger than our tent."

Jonathan is delighted. They shower and when they lay down, they are so very tired that Jonathan falls asleep, immediately. Katherine hears soft sore from Jonathan, and a moment later, she too is asleep.

They are happy that they won't need to awaken at five the next morning. When they walk outside, they see that a rainstorm has passed through the area. Morning has dawned bright and fresh. They devour a breakfast of ripe, juicy fruit. Limes squeezed on the papaya are sweet, and the juice from the mango drips down their chins.

"What are you ready for today?" Jonathan asks. "How would you like to rent a boat and sail around the islands? We can hire a person to sail us for the day. It's supposed to be beautiful."

"I can't wait. Let's get going."

They walk into town and make arrangements. An hour later, they meet the boatman and climb into a long narrow boat, with sails painted red, orange and blue. The boatman sits on one end of the boat, while they sit at the other end in a seat barely large enough for the two of them. Katherine has no choice but to lean against Jonathan.

Her thoughts come fast and furiously. She talks to herself internally. *He is nothing physically like Bernardo who is round and large. His body is lanky, bony. So different. I like that. Kind of like there is no padding to protect him. I never imagined I'd be sitting this close to another man. I wonder if I can trust myself to behave. It is getting more difficult all the time.* She bites her lip. *Remember what the monk taught me. Don't run from my fears.*

Her mind clicks back into charge. At least she hopes so.

Jonathan gazes out to sea. Both of them understand why filmmakers choose to film the beaches of Thailand for locations. Small islands rise from the ocean floor with mystically shaped cliffs and beaches.

Katherine looks through the lens, and begins to muse again. *This must be my wild mind at work. I've always been faithful to Bernardo; even though I am sure he has not always been faithful to me. I learned to accept his adventures as part of his work and his heritage. I never let him know I suspected him of being unfaithful. It was easier for me in a sense. I knew he would never leave me. He has always loved me. Now I am beginning to understand his temptations. I know that when people go on locations they get close and crazy. Actually I met Bernardo on location, now that I think of it.*

"Why so serious?" Jonathan asks, interrupting her thoughts.

Brought back to reality, she replies, "Do I look serious? Guess I was solving the problems of the world for a moment there."

The boat approaches an island; a sparkling white beach stretches out before them. The boatman pulls up to the shore. An ice chest stands full of beer. They order lunch for themselves and the boatman and sit on the beach while they eat. The whole day feels as though they are in slow motion. The only sounds they hear is the lapping of the waves, and the birds singing in the trees. They lean against the trunks of the palm trees.

On their return home, they shower and walk back into town for dinner. They find a small place and wander in. and order fish cooked on a barbecue with coconut milk and little hot peppers. The glass noodles are slippery and difficult to eat with chopsticks, but they persist until they have cleaned their plates. Hand in hand, they walk back to the cottage, a little tipsy from the beer. They sit on the beach while the music of the village fades into the background.

It appears to be wise to wear themselves out and be exhausted at the end of the day so that they will not have to deal with any emotions that might arise due to their closeness. The following day they rise late again and make plans for meditation.

"We must meditate, even though we are on vacation." They have already begun to miss the routine. Jonathan is happy to get busy. "Let's make a place to sit, right here in the sand." They take their dishes inside and rinse them. Scouting the area, they find a protected place behind the house. They arrange the area, find flowers and arrange them in a jar. They sit down to meditate. It is much different than meditating in the center, but the ritual is helpful, and they feel more centered when they are done.

After the meditation, they stroll along the beach. Jonathan wants to ask Katherine something. "There is a question that I have asked myself for years, over and over again. Sometimes I answer it truthfully and other times I find myself unable to do so."

"What is that?" She asks.

"Have you ever asked yourself what you would do, if you had nobody to consider besides yourself?"

Katherine turns quickly, and looks at him.

"Sometimes I have thought about that, but I could never imagine myself alone. I always include my family in my decisions. It's a tough question. Don't you think?"

Jonathan is hopeful. Maybe he can inspire her to think about that. "Another way to ask the question is to ask yourself this. What am I pretending that I don't know?"

He continues. "When I first asked myself those questions, it was as though I couldn't allow myself to even imagine it. We have been brought up to be responsible, to never let others down. I couldn't allow myself to go there.

Katherine smiles and says, "I'll have to think about this and observe what comes up. It might be lots of fun, in a way. Just because I believe people will react in some way, it doesn't make it true. And anyway, it will be good for the muse character. Won't it?"

"I agree with you wholeheartedly. Yes, and it will help you to learn to be true to yourself. As for me, once I allowed myself to do this, everything fell into place.

"I wish I'd been able to know my father while he was still alive, but his death was a turning point in my life. He left me the house and the money, and, in an instant, my life changed completely. I'm sure we all harbor abilities that we're not aware of until they are brought out by circumstances in our lives." He is quiet for a moment. "I have to admit that for most of my life I'd gone along, wanting to do the right thing, to make no mistakes, to be a good person, a good husband and a good father. I guess I learned that from my parents. You know …please them or they won't love you."

"I guess we miss out because of our fears." Katherine is reminded of her own situation with her parents. "I know it is sometimes that we don't want to hurt anyone, but we care so much about others that we forget about ourselves. It's not the other person's fault; it is ours, for not respecting our own needs. I try to teach the twins to be independent. But sometimes I haven't taken my own advice."

"Okay, let's make another pact. Remember what the monk taught us. Let's give ourselves the freedom to let our wild selves out of the bag. Let's allow our minds to run free and have a true adventure of the soul."

Katherine replies happily in return, "Let's go."

They shake hands in agreement; threw down their towels, run into the ocean, and swim far out toward the horizon.

KATHERINE'S DIARY

Our vacation is nearly finished. We head back to Bangkok tomorrow. I hate to leave this place, this experience behind. It has been an amazing thing for me, to be at the other end of the world, so far from everyone I know. In a way, I'm invisible. This is a new kind of freedom. I must congratulate myself. Even my thoughts have been given freedom. I must confess at times I lust after Jonathan in my heart. The other side is that I mustn't give in to my attraction...but is it only lust? If I ever truly let myself be with him physically, it might change everything and become difficult. I might have to run away. REMINDER: How can I be his muse, if we become intimate? I admit I am confused. My wild self is feeling very wild. I do need to get acquainted with this side. Maybe I can do this some other way. I must have learned some skills, being around the movie business all these years. I can play the role of the muse. I can play the role I choose. What role is that? It is up to me, I don't have to be just one character. That is my choice. I read a book about a young woman who hangs out with Sherlock Holmes. She is adventurous. I could be a detective. I could be Collette; she was loved by both sexes, attracted to younger men. I could wear men's clothing. I can imagine myself living in one of those Rosamund Pilcher cottages, a sensible but romantic Englishwoman. I could be Auntie Mame and do whatever. I have to laugh at myself. I don't know if I should share these thoughts with Jonathan or not. Maybe it will be better to surprise him. If I tell him what I am considering, it might spoil the whole thing. I wonder how he will react.

I need to take more photos. This is my own rebirth experience, and I want to record it. One can never record their first birth, but the second birth, or rebirth, makes it possible.

I met a woman in Ayutthaya at the pool. We had lots of time to talk one afternoon. She shared her adventures. She had traveled with all sorts of men, to many far away places. Now she has settled down with her present partner. I loved hearing her stories. She inspired me to do what I have done, in a way. She once hiked to India over the long trail pilgrims make to Kashmir. She no longer does exotic trips, but she has her photos and memories. Lucky woman. She has been to Maccu Pichu, to deepest parts of Africa, and lives to tell her stories in photos. She told me about her favorite trip, to Bhutan, a county, whose success is rated not on national gross product, but on gross national happiness. That is fabulous.

I've never been brave, never had to be. Maybe I'm doing this all backward. I've always been cared for. Although I am sure I can be strong, nothing has really challenged me and made me willing to step into the unknown. I've been sheltered, first by my parents, and then by Bernardo. I may be a late bloomer at my age.

I believe it is time to follow my own path, even though I'm not sure what that means yet. It is scary. What could come up? What is my true identity? That famous philosopher (I forget his name) writes about searching everywhere for yourself and in the end, you find you were there all the time. Was it Teilhard de Chardin?

I see now that real happiness comes with growth. Thanks to Jonathan, and my life at the moment, I'm growing rather quickly. I know it's up to me to allow myself to be in the right places and situations so I can carry on with my journey.

I understand what truly radiates from people is more valuable than their caresses. Sadly, for the most part, we settle for physical relationships, without going any farther. Jonathan is filled with a current of life that attracts me.

Bernardo has energy also. The difference is that Jonathan doesn't overpower me. I feel there is room to grow when I am with him. It's not Bernardo's fault that I have let him do what he does. I have not bothered to develop my strengths, and so I've gone along with whatever he asks Why? Time to ask myself.

I feel like someone who has been on a long trip. This trip is inside. For some odd reason, I gave up early in some ways. I sat down to rest and enjoy while everyone else went on ahead of me. Now I have to hurry to catch up. I understand that taking the easy path never gets you to the top, or gets you there too late. I'm not sure what is missing. Is anything missing? I believe Jonathan is looking for joy, boundless joy. He had locked himself up too, yet somehow his father released him.

In England, I felt sorry for myself, when I found I was not needed. Somehow, it didn't seem fair. I had plans; Bernardo and his needs would be my life. You know the old joke, tell God your plans, and then He laughs at you. In reality, the fact is, he didn't need me and that has been the greatest gift I've ever received. What I do with it is up to me.

Bernardo...............................Jonathan

I feel confused and giddy. On one hand, I feel as if I have no right to consider a relationship with Jonathan. Still I feel like a teenager with a crush. I never tire of him. Never get enough of him. I wonder why this has happened. Is it a test? I feel so happy, so full of joy. And truthfully, I believe joy is a pretty good way to go.

I'll try to keep my mind on the goal, not the obstacles. I must relax and let nature take its course. If I live in the moment, it will all work. I hope all my reading and studies can help me now. But that's just my head. My heart is what is confused. It's the one part of me that's not letting me off the hook. No matter how much I try to rationalize that this is only a friendship, it is beginning to feel like more than that. I picture the mind like a computer. I put in the information and experiences, and somehow it is supposed to come out with a clear logical explanation. Right now, my mind isn't working like it is supposed to. I am not clear; I am confused. I am high on my life, and I love the way I feel. I don't want to hurt anyone. If I go with my feelings, what will happen? Can I live with that? It becomes more complicated with each passing day.

The way I must enter
Leads through darkness to darkness
Oh moon above the mountains rim,
Please shine a little further
On my path.

<u>The Ink Dark Moon</u>

BACK TO THE BEGINNING

During the train ride, there is time to converse. Jonathan asks, "Katherine, how do you keep in touch with your family?"

He is surprised when she says, "I haven't contacted them at all."

By now, she feels safe telling this man anything. When she first arrived in Chiang Mai, she would not have felt comfortable telling him this. "The day Tony brought me here, I gave him a number to call Bernardo or the kids if there was any emergency. I also left Tony's number, with Emily, Bernardo's secretary, so they could find me if anything happened. Tony could call Kai. She would know where to find me. "

Jonathan is surprised.

"I'm surprised at myself too, normally I would be calling home all the time, but this trip is different; I promised myself a true retreat."

They have not yet discussed their experiences at the retreat. Katherine is curious, and listens carefully when Jonathan begins to share what happened to him.

"What a gift the retreat has been for me! I desperately needed that. I needed to be reminded that real happiness is growing, moving forward in my life. I get stuck and tend to go into a deep depression to try to avoid my feelings. It is difficult to recover from that. Fortunately, something usually jolts me back to movement. For instance, you show up. When I went to pray to the Buddha for inspiration, I was a wreck. I know there is a higher power now. When you appeared, that was confirmed. One of these days, I'm going to have to surrender this ego, and let the higher powers run my life."

"Were you ever religious ?" She asks.

"Not really. I was a pessimist before I came here. On the other hand, underneath, maybe I really wasn't one. I was waiting for truth. Somehow, I can now see I was at least able, and prepared to move physically, mentally and emotionally when opportunity arrived. It's letting go of control that is so difficult."

Katherine smiles. "I think you are right. Some of us take it easy and unintentionally avoid growth. It is not on purpose; it just doesn't seem to occur to us that we might be happier if we worked harder at our lives. Perhaps we actually are content, we have enough at the moment. It never dawned upon me to want more until this last year when my whole life changed, and pushed me into a different frame of mind.

"Now I feel like I want to reach the top of the mountain on my own. But I also feel hesitation; I don't want to make mistakes. The truth is, we always make mistakes, or apparent ones. I understand now that the path itself is important, not the destination. The path I am traveling right now feels right to me. Thank you, Jonathan."

She gazes into Jonathan's eyes. He blushes slightly.

"Oh, Katherine! No change is worthwhile, unless it is an ascent, and that's difficult to keep doing every day of your life. Sometimes I get so tired and weary and I want to give up. Before you arrived, I longed for someone to share my life and inspire me. I had no idea it would be you. Finally, I decided I would forge ahead, give up searching for happiness; just see what came up. In doing that, I have found joy. You have made me aware that I truly have the capacity for joy. What more can I ask?"

He smiles and reaches for her hand. "There is far more to this relationship than we can imagine. How on earth did we come all the way across the whole world to meet again? That has to be the first sign that it is right. Since you came, I feel as though I have been unwrapping Christmas presents in every moment. Each one gets better and better. Wonders wash over me all the time now. I have to remember the teaching of the monk about how not to try to hang onto the moment, and to accept the gifts as they come. It's magical, I tell you."

Katherine can sense a new behavior in Jonathan. He appears to be enchanted. Sometimes she feels self-conscious when he watches for her responses in different situations. She must remind herself that she is the muse. She senses that he breathes her in. It is his way of learning and creating the character for the book he is writing. But often, it feels deeper than that, and she responds with her heart, although she tries to hide it from him.

The train chugs lazily into Bangkok. Jonathan has some surprises in store for Katherine. He has planned some interesting side trips before they returned to Chiang Rai. He can see she is pleased, and he is excited and happy that his plans had been well received. Their relationship has been cemented in some unexplainable way during the time they have been together at the beach.

"First we take a bus to Kanchanaburi, and tomorrow we will head to the Cave Temple of the Golden Dragon. We have an appointment with the 'Floating Nun'. She meditates while floating on her back in a pool of water, and then tells you what she sees in your future."

That sounds perfect to Katherine. "Let's have lunch." They stop at a noodle restaurant on their way to the bus.

Over lunch, Jonathan explains more about the Floating Nun and her powers. "She began floating many years ago. She is nearly seventy-five and she is passing her tradition on to younger disciples who come from all over Thailand. If we are fortunate, she will give you blessings, along with reading your future."

"I can hardly wait." Katherine recalls her Tarot reading. Their tourist cottage overlooks the river. The tiny building stands on stilts above the water, and has thatched roof. They stow their bags, and wash off travel dust. Katherine walks down the pier to photograph the sparkling lights reflected in the water; ripples give them a mysterious appearance. She is sure these shots will be amazing.

Dinner consists of whole spicy chicken, sweet sticky rice that they can pick up with their fingers, spicy green papaya salad, and ice-cold beer. The chicken is grilled before them, served with two sauces, one the usual sweet and sour, and the other, roasted red pepper sauce.

The next morning, they climb a series of steps with dragon-sculpted handrails leading them up a craggy mountainside behind the main sanctuary. They pass a tower similar to the red brick wats in Ayutthaya. A path takes them to a complex group of limestone caves. They follow a string of light bulbs through the front cave and emerge above the wat. A spectacular view of the mountains and the valley below is revealed. One section of the cave is so low that it requires them to crawl and almost duck-walk.

"Glad we didn't wear our best clothes."

By the time they arrive at the grotto, the nun is ready to float in the pool. She smiles at them and then climbs into the pool and closes her eyes. Her clothes float in the water and she hums from time to time. The water is steaming and not very clear. Katherine is certain this must be the original Floating Nun; withered and tiny, she looks well over seventy years old.

"It's probably all that time spent floating in the water," Katherine thinks to herself.

They wait silently for a long period of time. Finally, the nun emerges from the pool. Two women appear and wrap her in a dry robe. She motions for Katherine and Jonathan to come and sit beside her. They understand that it is unusual for her to actually speak with them. A young woman sits beside her and translates.

The little nun takes Katherine's hand. Her hands are cool after spending the time in the water. After a few minutes, she begins to speak. She looks directly into Katherine's eyes.

"You are new, reborn, fresh and flowing. There has been a death of the old self, as when one is born. It will take a while to learn the new ways and it will not be easy, but eventually, it will come. It is time to trust yourself, and let go of the old picture of your life. You have support from unusual sources and will discover much about yourself that you never knew existed."

She smiles at Katherine. "You may be confused at times, and there will be major changes in the future that will be bewildering, but will eventually lead to greater happiness after a period of time."

Next, the nun turns, peers into Jonathan's eyes and takes his hand in hers. "You are in a perfect place now. After many years of, merely enduring your life, not knowing what to do, I can see a gift has been made to you by someone who had love for you, but was unknown. Now you are in a position to do what you most desire. You will be successful, perhaps famous."

She smiles and once again looks into his eyes. "Your heart is being broken open right now and that is good. You need that. You are learning to feel deeply, to discipline yourself, and that will help your work. Go slowly, stick to what you believe in, and eventually you will reap your rewards."

With that, the diminutive little nun rises and slowly walks away, leaving Katherine and Jonathan alone.

Stunned, they are silent, trying to digest what they have heard and to understand what all it means. They realize it will take time for what she has told them to sink in. They stroll back down the path and explore ancient buildings on the grounds.

"How does she know?" They both ask abruptly in unison, laughing out loud.

The next day, they are off to see the new museum in Kanchanaburi. It is familiar because of the film they had seen long ago, <u>Bridge on the River Quai.</u> It was a tragic part of World War II. It is estimated that sixteen thousand POW's died there, along with nearly a hundred thousand coolies. The Imperial Japanese Army brought the materials for the bridge from Java during their occupation of Thailand. It was built to link Thailand to Burma, and was called the Death Railway. The allies bombed it in 1945. The museum tells the whole story. It has been a serious day for both of them. The weather is cool compared to Bangkok, and they enjoy the break in the temperature.

In the afternoon, they head for Bangkok, where they plan to tour the city before they return home. Although Katherine has been there a couple of times with Bernardo, in addition to the day she went to buy the books, she has never really become acquainted with the city. This will be Jonathan's Bangkok.

They check into a small guesthouse and decide to take a boat ride around the city. The view from the river is quite different from the view of the city she had from the balcony of the Shangri La Hotel (where Katherine and Bernardo stayed when they first arrived.) As they slowly move along, the river Katherine is engulfed by the life of the people who live there as though immersed in a film. She feels the breeze on her skin and inhaled the smells; everything is in reach, it is so close to them. At the floating market they see wooden canoes laden with multicolored fruits and vegetables, paddled by Thai women who wear indigo-hued clothes and wide-brimmed straw hats. Buildings encroach right down to the river. Naked children jump into the river and there is a gathering of dogs. The dogs all sit together on a pier and seem to be having some sort of a meeting.

Jonathan whispers in her ear. "I'm going to tell you a secret, Katherine. You see those dogs on the pier. They are the ones who actually run Thailand. The politicians don't realize it, though."

"I think you might be right; they look so intelligent."

After the boat ride, they eat a simple curry and noodle dinner, and head for Pat Pong.

"This is a place most women usually don't go, Katherine. I want you to understand some of the things I have learned about my newly adopted country." They remain in the taxi and look out the window. It is a gaudy atmosphere, and women call to them, and offer numerous kinds of sex. It is wild and sad at the same time; the realization comes to them that all these people must sell themselves to make a living. It is a reality of life in Bangkok for many.

Jonathan explains to her how he had become interested. "Rose mentioned a friend who needed to support her family, as is the custom in Thailand. She came to Bangkok and looked for a job. When she couldn't find other work, she ended up working as a prostitute so she could send money home. In a short time, she contracted AIDS. It broke Rose's heart; she is working on a project to help those young women, to keep this from happening in the future. The truth is tradition dies hard. The whole world comes to Thailand to get its kicks from sex. The sex market is huge, and nothing sells better."

The story makes Katherine shudder. "I can't imagine my own daughter having to live and die like this. There must be something we can do. Let's talk to Rose when we get home. I need a worthwhile project in my life. Maybe this is it." She sleeps poorly that night as she continues to think about the problems

They fly back to Chiang Rai. It feels like home to Katherine now. She is living in the moment and her thoughts seldom wander back to her life a few weeks before. It seems strange and unlike her old self, but she accepts it.

After unpacking, they hurry upstairs to see the meditation room that Jonathan has told her about. Entering the dusty room, now only used for storage, they see that, with a little cleaning, it will be a simple task to get it ready for their meditation. They spend the afternoon washing, cleaning, placing flowers and cushions around. They burn incense to clear the air. The space becomes sacred. They agree to have their first meditation in the room before they go to sleep that night.

After her shower, Katherine wanders out and sits by the pool. She is happy and peaceful.

"Dinner is ready," calls Jonathan.

"Coming," she answers, realizing how much of a family they have become.

"Aren't we funny?" asks Jonathan. "A few weeks ago, I would never have imagined myself here in this situation. Could you? But then a year ago, I couldn't ever have imagined I'd be living here in Thailand, let alone sharing adventures with a beautiful woman, sitting down to dinner with her. I never considered myself lucky. Now, to top it all off, I have the freedom to do what I always longed to do. Write."

After a couple of glasses of wine, Jonathan relaxes. He sits back and looks at Katherine. She experiencing some uneasiness but reminds herself of her role as muse. She decides to do something out of character.

"Can we go dancing tomorrow night? It's Valentine's Day. Do you celebrate that in Britain? The hotel has a lounge with an orchestra. I'm sure it caters to tourists and will have some sort of celebration."

He is pleased. Katherine is positively gleeful. She jumps up and dances around the room "I feel like dancing in Chiang Rai. I am ready to play. Are you game?"

"Oh yes, my dear, game as can be." He says, his heart beating faster and faster. He has forgotten for the moment that the nun had reminded him to go gently and carefully. It is with great difficulty that he will be able to behave, as he must if he doesn't want to frighten Katherine away.

KATHERINE'S DIARY

He watches me closely. I turn around sometimes because I can feel his eyes upon me. His gaze is intense. He studies me, my female ways, everything. To be truthful, it excites me. It may well be that he knows more about me than I do myself, by now. The depth of my feeling for him surprises me. I don't know if it is right or wrong, but it is happening. In times past, I would never have allowed myself to go "there." The retreat gave me so much freedom. The possibilities have always been there for something like this to happen, I have never given myself permission to feel like this.

At times I feel intoxicated. Like one more glass of wine and I'll be over the edge. But it hasn't happened. When I am truthful with myself, I do feel remote from Bernardo right now. It has been this way for a few months. I was wrong to think I could walk right into his life and fill myself up at his expense. Although he loves me, the most important thing is his directing. Even when he finishes a film, he is already on to the next one. He keeps himself so busy, as though he is afraid he won't be able to get enough done in this lifetime. The kids always kept me busy, and I never had to think about how I felt.

Being here with Jonathan has given me the capacity to look more clearly at my life, and feel the differences. I think back to my parents' marriage, and realize that it was more like the marriage Bernardo and I have. My father was the boss, the star, the decision maker. My mother went right along with him. She made his life her work. Up until now, I have followed in her footsteps.

I've never been the focus of anyone's attention the way I am for Jonathan. I'm not sure if I actually understand this relationship, but it appears to be a gift with perfect timing. There may be strings, but I'll deal with that later. I have to look at my life with open eyes. I never imagined being in this place. I assumed my life would continue as it has for twenty-five years. If I hadn't taken this time by myself, would I have known anything different?

I haven't had time to absorb what the nun told me. "A new life, death of the old life or self." I can feel something very deep is happening every moment. I am surprised at the person who is emerging from within the old Katherine. The phoenix is rising. Never in my life would I have imagined that I could come here on my own. This freedom to be in a place where nobody knows me at all. Jonathan will probably notice a difference as I free up myself, but he really can't compare me to the old me.

I feel as though someone has cut an opening in my brain, my emotions, and my heart. The channels are clearing out old debris and memories. I no longer have the inner map; I have to trust. I'm learning to think with my heart and feel with my mind. The nun said "major changes," what does that mean. Can anyone actually predict the future? Can she be telling the truth? Sometimes, lately, I imagine life with Jonathan, yet I don't believe I would ever be able to leave Bernardo. Still I wonder if Bernardo really, ever hears me.

Jonathan listens to me intently. Of course, it is different for him; he is not my husband, nor indeed my lover. Once sex enters a relationship, everything changes dramatically. He is a true friend, and that makes the difference. I realize men and women seldom are friends without some sort of attraction. I feel his attraction, yet I'm happy we agreed not to get involved. It gives me freedom to be who I am. I don't have to please him, just to inspire him.

My kids would say, "Chill, Mom." I must stop taking this so seriously. It's time to have fun, and not be so self-conscious.

The best thing I learned at the retreat was to be in the moment but not to try to hang onto it. If I'm able to stay in that frame of mind, everything is always perfect.

The nun said I would be bewildered by major changes. What can that be? Already I am trying to figure out my future. Stop!! At least she said there would be happiness after a period of time. I'll try to concentrate on that and let the rest go.

FINDING PURPOSE

"Jonathan, I need to talk with you, I need to ask you some questions. Questions about how you see me. Would you be okay with that?' Katherine desperately needs a sounding board.

"Katherine, I'd be happy to do anything you want me too." Jonathan is pleased that she has come to him with personal concerns.

"How did you see me when I first came? Have I changed in the last few weeks? I feel like a different person.

"Do you want me to be honest about what I see?"

"Please don't coddle me."

"Okay here goes. When you first arrived, I saw a woman endowed with charm, a mild temperament and grace. You were someone for whom compliance was not a strain.

You always attended to the needs of others. Neither of us had thought about taking up a spiritual practice. I am sure you didn't want to be thought of as pushy, or ambitious, you would rather be thought of as feminine and caring. I believe that if you had not come on this trip, if you had happily gone on doing what you normally do, you might have been able to endure, but a rocky ride would have come later."

"Go on."

"The mind's contents become disconcertingly visible. You are fortunate that you decided to do this retreat for yourself. The way you have taken to the meditations make me sure you have had an inner life all along, but you never expressed it outwardly. Examine the way you were able to look into the heart of the matter that was troubling you, instead of blaming another"

"I never blame anyone else."

"I know that, and I admire that in you. What I love is that you have been able to light the fire from the embers inside and now you are burning so brightly."

Katherine feels very good, very happy to hear what he has to say. She knows she is changing, rapidly and drastically and the reflection Jonathan portrays is reassuring.

They settle back into a routine. Katherine asked Jonathan to invite Rose over so they can question her and find out how Katherine can possibly help the young women in Bangkok.

The sad young women on the streets of Bangkok have had a deep effect on Katherine; she wants to do something to help. How can she make a difference? Rose is happy to respond and explains that many young people are dying of AIDS. It is an epidemic in Thailand. Katherine is aware that she will be unable to change the whole country, although perhaps there might be something she can do.

After lunch, they get down to business. Jonathan listens and observes while Rose explains the customs of her country to Katherine.

"Daughters are required, by custom, to support their families. Often they have to go to Bangkok to get work. If they are unable to find work, they often fall into a life of prostitution. Their life span is so short."

"It is not as though people frown on that profession. You do what you can do. You see girls coming out of temples on their way to work as whores. It is as though religion has one place in our lives and responsibility, another. In the end what is left are ruined lives, death, and babies in orphanages."

Rose knows of a woman who runs an orphanage in Bangkok. "The woman, Silvere, has contacts with dying mothers and might be of help."

When the netted fence of spider webs
Darken my ruined house
Can hold the wind in its strands
That's when these troubled thoughts
Will blow away.

<u>The Ink Dark Moon</u>

BACK TO BANGKOK

Rose brings the information a week later. She gives Katherine the phone number of Silvere in Bangkok In the meanwhile they have taken a few side trips, but Katherine has lost interest in sightseeing. Her focus is different now. They meditate twice a day; Jonathan writes for a few hours.

Jonathan is torn between spending time with Katherine and, on the other hand, doing what he has come here to accomplish. At times it appears that he is ready to give up writing the book altogether.

He makes an intimate confession to Katherine. "In my dreams, I make love to you, but in reality, I know there is no way anything can work out between us. I know you are faithful to Bernardo and I won't try to convince you to be otherwise."

Katherine is deeply touched, and to be honest, a little more than excited about his feelings. She senses that he understands she is also very attracted to him.

Sometimes Jonathan disappears for a day or two. At other times, he is unable to open to her. He appears to be far away, lost in his mind. Katherine understands that he is trying to distance himself from her, when his feelings became too intense, too emotional for him to deal with. Occasionally he shuts himself in his room and pours his emotions into his work.

"We'll leave for Bangkok next week. Silvere will talk with us and find us a guide. She will do anything to help her cause."

The numbers about prostitution in Thailand astound them. Although it is against the law, it is suspected that there are at least 200,000 people engaged in the sex industry, including women, men and children. It is said that the revenue from the sex industry is fifty percent higher than the budget of Thailand. Will they ever be able to make a difference?

"The truth is," Jonathan, surmises, "there has always been a market for sex as long as there have been records kept. Money pours in from people looking for Nirvana in someone else's crotch, unmindful of the cost to humanity. Slavery still exists. Do you think you will be able to handle seeing all of this?"

"I don't know, but I hope so. I just know that when Rose told me about what happens, something broke open inside of me, and I feel compelled to do this."

They stay in the same guesthouse where they had stayed on their previous trip. It is near the orphanage. When they meet the gorgeous woman with the silver hair, they sense her love and dedication to the children. Silvere has always taken photos of the children when they arrive at the orphanage and continues to photograph them as their health improves. When parents from all over the world finally adopt them, they have a record of their short lives.

Katherine begins taking photos of the newest residents of the orphanage. The babies in their cribs with their huge, dark eyes look straight into the camera as well into her heart. Each one is longing for love and acceptance. Katherine wishes she could take them all home with her. She knows even that will not make a difference. The beds will fill again, quickly. It is more important to go to the root of the problem.

The other part of her task is more difficult. The babies have a chance for a better life if they are adopted, but the women and young boys they see in Patpong are never going to have a chance. Nobody will adopt them or change their lives for them.

With their guide they are able to enter places they would never been able to see, like nightclubs where magenta lights flash, where the girls do their bum thrusts and their tit wobbles to the music, doing anything to entice the tourist. Most of the girls have a working life of ten to twelve years before they become ill, or succumb to physical ruin. No longer able to work, seldom do they find a caring "Mamasan" who might help them get prepared or get educated for their future.

Most of the young women with their ancient eyes are beautiful. The depth of their pain cannot be felt, only imagined. Katherine shoots roll after roll of film that week. She photographs girls wearing dresses with colored tags on their backs, denoting their asking price for the night. She sees people high on Yaa Baa, the mad drug, more powerful than heroin. Others imbibe beer and smoke ganja.

Later at night, the half-naked bodies are clothed in tee shirts and jeans, as the girls head for home. Pine-Sol scents blend with stale beer, cheap perfume and cigarettes. Most girls have at least one child at home.

Katherine has no idea when she will be able to return to Thailand, so she photographs everything that she might be able to use in the book, anything that might make a difference in their wretched lives.

When they say goodbye, Silvere hugs them both, and as the tears fall from Katherine's eyes, she promises to be in touch, and as soon as possible, to bring the plight of these people to the world.

They fly back to Chiang Mai, and Katherine puts her film away. She needs to give herself a break, to distance herself from all the horrors they had seen. Feeling raw, and aching for the people, Katherine realizes that because she had never been trained in photojournalism she hasn't the ability to set aside her feelings yet. The photos will tell the whole story, but she will also need to put words to the pictures. She has no idea what would happen, but she plans to put her heart and soul into it.

"Jonathan, thank you so much for taking me," she say one evening while they sit watching the sunset. "Before we returned to Bangkok, I was permeated by the beauty of this land and the people. Now I have been penetrated deeply by the darkness, the hopelessness, and also the acceptance by the people, by life as it is. In spite of all the bad things that happen, I feel a kindness in most of the people, and I'm grateful for the love they offer in their own way. It is impossible not to be compelled to make a difference." Love, not reason, should make decisions.

Decisions based on reason not love are karmic.

Therefore let the heart be your intelligence.

The heart is unreasonable.

The heart is mad.

And the heart is the ground that I call you to walk on.

The only way to overcome the murderer,

that is the comos, is to love.

Allow the heart to break and be that sign.

Be a feeling being.

Then you cannot be murdered,

you cannot be a fool,

you cannot be deceived.

Love is the victory.

Love is the meditation.

Love is life.

You simply must become willing to love.

Allow God to be.

To love is to be truly religious.

To consort with the Living One.

Adi Da Samraj

TIME TO SAY GOODBYE

Three months have passed too quickly. It is now time for Katherine to return home. No matter how much she wishes she could stay forever and to continue her relationship with Jonathan, she has made a promise to herself, a contract. She has always prided herself in keeping her word once she has given it, never letting others down. That part of her has not changed. She doesn't want it to, no matter how much she may suffer as a result of it.

She is well aware that the last three months have been the most important time of her life. She feels reborn and fully alive. She has gained an inner strength. She has expanded her talents and if she is truthful, fallen in love. The part about falling in love is the most difficult for her to admit. She realizes now that she is capable of deeply loving one man, while still loving another. For her own sanity, she keeps insisting to herself that the relationship between her and Jonathan is only a friendship, a partnership. There is no way she is willing to go deeper inside and totally investigate her feelings about Jonathan. She cannot allow herself that last freedom.

Jonathan is going through his own predicament. She is no longer just his muse. No. He has fallen deeply in love and could never deny that. He knows that he has found the perfect woman. He has never imagined that could happen to him. He had read about desirable women, tried to imagine them in his life, but he knew it had been wishful thinking. Now although he holds back his urges because of their agreement, at night, in bed, the anguish of parting leaves him nearly crazed.

When he comes out of his room for breakfast, Katherine feels his distress. Sometimes he doesn't eat at all. As their time draws to a close, both of them begin to pull away, to distance themselves, avoid each other so that they will be able to get used to being apart. Jonathan remains in his room for hours, writing his book. Katherine spends less time with him, knowing their situation has no happy solution. She is going to miss him too much when she leaves.

Sitting by the pool one afternoon, Katherine begins to speak. "I remember what the Buddhists say, about wanting things to remain the same. That it is the cause of unhappiness. I have never felt that more clearly than at this moment."

"I don't know what I am going to do without you, Katherine," Jonathan says softly. "You are so much a part of my life; you have crept right into my heart. I never imagined that this could happen to me."

She smiles at him. "I know we made the agreement in the beginning, but neither of us could have imagined what was going to happen. Could we?"

"No. We had no idea. It seemed like it would be easy enough when we first met. How unknowing we were."

Katherine continues. "In the beginning we didn't know each other. I had no idea, how much of me was missing when I arrived here. I wasn't feeling good about the way my life was going, or about myself. I am almost embarrassed to find myself feeling and acting like this at my age. My children went through this during their teens, you know, discovering themselves. But at fifty, I'm supposed to be done with this. I'm an adult. Or at least I thought I was."

"And I was such an old sourpuss, my glass always half empty, before. Even though I inherited this wonderful place and had the opportunity to write for the first time, I was stuck. All at once, I understand serendipity. It is so amazing that we ran into each other on the train in Wales, and then reconnected all the way across the world."

Katherine nods her head in agreement.

He continues, "I had no idea what an important meeting that was. I had seen lovely women before, but there was something different about you, something that stayed with me and didn't allow me to forget you. You were my muse long before I ever realized it."

Katherine sighs deeply. "Ah, yes, the muse. I think that is the only thing that is going to save me. I mean, I have been able to inspire you to write a best-selling novel."

"That remains to be seen."

Katherine adds. "I know it's true. One of the reasons I'll be able to leave you is because I realize that with me here you are unlikely to finish your novel."

"Sadly, that may be the truth."

Tears fill her eyes. "How will I be able to endure waking up each morning, knowing we won't have our talk over breakfast? I wish I could share my experience with Bernardo, but we know that is impossible. Even though he may not always have been true to me, he is terribly jealous at times."

Jonathan attempts to make it easier. "It may be best to cut off our relationship completely when we say goodbye. Just forget about "us". Just go on with our separate lives, diminished or not."

"It makes sense to do it that way, sounds easy, but won't be. I have never lived so close with, nor spent so much uninterrupted time with a man. Not even Bernardo. This is different. I don't know how to explain it, even to myself. I feel I have found my soul mate in you."

"What do you think our karma is?" Jonathan tries to make her laugh. "Who were we in another life? Do you think I could have been your mother?"

She laughs. "Oh, very funny. I don't want to be so serious, yet here we are, as dramatic as the kids. I can remember the drama that accompanied the beginnings and the ends of their romances. I don't feel much different myself. I wonder what they would say about the way I'm behaving lately. I have a feeling that children prefer their mother to remain their mother and not go off on a romantic fling."

Jonathan closes his eyes for a moment. "Do you think that all there is between us is the possibility of a fling, my dear?"

"Oh, no, not at all. I'm just trying to lighten up, when in truth, my heart feels heavy and broken."

Jonathan stands up and pulls her to her feet. He looks deep into her eyes and embraces her. They hold each other as they stand in silence their sadness penetrates their hearts. What began as a light-hearted adventure has turned into a deep relationship. They are both deeply affected. Jonathan, in the beginning had seemed dour, but now his shell has dissolved. He is feeling pain that he has never before allowed himself to experience. In this moment, they have truly learned about the wound of love. That wound where one loves so completely, that one becomes capable of opening and feeling the loss of that love. Without that vulnerability, their love will never be complete. Jonathan has learned what depth the pain can reach, and he understands, clearly at this moment, why he had never before allowed that to happen to him. This time, there is no way he can back out, or hold back. This is a fine ecstasy, the deepest pain he had ever felt, and he wonders if he will ever be able to recover from the loss.

KATHERINE'S DIARY

I am no longer the woman I was when I left for England last fall. I have my defenses like layers of an onion. I never questioned the conditions of my life before. I had no idea what was in store for me. Before I came here, I imagined myself spending the rest of my life at Bernardo's side. I thought I'd be able to work with him, to take care of him. I figured I'd be a wife and mother, and always be there for my family.

How wrong I was. The changes have been subtle. I never noticed while they were happening. Now, I cannot avoid looking at myself. Never could I have imagined how different my life would become. Never in my wildest dreams could I have imagined the changes that have taken place inside of me. I rejoice in being a woman. I feel light-hearted, giddy, and carefree. Even as my world seems to fall apart, I have a sense that it is being rebuilt from within. I hope I will have the courage to be true to myself, and to follow what for me is an unbeaten path. I am sure this has happened to many women before me. The truth is I would never have allowed this knowledge to penetrate me when I was younger. I thought I was so wise. Now I see how mistaken I was.

This isn't easy. Sometimes these lessons break my heart. Thankfully, now, I seem to have found a higher power. The meditation helps so much. There must have been a pattern set somewhere inside. It seems to be there now, to give me strength when I feel ready to give up. I have no idea what the future will bring. What I do believe is that I will have the strength and faith to live fully, without fear, from now on.

I always believed that, if I did things right, and lived in certain ways, my life would work. I bought into that. How wrong I have been. Life is all about learning about yourself, peeling off the layers, dropping old beliefs, and seeing more clearly. I thought I would get to a certain point in my life and just be able to relax. What happened? Am I getting senile? Sometimes I tingle all over. Who is this woman I have become?

Which shouldn't exist
In this world,
the one who forgets
or the one
who is forgotten?
Which is better,
to love
the one who has died
or not to see
each other while you're alive?
Which is better,
The distant lover
you long for
or the one you see daily
without desire?
Which is the least unreliable
among fickle things—
the swift rapids,
a flowing river,
or this human world?

The Ink Dark Moon

KATHERINE'S PAST

Katherine wants to tell Jonathan more about her life with Bernardo. She has sensed that Jonathan doesn't really care to hear about Bernardo. Nevertheless, Katherine feels compelled to tell him a few things before she leaves.

"Let me explain a little about earlier life. Jonathan. And maybe, if I share a little about my relationship with Bernardo, it will help us both to make sense of what has happened now. Do you mind?"

She has no idea if Jonathan is willing to hear, but he sits back and relaxes. "I'd be happy to listen."

"When I married Bernardo, I was able to put down roots for the first time in my life. I happily gave up my career without any regrets. In exchange, I had a fabulous, exciting husband who wanted children, and my dream house in the country. Soon I had my twins. Seasons came and went, and I loved being at home. My life was full and I was happier than I imagined I could ever be.

"I knew and accepted the fact that Bernardo would always be busy, often on location. We visited him, wherever he was shooting when there were school vacations. Time passed and the children grew up. It became more difficult to find time off from school to visit. We spent summers with him. I was patient; I knew in time the kids would be off to college and I would be there for Bernardo.

"I never worked in film again, nor did I have any desire to do so. When the kids grew older, I created my own projects. I photographed old, empty houses in winter. I climbed over snow banks, waded through icy brooks. Those houses, full of people during the summer, were deserted once the leaves fell. To me, they felt so lonesome. I imagined they longed for the people to remain there. I called my book <u>Where are the Winter People?</u> After I had taken the photos and developed them, I realized the book would need some poetry and I surprised myself by being able to write a poem for each photo. It took me a long time, but it was an artistic success. It was well received, if not a best seller. I gave a book to all my friends for Christmas. I've never attempted anything like that again.

"As the years went by, Bernardo's star rose higher and higher. A few years ago, he developed a problem with his health. He had prostate problems. I had never even imagined he would ever be in ill health. His operation was a success, but since then, I noticed him slowing down. It might be his age, too. When I joined him on location in October, I hoped I could be of help, but I soon understood it took a lot out of him, when he tried to work and also be attentive to me. Work took all his energy.

"The time had come for me to find what I was meant to do. It wasn't about taking care of him, but taking care of me, so he could relax."

"By the time we reached Ayutthaya, I was well aware that I needed to change. A woman I met on location became a mentor for me. She has lived her life with a busy man and learned to make herself happy. We became very close on a quick trip to Chiang Mai. On my return, I made the decision to take a three-month retreat for myself. I never dreamed it would turn out this way."

Even if I
Repeated love's name
Forever,
Could outward life match
The intensity of our hearts?

<u>The Ink Dark Moon</u>

TIME TO FLY HOME.

Katherine's ticket home has her routed from Chiang Rai, through Bangkok, to the international flight to Frankfort, and then on to New York. She and Jonathan decide it will be better to spend their last night at a hotel near the airport, to start the process of leaving. Departure time is very early. Katherine hopes an unfamiliar room might make it easier. Both she and Jonathan are already mourning, painfully aware that there will be an immense hole in their lives where their relationship has been for the past three months.

To simplify things, Katherine has already mailed many things home. With only one suitcase now, traveling will be easier. Upon her arrival in New York, she plans to spend the night with Franko, and then head home to Connecticut the next day. She is unsure when Bernardo will return home. If things go as planned, he will have finished the film a month ago and will be in Hollywood, working intensely with his editor. In a few weeks they will be able to resume their lives together.

To be truthful, Katherine wants time to herself when she returns home. She is going to have to gently let herself back into her old life. She is familiar with the needed re-entry time that Bernardo always craves when he returns to ordinary life after a film. She is going to have to give herself the same freedom and space.

For the first time in her adult life, she has been truly on her own. It has taken her a long time to feel the need of that freedom. Now it has burst out like an explosion, although it doesn't show on the outside. There is no doubt in her mind that she loves Bernardo and her children. More importantly she has found someone else to love...... Katherine. She wants time to introduce the new Katherine to her family.

Katherine and Jonathan check into the hotel.

"One or two rooms?"

They exchange glances and smile. Katherine says, "One will do."

They are shown to a lovely room with a balcony overlooking the gardens. Walls of soft green and blue compliment the flowered fabric on the chairs and bedspreads. It feels like an indoor garden. Yellow orchids, cascade from a tall vase placed on the dresser. Two chairs by the open windows seem to invite the soft breeze inside. It ruffles the sheer curtains. The sky darkens. Heavy black clouds swirl ominously toward them. A storm is in the air. They sit on the balcony and watch the storm approach.

"Shall we go down to dinner?" Katherine asks.

"I have a better idea. Why don't we order room service, stay here, and watch the storm come in?"

"That sounds perfect to me." She realizes she doesn't want to spend her last hours with anyone but Jonathan. Knowing it will be her last Thai meal for a while, she is extremely extravagant, obviously trying to distract herself from her loss.

Menu in hand, she reads off her choices, describing each dish. "Ground beef salad for starters; it includes minced beef, cilantro, lime juice, scallions and roasted sticky rice with tiny red Thai chili peppers. Sweet pork cooked in coconut juice, a stir fried chicken with basil and green curry, a plate of vegetables with glass noodles and for dessert, lotus seeds, floating in a pool of coconut in a tapioca base with jasmine extract added."

Jonathan laughs. "Do you think we will be able to eat all this?"

"I don't care; indulge me. It's just something I want to do," she confesses. "I don't know when I will ever be able to eat like this again."

A bottle of champagne in an ice bucket has been waiting for them on their arrival. They open it and sit on the porch.

"I love champagne," Katherine exclaims. "Years ago I saved a bottle of expensive champagne; I waited for someone to come and share it with me, sure who ever showed up would be the perfect one. That was before I met Bernardo. When I met him, we drank red wine instead. I no longer have the champagne, of course but perhaps it was you I waited for. That particular bottle would be flat by now. This is perfect."

Glasses held high, they make a toast to their future. "Whatever may come?"

By the time dinner arrives, the bottle of champagne is empty, but the champagne has not erased their sadness. They have little appetite.

"What a waste, I can't eat right now," Katherine sadly picks at her food.

Jonathan attempts a few bites, but soon pushes his plate away. He puts his fork down. "Let's sit on the balcony............"

Jazz plays softly on the radio, and for a few moments, it is peaceful. Suddenly the energy of the storm fills the room. Thunder rumbles above them and shakes the building. The sounds reverberate in their ears. Seconds later, lightning cracks. Over and over, the thunder booms, lightning flashes. Suddenly the lights go out. They move into the room. When the storm has passed, the only sounds they hear are water dripping and jazz music that mysteriously continues to play softly on the radio. Amazed, they realize the radio must have backup batteries in case of emergencies.

"Katherine, I am trying to be as good as possible about this. I thought I could keep my emotions under control, but I'm unable to. It's impossible. The truth is I have finally found my love, the woman I dreamed about, the woman in the Japanese poetry. I can hardly bear that I am going to lose you." He chokes on his words.

Katherine's heart is breaking, too. She wants to make it easier. "Jonathan, try to remember that most of the great writers have suffered, and that seemed to be what brought them to their utmost understanding, their losses exposed their talent. You must remember that."

'Yes, well, maybe my priorities have changed since I met you. Maybe being with you is more important than being a writer."

She can understand what he is feeling; she is at the breaking point, too. "I know it seemed so easy in the beginning, to make promises to each other when we first met. We had no idea what was in store for us. The truth is, after all that has happened between us, now we are two different people. I came here to find out who I might be and I must admit, I am surprised at what I have discovered. I never expected to feel so free. I'm not sure how Bernardo will deal with the new me. I'll have to face that."

"Ahh, yes, back to those promises. I never had a clue my heart could melt so quickly, that beauty would walk right into my life and entice me as you have. I know, I begged Buddha to bring you. I had always heard that one must be careful what one prays for. I wasn't careful, and I have found the most wonderful woman in the world. How am I going to live without you?"

The storm has passed, but the lights are still out. Water continues to trickle from the roof tiles, bushes and trees. The music plays on. A candle flickers on the table. It is a scene out of an old Bogey and Bacall movie. They are the actors, trying to put on a good show, but in truth, their feelings are much deeper than that.

Miles Davis's trumpet solo works its way into their hearts. "Katherine, this song is one of my favorites." Jonathan holds out his hand to her. "Will you give me the last dance?"

"How can I resist?" He draws her into his arms. They move slowly in place. The heat of his body penetrates Katherine. She can feel his heart beating and she wants him desperately.

"Jonathan, do you remember when we made our agreement?"

"Yes, of course. What a mistake. "

"No, listen to me. You said you needed to know everything about me, so you could understand and create your character. Right?"

"True."

"Have I satisfied my part of the deal of our agreement?"

"I think so."

"That's not true. I haven't given you everything. I have let you down and myself too. I haven't lived up to what I promised you."

Her eyes fill with tears. She reaches for him. She has hugged him before but dancing is more intimate. She wants feel him deep inside, feel his pain, and satisfy her longing.

He closes his eyes as they move slowly together. When the song ends, they are still for a few moments. Continuing their embrace, she slowly leads him to the bed.

His eyes are volcanic as he anticipates her moves He reaches for her dress as she slips it over her head. Overtaken by intense excitement, they throw off their clothes, finally unrestrained; they fall into bed, where they both long to be.

A whole new world opens. It is as though it is the first time either of them has made love. They have never known such loving. Impossible to hold back any longer, their emotions are set free. Their pent up needs are released. Their loving is wild and breathless. They completely surrender to one another. What they have always sensed must exist, now exists between them. Heart to heart, flesh-to-flesh, deep in love, they adventure and explore. They are perfect lovers, reunited; filled with an agonizing joy. Flying Into the Sun. Together, they are more than they ever have imagined they can be, neither of them is capable of thinking of the future.

They gaze at each other, their bodies glowing with sweat and happiness. Brightness fills the room. Skies began to clear. The door to heaven has opened.

"Jonathan, to be honest, all my life I longed for someone to make love with where my heart beat in the same rhythm. Long ago, I gave up on that, figuring I'd read too many romances, yet inside, the small dream was tucked away, along with the hope that it could happen."

Jonathan remains silent.

"The moment we touched tonight, it happened. Your love opened a wound from which I may never recover. I've never been so vulnerable. Before tonight, I tried to keep up a shield. I was sure I could stand back, enjoy our relationship and then leave for home, and remain untouched. I am not untouched, I am touched completely."

Jonathan reaches for her and wipes away the tears that fall softly. His eyes are also filled with tears.

Wisely, he reminds her, "No matter what we believe, we never truly love completely, because we know our loved ones are going to die and we will be left behind, deserted. We refuse to acknowledge that loss, so we withhold a part of us that we might give. Therefore, we never love completely. Tonight, for the first time, I totally understand what that truly means. With you, I have allowed myself to feel the wound of love. I will carry you with me all my life. Parting from you feels like a death, but we must part. At least, for once in my life, my dreams have come true."

She tries to smile, but is unable. Jonathan can say no more. He draws her into his arms.

The alarm rings too early for them. They shower and are off to the airport. Jonathan has to be the strong one today. Even if he wants her to stay, they both realize they need to be free to allow the future to manifest in whatever way it might. He cannot not ask her to stay. He would never forgive himself, if he were to break up her family and ruin her life. If there is to be a change, it will have to come from Katherine.

"Katherine, I have been a somewhat patient man all my life, but you have awakened many things inside of me. We need to let this all sink in. We have to give ourselves time to sort out our lives. In the meantime, I will be writing."

They slowly walk to the departure gate, and too soon the call for Bangkok comes over the speaker. They sit close together, holding hands, not wanting to release each other until the last moment.

"Last call for boarding!"

When they embrace, he reaches for her face and holds her softly, looking deeply into her eyes. He imprints her on his heart. She turns, and walks numbly toward the attendant, hands him her ticket, looks back for a moment, then slowly walks away, down the ramp and into the plane. She wants to run back to his arms, never to leave, yet she knows she cannot do things that way, or she will never be able to forgive herself.

He watches the plane as it taxies out and takes off.

So in tune with each other, they can feel each other calling out with their whole being and earthly passions, "Please come back."

In this world
Love has no color—
yet how deeply
my body
is stained by yours.

<u>The Ink Dark Moon.</u>

HOME AGAIN

Katherine lies back in her seat and closes her eyes. Numb, trying not to feel anything, she is unable to open to her pain and loss. It is like she is in shock and needs a neutral safe place for the moment. Fortunately, her seat partner is a woman with a noisy talkative child. They keep her busy with conversation and questions. She feels like a zombie, but they are unaware.

On the second flight, she sits alone. The pain of leaving Jonathan seeps into her consciousness. She is heartsick and lost. On the other hand, she feels more aware of the universe than ever before. Not ready to deal with everything, she falls asleep. While she sleeps, she dreams. She relives her last few hours with Jonathan. Happy to once again feel the moment she gave herself permission to surrender to Jonathan's needs and desire, and to be truthful, her own.

She is more attached to Jonathan than she has ever imagined she could be. She yearns for him, the feel of him inside of her, his body beside her, his lips on her lips. She wants him, more than ever, and begins to wonder if it had been preordained that they would find each other. Her body still vibrates with the excitement and feelings she has discovered with Jonathon. She has been able to open totally to another being.

Katherine orders wine with dinner and is sleepy again. She gratefully closes her eyes afterward and sleeps much of the rest of the trip home. She awakes when the stewardess hands her a warm, moist cloth to wash her face. She is groggy and weary from the long trip. On the flight from Munich to New York, she is able to write in her diary.

KATHERINE'S DIARY

What will happen now? I feel like a different person. I've become aware of an unknown part of myself. This wildness has been hidden deep inside me. I never gave myself such freedom to act on my feelings. I don't know why I was like that. I didn't question it. Maybe my parents expected me to be good and I never wanted to be different. Now I can no longer depend on my life being orderly. Everything is out of control. I've moved to a different level and I have no idea what will happen next. It is important to get home, and get grounded and see how I feel. I have been gone nearly six months.

The old me would never in a million years have slept with Jonathan, no matter how much I might have wanted to. I never thought I'd be capable of being untrue to Bernardo, but last night felt so right. The whole experience was amazing to say the least and I wouldn't trade it for anything, now that it has happened. To be truthful, I wish I were back in Jonathan's arms right now! I know that is impossible. Already it seems like a dream. Will I be able to put that dream behind me in the future? Is there a new me, alive and stirring, or will I disappear, wimp out and let the old Katherine back in?

This heart
Longing for you
breaks
into a thousand pieces—
I wouldn't lose one.

The Ink Dark Moon

NEW YORK

By the time Katherine's plane lands in New York, she is totally exhausted. Franko meets her at the airport and they taxi back to his apartment. She begs off talking that night. All she wants to do was fall into bed with her thoughts and memories. She needs time to sort them out before she talks with her old friend.

In the past, Franko has urged her to have adventures of her own, especially when she had confided in him that she was worried about Bernardo being overly occupied with some actress he was trying to direct. Katherine had balked. Now that she has opened her heart and shared everything with Jonathan, she isn't too sure that she wants to share these deep feelings with anyone else. She wants to savor the love that has grown between them and to talk about it might make it sound trite to someone else. She doesn't want to feel it is only a romance. She is well aware that it is much more than that. She also knows that she cannot go running off like a schoolgirl in love for the first time, even though she feels that way.

Katherine is well aware that Bernardo has always been the center of her life. He has made her the center of his home life too. He would be crushed if she ever left him. His health seems to be failing a little, his age catching up with him. He has always been good to her in his own way, and she knows he loves her deeply. She also loves him, and their relationship of over twenty-five years is important and binding. She cannot walk away from him. Looking at the big picture, she is well aware that there is more to consider than her desires and what she yearns for at this moment.

In Franko's spare room she crawls into the bed with a multitude of pillows and the softest down mattress in the world. Immediately she falls into a deep sleep.

"Okay, tell me all," Franko demands the next morning, his mouth stuffed full of bear claw fresh from the bakery. He knows they are Katherine's favorite. "You seem different to me. What happened over there?"

She wraps her hands around her coffee cup for warmth and takes a sip. "I'm not sure I can tell you yet. To be honest, I don't know if it's that I am unable to, or just not ready." She hesitates. "You know when you read a great book, how you live in it. You become intimate with the characters and the situation so that when it comes to an end; you hate it and want to continue your experience?"

"Yes."

"It's sort of like that. I don't want my experience to end. I want to hang onto it, not start a new book. I fear I will never find anything so wonderful."

"Give me a hint, at least." Franko teases her, hoping for more, much more.

"I feel as though I have been on a different planet for three months, like it wasn't even me...... at least, the me I know." She closes her eyes, allowing herself to remember. "It was as though someone handed me a new script and told me to play my part, to create this new character, no holds barred. You know what I mean?"

Franko smiles. "Yeah, sure."

"I jumped in and did it. I forgot about my past and my future, and just lived in the moment. Nobody knew me, and I was free to be who ever I wanted to be. I never had a chance like that before in my life."

Franko smiles again. "Didn't I keep telling you it was important to get out of Bernardo's shadow? I've been telling you that for years. You had to learn to cast your own character. Sounds like you heeded my advice. I know you are worn out from the trip, but nevertheless, you look wonderful."

"Thanks."

Franko is relentless. "Who is he? Is he a dream man? How did you meet? What happened?"

"Whoa! Wait a minute!" Katherine laughs at him. "I'll explain when I can. So much of what happened is still a mystery to me."

They sit in Franko's cozy living room all day long, sending out for food, drinking wine while Katherine shares as much with Franko as she feels she is capable. She tells him about the agreement she made with Jonathan when they first met.

"What does he look like? Is he tall, dark, and handsome? What is he like?" He is thrilled.

"It's sort of hard to describe him. He is nothing like Bernardo. He is tall and thin, rather lanky. Not handsome really, but I find him attractive in a serious way. Sometimes he has this pissed off look...sort of dangerous, but I found it sexy. I couldn't read him sometimes, and he does the unexpected. He is balding a bit, his hair is dark gray. He is moody and possessed when he begins to write. He'd disappear for hours. One time I didn't see him for a couple of days." She smiles to herself. "Yet I have to admit, he is the most attractive man I've met in years. There is something about him. Did I tell you he is Welsh?"

"Does he have that wonderful accent?'

"Oh yes. I love listening to him read poetry. His voice is...it's very sexy."

"How about the rest of him, is that very sexy?" Franko breaks into wild laughter.

"No comment."

"Okay, I'll cut you some slack. I can see you are fading. How about you take a nap and we go out to a little café near here for dinner. I'll drive you home tomorrow."

She happily agrees and goes to her room.

****

The next day, she dozes much of the way during the trip to Connecticut. She is still suffering from jet lag, so she plans to give herself time to recover in the following days.

The countryside is coming alive. She has been gone so long. It was autumn when she left for London. The trees had been orange, red, yellow and green. The air had been crisp, the flowers cut down, and the gardens put to sleep. Now she sees daffodils peeking up in flower gardens, and tulips in bud. Things have changed completely since last winter. So has she.

Gloria, the housekeeper, meets them at the door and takes Katherine's bag. "I'm so glad to have you home." She brings them a cup of coffee in the living room, and after Franko is finished, he is on his way home. He has an appointment back in the city that evening. He knows she needs to decompress.

"Call me when you feel like talking. Better yet, come back and visit when you are recovered from the trip." Franko waves as he drives off.

Katherine is relieved to be the only one at home. She walks back inside, pausing for a moment to take stock. The two Goldens come to greet her, waging their tails, but they follow Gloria back to the kitchen. Katherine understands. She deserted them for six months. She cannot blame them. They will remember her in a while.

The house is warm and cozy. Gloria has set a fire to take off the chill. Piles of magazines and mail have accumulated while she has been gone. They are carefully arranged on shelves in the den. In the entrance hall a large flower arrangement with a card from Bernardo sits on the table. She will call him this evening.

None of her boxes have arrived, so she has little to unpack. She calls the dogs, and takes a walk around her garden. She loves spring, especially when the little plants peek through the earth. The tiny buds of red, yellow and green on tree branches look ready to burst into light green bloom at any moment. Forsythia already offers bright, yellow blooms.

The change in air soothes her body. She has been so warm during her time in Thailand, where the sweat poured off her skin. Often it had been warm enough to make breathing difficult. She sits on a stone bench beside the pond, still weary. Her skin breathes in the coolness and she is grateful. Yet, perversely, somewhere deep inside is a longing to be back in the heat and all that went with it.

The aroma of roast chicken and freshly baked bread greets her as she walks back into the house. The dogs head for the kitchen, hoping for a tidbit. Gloria tries her best to make Katherine feel at home. For dinner, no noodles, no vegetables sliced small, or teeny, hot red peppers to remind her of her loss. Most things in her home would never remind her of Thailand. Only the feelings, emotions, and thoughts, circling through her mind will remind her of Thailand, and what she left behind. For a few moments, she wonders how she will be able to deal, once her family returns.

My body—
so used to you
even to think
of forgetting
too sad to consider.

The Ink Dark Moon

BACK TO NORMAL

Katherine calls Bernardo, but he isn't available. He's in meetings until very late. It is three hours earlier in California, so by the time he gets her message it is too late to call back. He doesn't want to awaken her, besides; he is exhausted.

The next day they speak to each other for the first time in three months. It has been so long and Bernardo is happy to hear her voice again, but he immediately reverts back to his pattern. "How is my little adventurer? I've missed you. Tell me about your trip. No, not yet. We'll talk all about everything when I get home. Are you okay?"

Bernardo is back in charge.

As soon as he begins to speak, Katherine feels bombarded. She tries to cover her reaction. After all it is she who has changed, not Bernardo.

She says," It sounds so good to hear your voice again. You sound wonderful. I can't tell you how grateful I am for these last three months." She wants to warn him about the changes that have taken place inside of her. "To put it simply, I feel as if I've finally grown up."

"What do you mean? You have always been grown up!" Bernardo is puzzled.

"No, not really, I had so much to learn. I've always depended on you to tell me what to do and how to live. I never took responsibility. I understand now that I have been a burden. You have so much else to do. This time for me was the best thing I could have done for both of us."

"Oh, my darling Katherine, you have never felt like a burden to me."

"Bernardo, you're so good to me. I realize you would never think of me in that way, but on this trip, I had to face the truth. I can't wait until you are home; we have so much catching up to do. When do you think you will be able to return?"

"In two weeks we should have the major editing done, and I'll be able to come home for a while. Later on I will have to return for the scoring. Maybe you can come out here with me then."

"Are you pleased with the film?" She asks.

"I'm pleased and excited, but the producers are very difficult. They are young and geared to a young audience that has no patience. They want things to happen quickly, too many fast cuts. I want time to build up the suspense, let the story evolve at its own speed. We argue daily about this. I'll explain more when I get home. Maybe I'm getting old. You know I usually love this part of the production." He sounds disappointed.

"Oh Bernardo, don't even think like that." she quickly responds, hearing something different in his voice. "They'll see it your way, it always worked. You know your style is unique and your films are beautiful."

"I'm anxious to get home to my beautiful wife, and the springtime. I have to run now. I love you."

"I love you too." But he has already hung up the phone.

She sits back and closes her eyes. Bernardo sounds very tired, even though he has tried to cover it up. Katherine senses that from now on she will have to take control of her own life and not add stress to his.

The next morning she feels lazy; somehow it is good to be home. No matter how wonderful travel is, and how many wonderful things have happened, underneath it all she always had the faint feeling that she could not settle completely. There was always the awareness that eventually she would return home. Familiar ways beckoned from the depths of her mind. One thing for sure, her own bed is always the best.

Downstairs she pours a perfect cup of coffee. "Gloria, thank you so much for taking such good care of everything. The place looks great."

The dogs, now alert, remember her, and when she rises to go for a walk, they happily follow her through fields, and down the familiar paths that surround her home. Trees, with the exception of the towering pines, are not yet in bloom. The pond is still, but once in a while a bubble works its way up to the surface. She wonders if it is a sign of fish or frogs. It is too early for the peepers who sing at night. They will come later in the spring. Sometimes their singing wakes her up at night. She loves their rites and imagines they are singing their own "Ode to Joy."

As the days pass, Katherine has no desire to leave the house, to visit anyone, or to shop. She leaves that to Gloria. The only place she ventures is to the photo shop, where she gets supplies for her darkroom. She does not want to share her photos with anyone yet. After being gone for so long, it is difficult to completely settle in. The dogs do their best. They come, snuggle up to her, kiss her and wait for her to pet them, as though they understand that she needs to be grounded again.

A few days later, her boxes arrive. Excited, she unpacks and puts everything away quickly. Although she is tempted to linger on her thoughts, she knows she must get busy in the darkroom before Bernardo returns. The moment she begins to work on the photos, she is filled with apprehension. She is opening Pandora's Box. All sorts of things run through her mind. Will she be drawn back into the last three months, unable to exist in her present life? Her thoughts drift back to

Thailand. What is Jonathan doing? It is already a day ahead. Is he sleeping while she is awake?

The next morning she begins work in earnest. While photos float in the developing solution, slowly coming to life, she watches. She is back in Thailand. These are the photos of the time Jonathan took her on their first trek. Her heart slows to a stop. She closes her eyes and dreams herself back to that last night they spent together. At last she begins to weep with longing and gratitude for what has happened, no matter how painful it is now.

She truly understands the teaching about how unhappiness is caused when one tries to hang onto a moment, or anything, no matter how wonderful or perfect. Being human, she is unable to convince herself that she wouldn't want to be in the same situation again.

There are hundreds of photos. She is surprised at how many she has taken of Jonathan. She has caught him in every pose and mood. In the photos he reveals the deepest parts of himself, and she treasures that. He never minded her photographing him, although he always joked about its being a waste of film. On the other hand, somehow he seemed to want to reveal himself to her. In studying him, while focusing for a photograph, he had begun to give her an opportunity to learn about herself. She reminds herself that it would be best to put the photos of Jonathan aside until she has time to explain what had happened to her in Thailand. She is not sure what she is willing to tell Bernardo about him.

Bernardo arrives two weeks later by limo. Katherine offers to pick him up, but he tells her he would rather take the limo. It will be easier for her. He is back to fathering her, no matter what she says. She wonders if he even hears her.

Katherine is shocked when she first sees him. Bernardo is thin and looks exhausted. Normally he is full of vitality and energy. This is different. She sees the toll the film has taken on him; she longs to take him into her arms and revive him, but she knows that it would offend him. The Italian Stallion never wants to admit weakness. Instead, she throws her arms around him and they embrace. They walk into the house, hand in hand. The late afternoon has turned cool and she has a fire waiting for him. They sit and talk.

"You look lovely. You're wearing my favorite dress." Although he tries to show interest in their conversation, she feels him fading.

"Are you hungry?" she asks. "There is soup and home-made bread ready. Are you ready for a nice glass of red wine?"

He nods.

'I'll bring it up to your room. Why don't you relax?" She is glad she has planned for something like this.

Bernardo is relieved. "Yes that sounds fine. I must admit, I'm weary tonight. I'll go upstairs and take a shower."

Katherine goes into the kitchen to prepare a tray. She is worried about him, but doesn't want him to see her concern. She carries his dinner up to him.

The walls of his room are deep red with off white trim, rich and warm. A velvet quilt Katherine made for him years before covers the huge bed, imported from his family home in Italy. A bright fire in the small fireplace warms the room.

"This feels wonderful." Bernardo is already in bed, propped up by pillows. She pulls a small table up beside the bed, and places the tray upon it. She pours a glass of deep red wine for each of them, then climbs onto the bed and sits beside him. She begins to rub his neck and shoulders, feeling how tense he is. He puts his arms around her and draws her to him.

"Thank you so much; this is just perfect." He sits back and takes a sip of wine. A moment later he begins to eat the soup. "I missed you so much. I don't ever want to be apart for so long again."

He eats slowly. When he finishes, he brushes the crumbs off his chest. He lies back on the pillows, and pulls the blanket up beneath his chin. Katherine moves closer to him. He places his hand in hers. His other hand is on one of the dogs, which has jumped up on the bed to lie beside him. A moment later, he falls fast asleep between the two of them.

After a while, she gets up, carries the dishes down to the kitchen and cleans up.

KATHERINE'S DIARY

I wanted the evening to be special for him. Perhaps I felt a little guilty. God knows I wasn't sure what I would feel. I have changed dramatically, but I don't think it shows. I love Bernardo so much and I wore one of his favorite dresses, the one he calls sexy. It's black, low cut and usually excites him. I wanted him to find me desirable. I wanted to respond to him, to resume our old relationship. I was shocked at his frailty, to see how much he had aged in three short months. All at once I can no longer think about exposing my new self. He needs me more than ever, at this moment. I knew I would never be able to leave him. Was the trip to Chiang Rai wrong? I've been so happy about all that happened to me, and now I feel confused.

I went back to my room after I cleaned up. It's funny; I worried so much about how it would be to make love to Bernardo again. I didn't have plans to ever be with Jonathan again, but I was nervous anyway. I didn't want to compare my experience, and I wouldn't. It was an entirely different relationship. It will never happen again. But to be truthful, I was concerned about how it would be with Bernardo now. I know this happens to many people. They have affairs and they seem to be able to continue with their marriages. I doubt they ever confess their experiences. I will never let Bernardo know what I have done.

I looked in the mirror, catching my reflection. We all have so many different personalities within ourselves, and these roles change with the circumstances. No longer the adventurer, I have returned to my role as Bernardo's wife.

I began to relax; it was going to be all right. When I discovered how weary he was, how frail, I was aware there was no choice about what I would do. Our life and family are by far the most important things in my life. I owe it to him and he needs me after twenty-five years. We are old friends, lovers, parents and so much more. He has loved me in his own way, all this time. I began to remember how it was when we first met. He was bright, intelligent, exciting. Always romantic, he drove me crazy when we first met. We were so in love.

The next day, after a good night's sleep, he felt better. Our lovemaking hasn't changed since I became a brazen hussy. No, just kidding. It assures me that I made the right decision. I feel happy now. I never want to lose what I have with my big bear of a husband.

Is love a reality
or *a dream?*
I cannot know
when both reality and dreams
exist without truly existing.

The Ink Dark Moon

LIFE GOES ON

For Katherine, things are back to normal. That is as normal as it can be. The twins come home from college for the summer. They have changed; they have grown up during the school year. They look older. Callie's light brown hair is full of blond streaks from the sunshine. She is beautiful. Ezra's hair, down to his shoulders when he left, is very short. They are tan, healthy, full of enthusiasm, and self-assured. They too have changed.

Dressed in Hawaiian garb, they cannot stop talking about their experiences in Hawaii. After a few visits with their old friends at home, they find the new friends they have made in Hawaii have become more important to them. Because they are twins, they have always had special relationship, and no great need to be close with other friends. In fact they tell Katherine they have decided to settle in Hawaii after they graduate from college.

Bernardo is more his old self while the twins are home. He is happy to be reunited with his whole family, and so is Katherine. During the summer he flies back and forth to California, putting finishing touches on his film. By fall he is done and the film is set to be released during the holiday season.

Although she has changed in many ways, Katherine finds it all too easy to slip back into her old ways while everyone is home. She is familiar with the routine, the expectations of her family, and loves to serve them. She realizes that these occasions will not happen often in the future. Life is changing before her very eyes. She understands that the twins have their own lives ahead of them, but she also sees that Bernardo is becoming needier, although he won't admit it.

In the hope that she can retain some of what she has learned in Thailand, Katherine joins a meditation group in town. She doesn't want to explain why she began meditating in Thailand, so by attending a meditation group, she feels free enough to create her own meditation hall in the small room next to her bedroom. She begins to sit, twice a day. It is important but not easy for her. She doesn't want to lose the spiritual threads she has woven in Thailand. She feels this will be very helpful in her future.

Callie and Ezra notice the change in their mother. They are amazed. "Spiritual life. Right, on Mom!" They are pleased. Bernardo doesn't seem to mind; he assumes it is just a passing interest.

In Hawaii, the twins have studied with some healers. They have learned many new things about different religions and spirituality in the world. They demonstrate massage techniques they have learned on Bernardo and Katherine. Katherine offers to be a practice model daily.

Even though Katherine believes her inner changes don't show, she seems different in some ways to Bernardo. "Katherine, you are like a fruit that has ripened. You have become succulent, robust and juicy. I like what happened to you. You were right to take your retreat. I believe it made you a new woman."

Katherine blushes and inside she thinks to herself, "and I thought I was so cool."

She begins to understand what is so different about her present role. Bernardo hadn't assigned it to her; she has chosen it for herself. Always interested in people, Bernardo observes her and finds he is even more attracted to her than ever before. On the other hand, he is weary and doesn't have the usual energy to be directing at home.

Welcoming Katherine's new strengths, he makes time for lovemaking and romance. In the past, Bernardo had regarded himself as the Italian Stallion; now he has become a gentle, patient lover. Katherine often is reminded of the song she loved about wanting a man with slow hands. She has one now.

At the end of the summer the twins return to Hawaii. Bernardo's film is set for release at Christmas time. Katherine puts her photography project aside because Bernardo seems to need her company more than usual. In December they go to New York for the premiere of the film. They spend the night at the Plaza. People at the grand studio party seem very young to Katherine. Has she grown older and failed to notice?

Murphy and her husband are there. Katherine hasn't seen her since Murphy left Thailand, last spring.

"Katherine, you look wonderful." Murphy hugs her warmly. "I heard you took a retreat. I hope I had a little influence. I sensed how important it was for you to find your own way."

Katherine is happy to be able to share a little of her trip. "Oh, Murphy, the trip we took to Chiang Mai was the best thing I could have done. It literally changed my life. I went off on my own for three months, right after you left."

"Yes."

"Something happened to me up there. Something I can't explain. It was like I had a call to return and when I did, my whole life changed. I found my way, strengths I was unaware I had, and a new passion for life."

"Tell me about it. What have you found?"

"You knew I was lost when you were there. Floundering actually. I needed some meaning for my life. During my travels, I met a woman in Bangkok who cares for orphans. Thousands of young people live in devastating circumstances there. I realized I couldn't help everyone, but I decided I want to help the orphanage. I took a lot of photos and I plan to use them in a book that will share the plight of those people. Maybe in some way Bernardo will be able to help too.

"I had no idea you would find such inspiration, but it sounds like the right thing for you to do. Let me know if there's anything I can do to help."

"Don't worry; I'll be in touch for sure."

The morning after the premiere, newspapers are delivered to their hotel room. Over breakfast they read the reviews. They are not as good as they had hoped. Bernardo is proven right when the reviewers allude to the facts that there are too many quick cuts. Bernardo had been angry when he saw how much the producer along with the editor had changed the film after he left thinking it would be the final cut. This has never happened to him before.

Bernardo nervously walks back and forth. "The movie business now caters to young people. Young people who don't care about the quality, the pace of a film, run it. They are used to MTV and fast cuts. I hate that style of editing and I refused to do it but I made a mistake in not having it in my contract the approval of the final cut. They won't do things that way anymore. Scenes I spent days photographing have been reduced to quick shots in the film, making it impossible to get a feeling of place. It's a good thing David Lean is no longer alive; he would have gone crazy! The story jumps here and there, leaving the viewer unable to settle into one place before being ejected into another. It isn't supposed to be a cartoon."

Katherine begins to understand what has happened. The film does not fit Bernardo's creative imagination. The truth is that times have changed. If he doesn't go along with the young people in charge, he is seen as difficult. Bernardo has always done things his own way in the past. He is too old to change. It is evident now, that few jobs will come his way, no matter how great his past accomplishments.

He laments over and over, telling Katherine how it is. "Sadly, now most of the time writers in Hollywood are finished at fifty. Many talented people are left behind because they refuse to sell out. The movie business suffers for that. Perhaps the public is unaware, or just doesn't care. When the corporations took over Hollywood, the art was sucked out of the business and now talented artists go unappreciated. Where it was once a family at work, now the main focus is to make lots of money. The young audience will go to see anything. Integrity no longer seems to matter."

Katherine fears that Bernardo may never again have the opportunity do the work he loves. Making movies is his life; the main reason for living. He would never accept or believe that his directing days were over. She says nothing, just squeezes his hand.

A snowy January arrives. Bernardo is at loose ends. He isn't used to being without an upcoming project. Ordinarily he has a project to go to immediately. He turns to Katherine, needing her company and he wants to spend their days together. She has finally gotten the wish she made when she left for London, He needs her. Yet ironically her needs are now different. He waits for her to come home when she leaves the house, sometimes calling her on his cell phone. He sits in the garden watching her work. Other times he visits his old friends in the neighborhood. Sadly, many of them are working and have little time for him. Besides, it only makes him feel worse. As spring comes, he follows Katherine around the garden, trying to drum up some interest, but his body begins to ache and he cannot bend for long. He is short with her when she tries to work in the darkroom, always calling to her, "When will you be finished?" He desperately needs a new project.

A publisher asks him to write an autobiography. Bernardo jumps at the opportunity and asks Katherine to work with him. She longs to work on her own project, but senses it is not time to push that. She gathers photos from Bernardo's work, and life, many that she has taken through the years. Being busy seems to brighten him a little.

Bernardo doesn't think about consulting Katherine when he signs the contract for the book. He always decides on his own projects, and takes it for granted; she will be there for him when he needs her. She has never let him down. Bernardo is the director and has always assumed everyone else needs to be directed. Although Katherine is happy to accommodate him while he works on the book, she prays silently that a new film project will show up soon.

In retrospect, she understands now she is able to do for him what she planned to do when she left for England. She wanted to be a part of his work, but hadn't been needed. Once again, that old saying that comes to mind, "Be careful what you pray for." Now she is pulled away from her own project. Maybe, when the book is done, Bernardo will reciprocate and help her with her project. She knows not to be disappointed if he is not willing to reciprocate.

Katherine continues to assimilate all she's learned in Thailand…about taking care of her own needs first. She feels her life pattern has changed somewhat. At the same time she strongly feels the pressure to support Bernardo. Something inside makes the importance of responding to his needs, the stronger drive. His infirmities have accrued though the years; natural with his age. He isn't helpless, but for the first time in their relationship, she feels their age difference. It has never mattered before, but now that she wants more independence, she is becoming aware of how much he needs her company and support. Life isn't working out like she hoped, and she has to learn to remain in the present.

That spring, they work on the book, locating film strips and the photos they need. They relive their adventures and laugh when they remember all the locations spent with the kids. What a wonderful education they have had through all their travels. Katherine had loved meeting famous actors, the beautiful locations, fabulous hotels, outstanding meals, she experienced all through the years. There are amazing memories for both of them.

One evening Bernardo finds the dining room transformed into a Spanish restaurant similar to where they often ate at when he shot a movie in Madrid. They drink Spanish wine; eat tapas, paella, and tasty Spanish dishes, accompanied by flamenco guitar on the stereo. When they awaken the next morning, they are happy and laughing; content to be home and cozy, instead of somewhere far away on location. It is a very special time in their lives.

The book project drags on longer than they had antici- pated. Bernardo becomes weary of the project. His movie work is always over in a few months. He can go on to a fresh project. The book doesn't offer the excitement that directing a film does. Bernardo is a people person; this is all too solitary a pursuit for him. He has already lived the life he is writing about. It bores him. He is not interested in repeating it. He wants to be on to a new experience. Films are alive, new people, new stories, and new experiences. Bernardo is most alive when he is directing people, bringing out the best of their talents.

Katherine admires him. She sees how hard he tries. She is very aware of his feelings and prays for him to be able to find a project to bring him fully alive again. She sits in her meditation room and visualizes him happy, at work on a new film.

Early in June, Bernardo decides to spend a day with his agent, in New York City

Over lunch his agent, excitedly tells him about a book that is about to be published. An auction for the film rights will be held the following week.

"You must buy the film rights. It is perfect for you Bernardo."

"Give me a synopsis," Bernardo asks. "I could buy it and produce my own film. That way it will turn out like I want it to."

As he listens to a quick synopsis, the agent watches Bernardo's excitement mount and he strongly suggests that Bernardo buy the option. Film rights are often purchased separately from the book rights, so a first time writer is very happy to sell the rights at a moderate price. Bernardo trusts his agent. His instincts have always been exquisite and he has never let him down.

"Take carte blanche! Go for it! Let's get this book. I need a project badly." Bernardo is ready to throw caution to the wind. "Go ahead; bid for the film rights. "

The agent says," There's a rumor that the book will be a best seller; even though it is the author's first I'll try to grab the rights immediately."

Bernardo desperately wants a new movie project. He usually writes the screenplay for his own films.

Back home, during the day of the auction, Bernardo paces back and forth. He knows how quickly a project can slip away if one hesitates. Years before, Katherine found a book for him in London, asked him to read it. She advised him to option it. He put off reading the book and forgot about it. By the time he read the book and realized it would make a great film, but it was too late. He had his agent inquire about it. To his surprise, the rights had been sold only a few weeks before. He learned from that experience not to hesitate. This time he wasn't about to let a very important opportunity get away. He needs to get back to work.

Two weeks later, he owns the film rights to <u>Mirroring the Fire.</u> He has kept his purchase from Katherine a secret. He wants to surprise her when the deal is actually sealed. Bernardo may be selfish, but he also knows human nature, and he realizes he cannot ask Katherine to make his life worthwhile. Nobody can do that but Bernardo.

Delicate sun shines into the screened porch this morning. Bernardo holds a contract in his hand. He waves it in front of Katherine's face.

"What's that?" she asks.

"Guess what, Katherine; I've bought the rights to a new book!"

Hardly able to believe what he has done without her knowing, Katherine is excited.

"How did you do that without my knowing?"

She is so happy that Bernardo will again have a project. She hopes he can regain his old self.

"It's called Mirroring the Fire. It's by a new author, Jonathan Burnett. It's his first book and it's supposed to be wonderful. It will make a perfect film. They are sending copies for us to read. My agent loves it, and you know I can always trust his intuition."

Katherine's heart begins to beats wildly. She wonders if Bernardo can hear it. She feels weak and can hardly believe what he has just told her. Jonathans book! How could this be?

This couldn't have happened unless Jonathan sat down the day she left, and had never gotten up, until he finished the book. What a coincidence, that Bernardo would come along and buy this particular book. Along with feelings of confusion, she feels a great thrill. She knows now that Jonathan has been able to finish his book and accomplish what he set out to do. She hopes she has actually helped this happen. There is no way she can tell Bernardo about Jonathan and that she knows Jonathan; especially how well she knows him. He would wonder why she never mentioned him before. She is quiet, trusting her intuition. This might well lead to all sorts of complications. She isn't ready to think about it just yet.

Copies of the book arrive by courier that very morning. Bernardo cannot wait to begin reading. He sits on the porch in a comfortable chair, pen and paper at his side. He has a ritual. First he reads through a book quickly, to get a feel for it the first time. It is almost always true that a book will need to be changed in some way before it becomes a good script. Bernardo is a master at screen writing.

It doesn't take long for Bernardo to fall in love with the woman in the story. He laughs, and makes sounds of joy, as he does when he is happy. Katherine brings him lunch, yet he hardly touches his food. He cannot contain his excitement.

"This woman is perfect. I have already fallen in love with her. I can't wait to bring her to life. Who will I cast? Oh, right, you haven't read it yet. When you do, let's discuss it. Why don't you sit right down and start reading at once? I can hardly wait to hear what you think."

Bernardo is back to himself.

Katherine hasn't had time to open the book, but she is sure that Jonathan has used some of their experiences in the book. Wouldn't Bernardo be surprised if she told him she was the inspiration for Jonathan's heroine? But there is no way she could do that.

"What is it that appeals to you so much?" she asks cautiously.

"It's not one thing, it's the woman. Everything about her." He smiles. "Do you think there could actually be such a perfect being?"

"Bernardo, remember this is fiction. The woman has to be a figment of the writer's imagination. Until I read it, I won't be able to comment with any accuracy. Nobody could be that perfect. Could they?"

"One can only hope."

Bernardo continues to read, and Katherine almost feels left out. She wants to savor her time and although she has wanted to read the book, from the moment it arrived, she doesn't want to appear too anxious. Truthfully, she wants to read it in private because she has no idea what her reaction will be. She keeps herself busy. After lunch, she takes a copy to her bedroom. She lies down on the bed and opens it. It is a galley print, so there is no photo or bio of Jonathan. In a way, she is disappointed. In her lab she has hundreds of photos of him, but she wants to see what he looks like now. Does he look different? She is almost afraid to read the book. How much has Jonathan revealed about them and all that happened between them?

She opens the book slowly and in an instant she is back in Thailand, fully aware that anyone who reads the book will feel the love the author has for his heroine. He has drawn a picture of a lovely being. Even Katherine is attracted to her. "Was that the way he saw me?" She asks herself out loud. He has combined some things she shared with him, along with the passion of the Japanese women in the poetry. She finds herself drawn into the story, losing herself. His writing has her spellbound. She cannot put it down.

Later that evening, over dinner, she assures Bernardo that she is equally as excited as he; she loves the heroine. "The book will make a great film." She cannot wait to get into bed that night and continue reading. She reads until after midnight and awakens later to find the book has fallen upon her breast.

The next morning, she pours steaming milk into the coffee cups at the table by Bernardo's bedroom window. She takes his coffee to him, where he sits in bed propped up by pillows. He is more excited than she has seen him in years. He is a changed person. He smiles, waving his hands, describing the scenes he can imagine. He appears as though he might break into song. She is so happy; she has missed that in Bernardo. He is coming back to life. His work is his life. Katherine understands that, and she is willing to do almost anything to support him. He needs the courage and energy to go forward on this project. It is the best thing she can do at this time of their lives.

Bernardo is as enthusiastic as can be. He sets up his office and orders a new computer. He always buys a new computer each time he writes a script. It is a ritual of his. He is up early every morning, writing, rewriting. "Come listen to what I have written. What do you think?" He asks for suggestions. After all this time, Katherine finally is a part of his work-life, and she loves it.

Two months pass. Bernardo works every day. He has an outline, but all of a sudden, he comes to a standstill. Puzzled, he is depressed. He has never had writer's block before. Katherine doesn't know what to do.

"Katherine, let me run this by you," Bernardo says one morning. "I have an idea. I feel as though I'm going in circles, I need some help. What do you think about my calling the author and seeing if he would come and help me work my way through this block? He might be able to help."

She is speechless. Never could she have imagined this situation. It is all coming too close for comfort, yet how can she deny this man, now that he is finally is happy?

She hesitates, "I don't know if it is such a good idea. You always do such a wonderful job, writing your own scripts."

"Yes that has been true, up to now, but I've never had such a wonderful character to work with before. I don't want to lose her. She has such depth, but I don't know if I can get it all from book to script. I hate to admit it, but I think I am getting old. Hopefully, I am getting wiser too. I have this feeling I must hurry. I can't sit around and wait for inspiration." Bernardo takes a deep breath, as though to reach deep inside for strength.

"I need to call him."

"Where is he?" Katherine asks, trying to appear normal.

"My agent can locate him. I'd love to have him stay here with us for a few days so we can work together. Would you mind?"

She is at a loss for words, falling deeper and deeper into something she could never have imagined. She doesn't know what to say and mumbles, "Whatever you think is best."

The truth is, there is no way she could say no. Perhaps in the past she would have tried to save herself, trying to convince him that he is totally capable. This is different. She is confused, and it may be because she knows how important the project is to Bernardo. He has never asked for help before. Something inside of him has changed, and she must not be selfish. If truth were told, part of her longs to see Jonathan. If he accepts, she will have to walk a thin line, right on the edge and there is no guarantee what will happen. The universe has handed her a situation with no simple solution.

If you had
only stayed away
when I first missed you
I might have forgotten
by now!

<u>The Ink Dark Moon</u>

WHAT DO WE DO NOW?

Fortunately there is not much time to worry. Jonathan will be there within two weeks. Katherine hopes she will somehow be able to prepare. That is, if she can ever be prepared to see him again.

All too soon, Jonathan's car pulls up in the driveway. His lanky frame unfolds and he is on his way up to the front door. Bernardo waits for him, anxious as a child at Christmas. He opens the door, rushes out in his energetic fashion, and throws his arms around Jonathan.

"Here, let me take your bag."

"No that's fine, I can handle it." Jonathan smiles at him.

"Come on in then, I'm so glad you are here." Bernardo is like a young man again; happiness exudes from his pores. Here is someone to work with. It isn't that he doesn't enjoy being with Katherine; it's just that he needs many people around to be fulfilled.

Jonathan walks through the front door. Instinctively, he looks toward the living room and sees Katherine. She looks straight at him. His heart beats wildly. She looks even more wonderful than he remembers. He has never seen her in her own home. She holds out her hand when Bernardo leads him over and presents him.

"This is Katherine. She is so happy you are able to come. I've driven her crazy while we have been waiting for you."

Jonathan takes Katherine's hand. Somehow, without speaking, they have agreed not to let Bernardo know they have known each other before.

"So nice to meet you, Katherine." He looks deep into her eyes, fearing he will drown. He looks away.

Katherine recovers. "I'm glad you are here to work with Bernardo. He is so happy, and that makes me happy too. Here, let me show you to your room. You must want to get settled. We'll have lunch if you are ready. We waited for you." Bernardo is off to the dining room.

Jonathan follows her up the stairs. She opens the door to the guest room. It is a cheerful, sunlit room with jade green walls, and starched white curtains. Two brightly patterned wing chairs sit in front of the fireplace. Katherine allows herself to soften and feel, instead of locking her feelings inside.

She is happy to have him in her home. She is aware that he is pleased and feels comfortable, at least in some ways.

"Here's the bathroom. It has a great deep, long tub. Take your time." She is nervous again.

"Katherine, try to relax, if you can. I could have refused, you know. This could not be more difficult, but to tell you the truth, I had to see you again. I never get enough of you, and I am a selfish man. I will try to behave and not give Bernardo any indication of our relationship. Please trust me."

"Oh Jonathan, I do trust you. It's me I'm worried about! I have tried so hard to keep myself distracted, to forget you. I tried to remember the meditations and the teachings, to live in the moment, not in the past. I know Bernardo needs me now. When he returned, I realized how weak he was. I made a pact with myself to be here for him, no matter what."

"My dear, I understand. That is one of the things I love so, about you. I won't be selfish, but I will enjoy being near you."

"Your book has brought him back to life. I'm so happy he found it. It's strange, how we have been drawn back into each other's company. We meet in the strangest places."

"I'll second that." She smiles disarmingly.

"Whatever reason we have come together for, whatever difficulty it might cause in our lives, we will never be able to know all the answers. But the music that used to play inside of Bernardo was missing, and once he found your book, he began to sing inside again. He has always been the conductor, and he was lost without his music, his musicians."

"I hope I can make a difference for him."

They hear Bernardo's footsteps in the hallway and hurry out of the room.

"Gloria says lunch is ready." Quickly they descend the stairs.

Over lunch, Bernardo praises Jonathan for his work. He asks question after question. "Was she a real person? How did you imagine her? Who would you imagine playing her part in a film?" On and on he goes.

Katherine begins clearing the table. "Okay, you two, get to work." She wants to get away from both of them. Her emotions are in a jumble.

Later that afternoon, Bernardo is weary from all the excitement, and takes leave of Jonathan. "Ask Katherine to show you around the property." he says, "I need a nap."

Katherine agrees to join Jonathan. Bernardo has always depended upon her to entertain their guests. Normally, she does it with ease. This time she is a little shaky as she walks out the door with Jonathan. They set off down the path and the two dogs follow. It almost seems natural to take each other's hand. They reach and then pull back. This is going to be more difficult than they can imagine. They don't say a word; just walk in silence until they are over the hill, out of sight of the house. They come to the pond and sit on the bench that overlooks it. The bugs are buzzing, hopping across the surface. They can see the fish jump to the surface, trying to catch their dinner. It is lazy and calm, but inside they are anything but calm.

"Isn't it strange? We never made any plans to meet again; look at what the universe has provided for us. Thailand was never the same after you left. That was good, because all that was left for me was to write."

"I understand. I was astonished that your book was finished so quickly; published almost instantly. How was that possible? Most authors I've known try for years, before they find a publisher. That is, if they get published at all."

"Oh, Katherine, before you came, I had written parts of my story, sort of an outline. I didn't have you filled in. My heroine eluded me. Once you came and brought my main character alive, the book practically wrote itself." He smiled, remembering their times together. "It was as though I was still with you. I drank heavily and somehow that seemed to help my writing. I longed for you. For the first time in my life, I was lonely. I'd never felt like that before. The pain helped me become a far better writer than I ever would have been. Fortunately I have a good friend who is an agent. I think your story sold itself."

Katherine begins to share her side of the story. "I came home and had a few days to recover. Luckily I was alone; Bernardo was still in California. I was afraid to give in to my feelings, so I got busy trying to forget about you. When Bernardo arrived, he was so thin and he had aged. I was shocked and I knew at that moment, I would have to put my feelings aside. When it comes to my family, I am used to being unselfish, but when I admitted the truth to myself, all I wanted to do was run back into your arms."

Jonathan almost pulls her into his arms; he senses that is what she feels too. On the other hand, he knows it would be unfair. He takes a step back and looks at her. They are going to have to play at the act that they have never met, for the time being. It will be okay to let Bernardo see them become acquainted. He likes it when Katherine appreciates his friends. They draw back and continue to walk, circling the property and then return to the house.

"Time for a shower," Katherine says.

"That sounds good. Maybe I'll soak my bones in that beautiful old tub."

Once again, they are drawn toward each other, and then pull back. This is going to be very difficult. Katherine has learned to be true to herself, and now she is going to have to become a very good actress.

Bernardo is refreshed by dinnertime, full of enthusiasm. There is no problem with his energy, once he has napped. They drink lots of wine during the delicious dinner, and go to bed too late.

The next morning by the time Katherine arises, Bernardo and Jonathan are at breakfast. She sits down with them, enjoying her coffee. Soon they are off to Bernardo's office, where they work until lunchtime.

Katherine is happy to see Bernardo so lively, along with the fact that she is able to enjoy Jonathan's company at the same time, if a bit uneasily at times. She finds what is difficult to do, is not to drop back into her old relationship with Jonathan. They have been such close friends, but if they fall back into those ways, they will possibly reveal things that Bernardo would not be happy knowing. They remain especially polite and rather formal with each other.

Nothing

in the world

is unusual today.

This is the first morning.

The Ink Dark Moon

KATHERINE'S DIARY

I am basking in happiness like I've never experienced before. Never could I have foreseen that both of the men I love could possibly be in my life at the same time. Bernardo is ecstatic. He always has a love affair with his co-workers. This is definitely a love affair with Jonathan. Not sexual, I don't mean that, but the true love Bernardo always feels for those who support his vision.

His writer's block has disappeared. Jonathan, well acquainted with that problem, is so happy he can help Bernardo break through the block.

Things have changed in our house. The moment Bernardo began working with Jonathan he has awakened and nearly jumped up early each morning. His appetite is good; his energy has resurfaced. This is a very special connection.

I feel like a new person too. I've been trying to be faithful to myself. Now it is difficult. When they came together in my presence, I knew I would need to hide the love and warmth I feel for Jonathan and he does the same thing. It seems to be working.

Sometimes when I think about the whole thing, I know how helpless I am to change anything, really, so I have given up my concerns about the outcome of the situation. During the meditation retreat in Thailand, I learned that I must live in the present. Even though it isn't always possible in this situation, it seems to work from moment to moment. There are so many problems I can conjure up, but I choose not to do that.

Sometimes, I daydream that this life with the two of them will continue. It would be absolutely perfect for me. The three of us make a perfect couple. Society might not approve, but to be truthful, it feels right for all of us. Maybe the Mormons had something right, with the multiple partners, except in that religion it was multiple wives. I like it better this way.

Now that Jonathan is working with Bernardo, he has little time to spend with me. That is good. Bernardo is possessive with Jonathan and they spend most of their days together. From time to time, I leave them alone and take short trips to New York to see Franko. He is amused at my situation. I finally had to confess what was happening. Being gay, he has been through many unusual relationships and there is no way he would give me a hard time. I couldn't tell anyone else about what was happening. I told the twins that the author of the book had come to help Bernardo. I wanted to keep the situation to myself and not introduce any other ingredients. It seemed to be going so well, that I wondered about myself at times.

My life is so crazy. I could never have imagined anything like this. Never, ever. How did this happen? How is it that the two people I love are in the same house, in my life at the same time? I am happier than I have ever been. In a way, I understand that no matter how much Bernardo loves me, I am not enough to fulfill all his needs. I'm only one person, perhaps gifted in some ways, but not in all the ways, he needs. From the beginning, I understood that, and for the most part, never minded. There were times when Bernardo seemed very close with an actress on a film he was directing, but I never questioned him. Now I can understand, more than ever, how a person can love more than one person at the same time. I know now, different people nourish me in different ways. I have come to understand that this relationship with Jonathan is not only all about sexual attraction. But oh my God, it was amazing when we came together. I never realized that I was capable of feeling so

274

deeply, and responding with such passion and freedom. Imagine, at my age. Where had that person inside of me been, all my life? There is so much more to our friendship, an ease, a joy, a fitting together. I can't really explain it yet; maybe I never will be able to.

I'll live in the moment, and then the next moment. It is the only way I can live so close to him. My heart breaks open and lets them both in. I am totally vulnerable.

I trust Jonathan, and can feel he has also begun to love Bernardo. He is under Bernardo's spell, but it is more than that. It is so weird. I have no idea where this is going and I don't think I have any control over anything right now, except, maybe, me. That is all I can handle.

Years ago, I sat beside a woman on a plane. She was a widow, nearly sixty, flying to begin a second marriage. I remember her telling me, with a sparkle in her eye, and a big smile, that she could guarantee that love at this time of her life was just as wonderful as the first time she had fallen in love. At the time, I thought that was so sweet. Only now do I truly understand what she meant. I have no idea what the future holds. Nobody ever does. I never imagined that it would be possible to meet another man and fall in love; especially while I was still married and still loving my husband. Life is supposed to be simple when you follow the rules. Ha! What a joke. Dear God please help me to do what is right for all of us.

Be patient toward all that is unsolved in your heart,

and try to love the questions themselves,

like locked rooms and like books written in a foreign language.

Do not now seek the answers that cannot be given to you,

because you would not be able to live them.

And the point is to live everything.

Live the question now.

Perhaps you will then,

gradually

without noticing it

live along some

distant day,

into the answer.

Rainier Maria Rilke.

GONE

Without Bernardo actually realizing it, the love for the same woman has brought he and Jonathan close together, and nurtured their relationship. Bernardo is pleased to have been able to accomplish so much. His creative ability has returned; the script is nearly finished. The two of them work intently each day. They are not running a race, but unconsciously they understand that it is important to finish as soon as possible.

Without notice, Jonathan receives a call from Thailand. He is urgently needed to take care of some business. He has to return home to do it. They push themselves trying to bring the script to completion.

Once Bernardo realizes Jonathan must leave, his vitality begins to flag. He is no longer as energetic as he had been at the beginning of the project. He has given his all to this work, but as the end draws near, he is running out of steam. Jonathan has been like a transfusion for him. Somehow he doesn't appear to have the stamina to follow through on his own. He jokes with Jonathan, urging him to hurry back as soon as he is finished with his business. "We have become Siamese Twins, conjoined, and I am unable to live without you." Bernardo tries to laugh.

Katherine wonders if it is not a joke at all.

Jonathan calls for plane reservations. His rental car has been turned in weeks ago, so Katherine will drive him to the airport. He offers to call the limo, but Bernardo insists that Katherine take him. Bernardo is unable to bring himself to see Jonathan off at the airport. He is already suffering from the future loss of his friend. Jonathan and Katherine are relieved to have a little time alone, before they part. They are still a little bit in shock, when they realize how amazing the last few months have been.

On the ride to the airport, they try to make sense of what has happened.

"It is astounding what he does with people, Katherine. He has charmed and courted me, and I have fallen in love, in some way, with Bernardo. I understand why you feel the way you do, and how you are so devoted to him. He makes me feel important and gifted. I must say, I have truly enjoyed his company."

"People have always said that about Bernardo. I know that is why he is such a great director. Your book will become a wonderful film. How do you feel about that?"

"I have mixed feelings. Of course, I want it to be a success. When the book sold, I was thrilled. On the other hand, I can see how selfish I am. I don't want to be near the readers when they discover what I have written, when they fall in love with you, as I have done. I am jealous of each reader. I don't want to know what they feel. It is perverse... I understand that... but......... I don't want to share you either. "

He looks at her. "Writing the book into a movie changes everything. I don't know how I will feel sharing you on the screen. Who will play you? I can't imagine. On the other hand, I admire Bernardo and this is what he does. He has fallen in love with the character, and I don't think he realizes it is you. It isn't as personal for him. "

"Oh, Jonathan, how did it ever get so complicated? I am going to miss you so much. Why is it that I feel what we have had for the past months is all over? The spell is broken. When you return, we may not be able to recreate this Camelot, we've had."

"I understand how you feel Katherine. You know, when you are on vacation with people, or in a special situation and you become very close?"

"Of course. Look at us in Thailand."

"The sad thing is that if we try to recreate the same feeling on other occasions, it never turns out the same."

"That's true, but with us, nothing seemed to change, even though we haven't been able to indulge our feelings. In fact the tension almost makes them increase."

He looks at her. "I know. It's the situation that changes, not the people, really."

"It will probably do you good to have a break, Jonathan," Katherine says, knowing it will not be a happy time for her.

They pull up to the luggage drop-off. Katherine waits for him at the curb, while he gets out and checks his bags. Together they park the car. Neither of them wants to say goodbye, so they stay together until his plane departs. The closeness they have felt, without giving in to their physical attraction, has been difficult. The tension is high. Katherine's heart feels as though it is breaking. She wills the tears to stay tucked away. In the end, nothing has changed, the attraction and love they have discovered has grown, no matter how hard they try to quell it.

"Flight 6706 delayed. Please check boards." Jonathan's flight is delayed for an hour.

"You know we could take a little time and go to an airport hotel, my love." Jonathan tempts her with humor, but she doesn't laugh.

"Honestly, Jonathan, there is no place I'd rather be than in your arms. I want nothing more, in some ways. Yet I'd better behave and get back home." She is near tears. "It has taken so much time for me to get my feelings in order, to not show too much attention to you. I'm afraid to let down now, even a little. If I do, I might never be able to get back up.

Being with you again for all these months, was more than I could have asked for. I know how lucky I am to have two wonderful men in my life to love. I can't tempt the gods." Jonathan puts his arm around her. She continues: "Truth be told, I wish we could have been intimate, but I think we both knew that wasn't possible. I do feel wanton. I couldn't control my feelings and dreams at night, with you right down the hall."

"Wanton!" You? No, I don't think that describes you at all. Loving, warm, sexy, inviting, seductively open. Yes! All that and more, my dearest friend. Yet you are so much more than a friend, and my heart breaks too. You are the only woman I will ever truly love. When I found you that was it. You are the woman of my dreams"

They embrace and then draw back. During lunch, Jonathan fills her in on more about his life after she had gone. They pick at their meals. Fortunately, he had been able to finish the book quickly, even though at times he felt so morose, ready to give up and it seemed that the whole project was hopeless. Miraculously, he was able to get through his dark times and finish it.

His timing had been perfect. The agent had loved the book. He quickly found a willing publisher. It was as though the powers that be had arranged the book be available just so Bernardo would be able to buy it and bring them back together. What serendipity, almost like a fairy tale, but the ending is still a mystery.

Jonathan's flight is called. He takes Katherine into his arms and holds her close. In the silence, their hearts beat together. They stay that way, until the last minute. They both want to drink in all the love they feel.

"Last call!" They step apart.

As Jonathan walks toward the boarding door, he turns back to Katherine. "I'll take care of everything at home as quickly as possible. Then I'll be back to help Bernardo polish up the script. I am going to miss you terribly. Even if I can't have all of you, I'll take what is possible. I love you."

Katherine can no longer hold back her tears. They run down her face as she watches him depart. This is nothing she could prepare for.

He is gone.

She starts toward the car, walking slowly, not wanting this day to end. As she drives toward the turnpike, she cannot stop thinking and reviewing her life, since she met Jonathan. She knows she must turn things over to a higher power, or she will go crazy. She tries to numb her longing when the pain becomes too great. She turns it over and over but the pain keeps returning.

Finally she says a prayer, knowing she has no control over anything.

"Please dear God, let the outcome of this situation be the highest and best for all of us." It is the only way she can make it through these painful moments.

By the time she reaches home it is dark. She sees the light in Bernardo's bedroom and heads straight up to see him. He sits in his bed, eating his dinner on a tray.

"Are you all right?" she asks.

"I don't know, I'm just a little weary. Gloria said she would be happy to bring my dinner up here, and I took her up on the offer."

Katherine is worried. This is not like Bernardo. What had happened?

He continues. "You know, I already miss Jonathan. He has made such a difference for me. I know I couldn't have accomplished what I did, without him. I don't know what happened. I never had a block like that before. "

It is unlike him to admit his doubts, and Katherine tries to console him. "Maybe it will be good for you to have a break, time to rest. Jonathan will be back soon. I know you want to finish the screenplay quickly, but sometimes a little time out is good for you."

His eyes begin to droop, and she can see he is finished with dinner. She takes the tray from his lap and leans over to kiss him goodnight. He lies back on his pillow and is asleep in moments. She turns off the light and leaves the tray in the hall.

Katherine goes to her room. She doesn't want to take a bath; she wants to keep the smell, the memory of Jonathan's touch on her skin. She puts on a nightgown and climbs into bed. For the past few months' life has felt complete, if a bit unusual. Now it feels as though a piece of the jigsaw puzzle is missing. Fortunately, she is so tired, that she falls asleep immediately.

The next morning Katherine is still weary, and sleeps in. This has become her routine. Gloria usually brings the coffee and some toast up to her so she can quietly enjoy it. Today she enjoys a long leisurely morning in bed as she has often done while Bernardo and Jonathan were working together. She never wanted to interfere in their time together. She showers and puts on slacks and a loose silk shirt. She plans to go for a walk, after she tells Bernardo good morning.

Gently, she pushes the door to Bernardo's office open. She doesn't want to disturb him in case he is busy. But he is not busy; he is slumped over his desk. At first, she thinks he is just resting, but in a moment when she calls his name and he doesn't move, she runs to the desk.

"Bernardo, Bernardo!" She cries out. He doesn't respond to her touch; he isn't breathing. He is gone.

"Help me!"

Gloria rushes into the room when she hears Katherine cry out. She immediately calls 911.

Katherine takes Bernardo into her arms, hoping to hear a heart beat, but he is limp. He looks peaceful, as if he is just sleeping.

Sirens scream. Moment's later firemen and EMT's workers rush through the door. They take Bernardo from Katherine's arms and lay him on the floor. They try to revive him, over and over again. Later, Katherine understands that it all has been for her benefit. There is no life left in him. It is to no avail. Bernardo is gone. He is dead.

The ambulance waits outside, lights flashing. The red light is reflected in the room. The attendants bring in the stretcher and place Bernardo on it. They cover him with a sheet. It is so final, so quick. Katherine cannot stand it.

"Please, give me a moment with my husband," she begs.

She isn't prepared for this. She never will be. The door closes and she is alone with Bernardo. She embraces his body and puts her head upon his chest.

"Oh, Bernardo, I love you so. How could you go like this? It's too soon. Why did this have to happen now?" Her heart bursts open, and with it come the tears, and the realization that Bernardo will never be there for her again.

The attendants wait patiently. They have been through this many times before. The ambulance pulls away the lights no longer flickering. Katherine goes to her room and falls on her bed. She is stunned, in shock. It must have been his heart. Why didn't he say anything about that being a problem?

After a while, she gets up: she must call the twins. Heartbroken, they don't hesitate to rush home to her side immediately.

"I'll make the reservations." Katherine tells them. She makes arrangements at the funeral home. Keeping busy also keeps her sane; there is so much to be done.

Bernardo had always joked about his obituary. He had written one up, a few years before. Katherine looks into his files and finds it. Operating in robot mode, she sits down to complete it for the <u>New York Times.</u> Her feelings and emotions are still locked up inside. She must keep herself moving or she will not be able to go on.

There is no way to reach Jonathan; he is still in flight to Thailand. He didn't leave a number, believing there would be no reason to contact him. He had disconnected the phone in Thailand when he left. Most people there use cell phones anyway. Katherine hopes he might see the news of Bernardo's death in the papers. Bernardo is famous, after all. He might find a newspaper in an airport, but not in Northern Thailand where he is headed. Jonathan had planned to return to work here in a few weeks, so they had not made plans to get in touch with each other. Now there is no way to contact him.

Bernardo's agent comes to the house to help Katherine with the announcements and arrangements. She makes provisions for people to gather at the house after the funeral. She is amazed at how many people respond, and plan to come. Finally, she breaks down. Up until now she has been able to seal off her feelings of utter loss, but once she has a moment on her hands, that's it. Her heart sinks. Sadness envelops her. She aches with loneliness. She never imagined this could happen so suddenly.

When the twins arrive, Katherine tries to be the strong one and support them. They never considered losing their father, but their strength surprises her. Their youth bolsters them through the ordeal and they are a huge help. After the funeral, they greet all the people who come to their home to support them in their loss. Franko is also there for Katherine.

Flowers arrive from all over the world, cards filled with touching letters of condolence from many people who write to share their experiences with Bernardo. These remind her how important he had been to so many people. The outpouring of love and gratitude helps in many ways, but it cannot erase the feeling of loss. Bernardo has always been so large in life. Now there is a void that will never again be filled.

Shall I say how it is in your clothes?

A month after your death, I wear your blue jacket.

The dog at the center of my life recognizes
You've come to visit, he's ecstatic.
In the left pocket a hole.
In the right a parking ticket
delivered up last August on Bay State Road.
In my heart a scatter like milkweed,
a flinging from the pods of the soul.
My skin presses your old outline.
It is hot and dry inside.
I think of the last day of your life,
old friend, how I would unwind it, paste,
it back together in a different collage,
back from the death car idling in the garage,,
back up the stairs, your praying hands unlaced
reassembling the bits of bread and tuna fish
into a ceremony of sandwich,
running the home movie backward to a space

we could be easy in a kitchen place

with vodka and ice, our words like living
meat.

Dear friend, you have excited crowds

with your example. They swell like wine bags,
straining at your seams.

I will be years gathering up your words,

fishing out letters, snapshots, stains,

leaning my ribs against this durable cloth

to put on the dumb blue blazer of your death.

Maxine Kumin (from <u>Selected</u>
<u>Poems 1960-1990)</u>

Norton

KATHERINE'S DIARY

I've been so busy that there has been, so little time to think or feel. I guess that's why they have funerals, so some sort of closure can come before the breakdown. After the services, after the will had been read, after as much as possible has been done to set our lives in order, the twins returned to Hawaii. They offered to stay with me, but I wanted them to get on with their lives.

When the house was empty, I finally gave myself permission to fall apart. I lay on Bernardo's bed, sobbing and sobbing, staying there for hours. I would sleep, then awaken and continue to cry. I scarcely ate. Gloria kept after me and tried to be there in case I needed anything.

Sometimes, when I wake up, it seems as though Bernardo is only away on another location as he had been so many times before. That was the way we lived our lives. Then reality comes back, like a blow to my stomach, and I am aware that he will never come home again. I sleep in his bed, not allowing Gloria to change the sheets. His glasses and water glass remain on the bedside table, where he always kept them. I wear his robe when I get up in the morning and at other times I wear his sweaters, his jacket or his shirts. I listen to his favorite music and when I finally regained my appetite, I asked Gloria to prepare his favorite meals and serve his favorite wines. I cannot let him go yet. At night I sit in front of the fire and converse with him. I make toasts to Bernardo. I talk with him, as though he is still here. At times I can almost feel him near. I imagine I can nestle into his arms. But in the end all there is only emptiness.

Wishing to see him,
to be seen by him -
if only he
were the mirror
I face each morning.

The Ink Dark Moon

WHY?

Franko telephones Katherine daily. He senses she is having great difficulty. Two weeks after the funeral he decides to go up to stay with her.

"What's going on, my friend?" he asks. "I know you need to grieve, but it seems as though something more is going on than normal grieving."

Katherine looks at him, and suddenly she breaks into tears. "I can't give you an answer. I don't know."

Franko stays with her for a few days. For the first time in their relationship, he is quiet and patient. He just observes her and lets her be. She feels his love and appreciates him more than ever, but she is unable to give him the answers he seeks.

After several days, she begins to talk about how she feels. "I'm so confused."

"Wouldn't anyone be?" Consoles Franko.

"No, you don't understand. Let me explain."

"Please do."

"The day I dropped Jonathan off at the airport, I was so confused that I prayed for the highest and best situation for all of us. You know how happy I was with the two of them working together. I imagined it might continue." Her face grows sad. "And now, look what happened. I feel like I caused Bernardo's heart attack. I know it sounds silly, but somehow I feel that way."

"Listen to me. Just settle yourself down and listen. Don't go getting all filled with guilt because you prayed that way. God doesn't grant wishes or always answer your prayers in the way we expect. You never prayed that Bernardo would die. You know that. Believe me, you aren't that powerful. His death was always inside of him. We're born with our death inside us. To be truthful, I think he would have wanted to die on the job, while he was at work. He would have suffered too much if he had become an invalid. He could never have allowed anyone to see him ill. He would have been too vulnerable to let that happen. He never wanted to appear less than strong."

Katherine nods in understanding.

"On the other hand, can't you just imagine him in the hospital, directing the whole staff from his wheelchair, telling everyone to do this and that, whizzing in and out of the hospital rooms, up and down the halls?"

Katherine has to laugh, in spite of her sadness. "I would never have left Bernardo. I loved him too much. Maybe I feel guilty because of Jonathan. The truth is, we both loved Bernardo and Jonathan never expected me to leave him." She stops for a moment. "You are right, of course, but somehow, I still wonder if somehow I could have caused it."

"Of course you didn't."

"At times I still imagine that he is on location, and coming home soon. I think about our lives and the wonderful times we had as a family. How handsome and sexy he was, when I first met him. I know after the prostate thing happened, he started to worry about his health, but why didn't he tell me about his heart? Maybe I could have made a difference, somehow."

"Katherine, think about it. Bernardo's first priority was to finish that screenplay. Nothing was going to keep him from doing that. When Jonathan came to help, he was able to finish it, to give it his all. You know how people are able to do amazing thing under pressure; things they normally wouldn't be able to do. That's probably what happened to Bernardo. I am sure that is why he needed Jonathan. I can understand why he left him the screenplay in his will. Did you know he was doing that before the will was read?"

"No, but I'm happy he did. I think it was the right thing to do."

"Have you been able to reach Jonathan yet?"

"No, I have no idea how to get a hold of him. Neither does his agent. It is strange, but I have to be content with that now. Eventually he will get in touch, I'm sure."

Franko throws his arms around her.

"You know, Franko, I always have been taken care of. For the first time, I'm going to have to handle this myself. I long to have someone else take over and do everything for me. I wish Jonathan was here; but the truth is all my life, I have depended on others to make the big decisions; mostly Bernardo, of course. Until I went to Chiang Mai, I'd never made a life changing decision. Only now am I beginning to discover my own strength. I hope it will be enough to handle the challenges ahead. I could have been a help to Bernardo if he had lived."

Franko begins to muse, and smiles. "Remember how Bernardo loved to make up stories out of things he saw happening?"

"Yes, he was amazing. He'd have a whole lifetime figured out in a few moments. I think that was what made him such a great director. He intuited so much."

"Okay, imagine then, that Bernardo realized in some way what was going on within himself. Maybe he intuited that he would not be here very much longer. I think we do have an idea, when we are ready to go. He knew that when it happened, you would be on your own. You would need the strength to handle everything. Maybe that was why he so readily supported your venture in Thailand. Life works in mysterious ways. Haven't you done things without knowing why, and later it made perfect sense to you?"

"Sure, of course."

"Sometimes people need to leave but they need to know the one they leave behind is strong enough so they can go. I can already see that you are much stronger than you used to be. You wimp," Franko says, laughing.

Katherine begins to brighten up, even begins to laugh a little. "You may be right. It is time to turn around and look at the gifts Bernardo gave me, instead of focusing on my loss. Maybe he knew he could no longer look after me. I am sure I was a burden at times. When he realized I was strong enough, he was able to let go. It could be my growth signaled to him that I was ready to be on my own."

"It happens," he shrugs.

"I was shocked at how fragile he looked when he came home. He was so thin, and his vitality was no longer constant. He had always lived life to the limit. He was not the same, and he had to rest so much. I should have realized it was more than weariness. His skin even hung from his limbs, and he moved more slowly than usual. Remember how I could hardly keep up with him?"

"I never could either, even when I was younger," agrees Franko.

"When Jonathan came to stay, he seemed to regain his strength, his vitality, but the moment Jonathan left, he gave out. It was so sudden."

"Do you think he knew about you and Jonathan?"

"I hope not. We tried so hard not to let him know. But, as you said, he was amazing at reading people. Maybe subconsciously he knew. I hope not, or at least not all about us."

Franko is quiet for a moment. "It could be, even though he sensed something between you, he could see that you were strong enough to stay with him, to come home to him from the airport that last day when you dropped Jonathan off. Maybe you proved something to him. Even if he didn't know everything that happened, he may have felt Jonathan would be there for you when he was gone. You know how he loved to direct. It is such a mystery."

Katherine leans over and hugs Franko. "Thanks so much for your perspective. I have a hunch that it might be more accurate than we know. You've helped me so much. Bernardo was so very tired. I do know the only way he would have wanted to stay alive, was if he could live fully. As his energy ebbed away, it must have entered his mind, and he would have wanted to go before he was unable to make his own decisions. You know he was always generous and let me know how much he loved me. He would never have wanted to feel like a burden."

Franko changes the subject. "Don't you think Jonathan must know what is happening by now? Hasn't he ever called?"

"No. I can't imagine why. I have no idea what will happen between us now. I don't want to make any decisions about that right now. I'm aware that you need to give yourself at least a year after such a loss before making any major decisions. Maybe it's best that he is out of touch. I know I need to give myself time alone right now."

That night, exhausted but somewhat restored, Katherine lies down knowing that Franko's visit had helped her put things in perspective. She puts her head on the pillow. As she rolls over, she sees a book she hasn't seen before. Perhaps Gloria has rearranged her bed table when she cleaned. She picks up the book and opens it. It is a book of poetry by Rainier Maria Rilke. There is a short note on the fly page, written in Jonathan's hand, but he hadn't signed his name.

Instantly she knows who it is from. A bookmark marks a page. She begins to read.

> *God speaks to each of us as he makes us,*
>
> *Then walks with us silently out of the night.*
>
> *There are the words we dimly hear:*
>
> *you sent out beyond your recall,*
>
> *go to the limits of your longing.*
>
> *Embody me.*
>
> *Flare up like a flame*
>
> *and make big shadows I can move in.*
>
> *Let everything happen to your beauty and terror.*
>
> *Just keep going.*
>
> *No feeling is final.*
>
> *Don't let yourself lose me.*
>
> *Nearby is the country they call life.*
>
> *You will know it by its seriousness.*
>
> *Give me your hand.*

Rainer Maria Rilke.

She reads the poem over and over, weeping and finally falls asleep with the book in her hands.

Last year's
fragile vanished snow
is falling now again-----
if only seeing you
could be like this.

The Ink Dark Moon pg 88

KATHERINE'S DIARY

I write in here trying to gather my feeling. Perhaps someday I will understand Bernardo's death.

Pain comes and goes, sinking, then rising again to the surface. Awake, asleep, holding my breath, trying to remember to breathe. I let go of the tension, only to have the sadness return in a moment.

Foolishly, I believed that Bernardo and I would be together forever. What denial. I was so wrong, yet how could I have lived otherwise. I have no idea what will come next. I only want to escape the pain of my loss.

For twenty-five years, Bernardo was the center of my life and now the whole framework has collapsed. It is as though I no longer have a skeleton to hold my body up. I feel like a limp rag. There is nothing to look forward to. All the plans and ideas I had for our future are gone. The retirement years that I looked forward to spending with Bernardo, without his being involved in some project, will never happen now.

As I keep remembering our years together, I begin to allow myself to understand how, little by little, life had chipped away at Bernardo. First there was his operation, and then his heart holding him hostage, but he was unable to share his fears and problems. I didn't see what was happening. I didn't face reality. I didn't want to face the truth at all. I focused only on what I wanted to happen and that made me blind in a way. I should have seen how Bernardo's vitality was ebbing. I assumed he had given his all during the last film. He always did. But age must have robbed parts of his body that normally would have been able to heal. On the other hand, he wouldn't have wanted to live, if he couldn't work. I wanted more time with him, but perhaps he had no more time to give.

I meditate, and sometimes I can breathe in the love I feel for Bernardo and breathe out my sorrow. When I remember, I try to stop and take a deep breath, especially when the tears threaten to flow.

I feel disconnected from everyone and everything, by my grief. The twins call often, they are very concerned. They ask me if they should come home, and I tell them no. It will just take time, I tell them. Nobody can help.

In time, as I begin to meditate, I am able to move into my body again. I can feel my body withdrawing from the pain. Sometimes I grow hard as I try to numb my grief. Sometimes I feel angry with Bernardo for leaving me, without warning. Then my belly gets hard and the tender place at the center of my chest aches.

I still haven't heard from Jonathan. I wonder why, but after a while I realize it may be a gift. I have to get through this on my own. I understand this is the most important thing I can do for myself. I no longer depend on others.

I have joined a group of people who have lost partners. We all go through the grief process, and listen to others share their experiences. It gives me the strength to open to my own feelings of fear, anger, and sorrow and to share them, too. I never thought I would feel angry. I begin to understand that I am not alone in my feelings of hopelessness. One feels as though one is the only one suffering, and that nobody else can understand. I wonder if I will ever be able to trust anyone again. I feel betrayed. How could Bernardo have left me like this? I am surprised at my own anger.

I believe it is too painful to ever love anyone again. When a loved one dies, it leaves such a deep wound. I never want to feel that way again.

Because of my sorrow, I begin to have more insight into other people. I now have more patience and mercy for those who are in pain. The mindfulness I learned about in Thailand has a deep bearing on my life right now. The tools are more useful than I could ever have imagined. I am coming to understand that the pain I feel is universal. Although it all seems personal to me, many others share it.

As the weeks and months pass, I still reach over to feel for Bernardo at my side when I awaken. I can't bring myself to sleep in the middle of our bed. One night I tried to sleep in the middle and found myself back on my own side when I awoke.

Bernardo's death doesn't stop the flow of love I have for him. This confuses me at times. Yet it feels healing, and I accept it. I do understand that during the time I spent with Jonathan in Thailand, I was building my back-bone.

Sometimes I wish for Jonathan. I long for his support in my grief, but by now I realize he will not be here for me. I still wonder what happened to him. I long to be able to talk to him, and a moment later, I understand that it is better he is not here to distract me. I never have had the opportunity to become acquainted with the person I thought I had become in Thailand. I never have been able to test her, but I feel her presence as I go through my grief.

I sense the value of all that has happened. Perhaps there are no mistakes. Answers come to me during the day, during dreams at night. I am becoming aware of what I need to become.

Answers seem to turn up everywhere. I open a magazine and there is a quote from Arthur Miller. "Once we begin to see, we are doomed, and challenged to seek the strength to see more, not less."

Sometimes I begin to feel guilty. I will have the freedom to do things I never would have done if Bernardo were still alive. I am confused and amazed at the same time.

Again and again, thoughts of Jonathan enter my mind. Surely he must know by now. Perhaps he is afraid, now that I am on my own, that he won't be able to deal with the situation. I can hardly believe that; but who knows? Where has he gone? It is as though he dropped off the face of the earth. Has something terrible happened to him?

I have been so far down, for a long time now. I realize it is time to get busy. I've been self-involved for too long. Bernardo left the twins enough money so that each will be able to buy a home. For months, they have been begging me to come to Hawaii. They want my input about where they settle. That makes me feel good. I must get out of this self pity mode and go to see them. Until now, I haven't felt up to the trip. Today I made a reservation.

****

Hawaii is lovely and the warm breezes embrace me. I am reminded of Thailand, my time in Chiang Rai. By now I am sure Jonathan must have another relationship with a woman. I have never really been available to him. I can't expect him to have waited for me. I try not to think about him.

What a wonderful time with my children. Their enthusiasm rubs off on me. They are planning to buy a pineapple plantation. They want to build their own homes plus a guesthouse for me. That way I can visit them whenever I want and not feel like I am intruding. They asked me to move in with them, but I told them no way, although it did make me feel good; the fact that they want me. I am not ready to make the changes that would take yet. They have a whole lifetime ahead of them. They suggest I sell the big house, and find a smaller place, easier to keep up. I am not ready yet.

I told them about my project with the orphans in Bangkok. It has been so long since I have had the energy to think about it. I have to get back to that. I shared my book ideas. They were excited; they know I need something to do so I can get on with my life and finish grieving. They are young and resilient, and they know that I need to release Bernardo and get back to living my life.

They question me. "Mom, you are still young! What are you going to do?" I know they hope to hear a glimmer of passion in my voice. They have mostly recovered from their father's death. They loved him too, but already they miss him far less than I do. At their age, they have the capacity to get on with their lives, no matter what happens. I begin to learn from them and find the urge to get on with my life too.

When I left for home, I vowed to shape up. They were relieved. They feel somewhat responsible for my happiness. I know they would do anything for me. But that is not their job. I have to do this on my own.

When I came home, I began to get busy. The first morning I went to my dark-room and pulled out my photos from Thailand. I spread them out on the floor, and set up a schedule for myself. Unconsciously, I've been preparing for this project for a long time. I had planned to do it when I returned from Thailand, but when Bernardo came home and needed me; I pushed my own plans aside. Now it awaits me, like an old friend, and it will fill my days. I am learning that my grief will eventually dissipate. What will remain are all the good things about my relationship with Bernardo.

Nevertheless, there are times when loneliness creeps in and my whole being wants Bernardo back. I never knew anything could hurt like this. In my mind, I understand that it is my own thoughts that are making me sad, but I never realized that sadness could be felt in my whole body.

I call friends, when I feel sadness creeping in. That turns me in another direction. It makes a difference. We go out together for dinner, or take a walk. It always helps. When the sadness comes, it is too easy to dwell upon it. It is so weird how we humans operate. It is as though I need to be sad, because if I were to be happy, I'd be untrue to Bernardo's memory. I guess nobody is ever prepared for such a loss.

A string of jewels
from a broken necklace
scattering–
more difficult to keep hold of
even than these is one's life.

The Ink Dark Moon

BACK TO LIFE

One morning Katherine awakens and senses a difference. Things have shifted inside her; she doesn't know exactly why or how. No longer does she want to bask in her sadness. She is ready to clear up her life. Before Bernardo's death, she always tended to avoid uncomfortable memories. She must no longer do this. It is evident in the way she had dealt with her parents' home after their death. Even though she inherited the house in New Hampshire, she had no urge to return. After they died, she'd hired a caretaker and tried to forget about it.

The house deteriorates daily. It is time for her to clean it out; to sell it. Now she also has some incentive. She will donate the proceeds from the sale of the house and antiques to the orphanage in Bangkok. This becomes a driving force, moving her forward. Maybe she really has changed. She doesn't need the money; Bernardo left her more than enough money and security to live on for a lifetime.

"I've been waiting for you to do this!" Franko excitedly exclaims when she asks him to accompany her to New Hampshire. "There have to be some wonderful antiques. I get first pick! Right?" He can hardly wait.

She knows he will keep her spirits up, and he will probably discover a bundle of treasures for himself. His humor heals her; he won't let her sink back into the doldrums.

It's a bright fall morning when they leave the house in Connecticut, and head north to New Hampshire. Katherine drives the shiny, red convertible Bernardo gave her on her fiftieth birthday. The air is warm, and they feel like a couple of kids on an outing, a treasure hunt. They take the coast route, up Route #1 and drive along the ocean. They stop for lunch and load up on snacks for later.

Katherine had contacted the caretaker. He agreed to meet them the following day. Until now, she hasn't been ready to face the mess that she knows awaits her. Franko will be a great help. This big old house in the country has been a storehouse for her father's collectibles, purchased during a lifetime of traveling and working overseas. She has no idea what condition the house is in. All she knows is that there is a big job ahead of them, involving many decisions and lots of physical work.

The ride up north brightens Katherine's spirits. She likes a challenge. She is finally ready to appreciate Franko. Although he brings up what she doesn't want to think about and delves into her worries, he brings them up into the sunshine. Once she opens her mind to her imagined troubles, they don't seem so terrible. At the same time, she isn't sure she wants to face some of the things that will come to mind as she empties this house. She hasn't gotten rid of Bernardo's clothes yet. Getting rid of his clothes seems to her like erasing his life, in a way.

Franko listens to Katherine as they drive. She shares her anger about Bernardo's death, apologizing time after time. "I have no right to feel like this."

"What you are going through is only normal. Believe me, I have lost many friends and family," Franko assures her. "Anyone who has had a close relationship feels deserted when a partner dies. You are not a bad person; it is part of the healing process." Franko says this with force. "You know how a person acts when they are told they have a fatal disease? There are five steps you must go through. You can't avoid any of them or you are unable to deal. The stages go in order, no matter what you try to do. Denial at first, then anger, bargaining, depression, and finally, acceptance. We all have to experience each step, and in the end it becomes possible to accept what is happening, or going to happen. It works that way in divorce, sickness, and death, even the end of relationships. Each is a little death. The way you deal with a loss, relates to the uniqueness of the relationship."

"I sound like a self-indulgent, spoiled child." Katherine laughs more easily now. "I want everything to be my way, but I understand that the world turns in spite of how I feel. I know it's my job to deal with the feelings and become happy again."

She realizes that by now, she has actually also gone through these steps regarding her relationship with Jonathan, without actually identifying them.

They cross the border of New Hampshire at Portsmouth, and an hour and a half hour later they are bouncing up a dirt road, rough as a washboard. She turns off the main road and follows a long driveway that leads to her parents' house. The house is located up a winding road, on top of a hill, surrounded by ancient stone walls. Huge maple trees tower beside the road. Bright green fields are groomed, and wildflowers line the driveway.

"This is a gorgeous property. How charming!" Franko exclaims.

"So far, so good." Katherine says. "I have put this off for three years, since my parents died."

The house appears on the rise. It looks as sad and deserted as a house can look. The porch tilts, and there are a few boards missing. The gardens are overgrown, perennials and weeds mixing wildly. The roof needs to be replaced. It is obvious that nobody has cared for this place. Finally facing the reality, Katherine is shocked at the condition of the house. She begins to feel guilty when Franko asks, "What on earth happened to this house, Katherine?"

"I don't know," she answers meekly, now ashamed that she has ignored it for so long. Why hadn't she come to see it in all this time?

"We sent my parents the money to keep it up, but it doesn't look like they made any repairs. I remember that when I hired the caretaker, he informed me he didn't do contracting or repairs. He agreed to look after the books in the library though. He probably likes to read. I know I should have checked on him once in a while, but I just wanted to put it out of my mind."

Papers and leaves gather in the corners of the porch, flattened by winter snows that had fallen through the years. Broken branches litter the yard. A few flowers try to bloom in the garden. Cracked paint peels off the windowsills. The two friends walk toward the front door, and find the key under the mat. "Isn't it amazing it is still here, and nobody has broken in?"

Katherine opens the door at the front of the house, and they first walk into the mudroom; a small unheated room where her parents had stowed all their outdoor gear and wood for the fireplace. A sickening smell meets them. Franko wrinkles his nose and makes a face. Mouse droppings litter the floor and the musty smell of old neglected houses fills the air. Piles of newspapers line the mud room. Heavy winter coats hang from hooks on the wall. There are boots standing in a line beneath the coats.

"Looks like the coats are waiting for someone, doesn't it?" Franko tries to ease the depressing sight. "Do you think ghosts need to keep warm?"

"Achoo! Achoo!" They both sneeze as soon as they open the door to the living room. The house doesn't look any different from the last time Katherine was here years before. The only difference is everything is now covered in dust. Her mother had been an immaculate housekeeper. It is obvious that nobody has broken in.

"Oh girl, is this a bonanza, or what! There are antiques everywhere! I love this place, dirt, dust and all." Franko is ecstatic.

Two reclining chairs face the fireplace. Logs are still stacked and set for a fire. It is eerie. Katherine almost expects her parents to appear in the room.

She is still confused about the strange way her parents had died. Her trip home, for their funeral, had been a whirlwind. She had been on location in Africa with Bernardo so she and the twins had flown home for the funeral. As soon as her parents were buried, they rushed back to Africa. She wanted to escape the horror of the whole experience. She hired the caretaker over the phone and never returned.

The old house had never been a real home to Katherine. It is more like a museum. In truth, she has moved so much in her life, she never felt like she had a real home until she married Bernardo. He had filled a deep need for her. He had given her security for the first time in her life, and she always valued that. This house was a holding place for her father's possessions, a reflection of him. Although her father and mother had been very close, her mother always remained in her father's shadow. She had been there to support his life and work. In his line of work, he had needed her, but still, here in this house, her only private domain had been the kitchen. Her father seldom entered there. He expected to be waited on and served as he had all throughout his career.

Having become more introspective in the past year, Katherine now understands that her mother had never explored her own needs. Enough time has passed so that she can see her mother more clearly. She also realizes that women in her mother's time hadn't found it necessary to do much self-searching. Yet the example of her mother's lifestyle has set Katherine up for a pattern she has to overcome herself at this time.

She had often heard other women say they didn't want to be like their mothers. In spite of not wanting it to happen, most women, as they grow older, tend to resemble their mothers in some ways. The other side of that is that as they mature, they began to appreciate what their mothers have done for them, and how they played what cards of life had been dealt them. By the time women understand, they no longer judge their mothers. Katherine is in that place now. For the first time she can see her mother clearly, without being critical.

Lost in her thoughts for a few moments, she remembers how she has always been grateful for the most important gift her mother gave her when she was very young. She had been given a camera, and her mother nurtured her interest in photography. Living a childhood filled with many moves all over the world made her independent in some ways. She had to make new friends each year. They had lived in homes provided by the embassies, but they never owned a home of their own. Her mother had done her best to make each new place a warm, attractive home for them to live in.

"What on earth is this stuff outside, in the garden?" Franko's voice brings her back to the present. "It looks like columns from a temple, or something."

Katherine laughs, as she recalls her father's dreams. "He sent things home from all over the world during the time he worked in the diplomatic corps. In his imagination, he could see how he would use this and that, in some way, after he retired. It is sad to see how may things still lie in piles around here. Some have decayed with time and are no longer of use."

She takes Franko by the hand and leads him to a separate building. "Most of all, my father loved books. The first thing he did when he retired was to build his own library. It holds all his books. Some of them are valuable. He built in a heater and a humidifier so they would be safe in all kinds of weather. I did make sure the caretaker would watch over the library, if nothing else. He agreed to the task."

They can see that the caretaker has done a good job. There are no mouse droppings and the library smells warm and clean.

There are hundreds of books, filling shelves from floor to ceiling...everything one could imagine, history, travel, and science. Her father had loved them all.

Jonathan would be in heaven if he owned this, Katherine thinks to herself. As she observes herself, she is aware of how much she has tried to shut Jonathan out of her mind ever since Bernardo died. She has tried not to include him in her life and she still feels almost guilty when she longs to turn to him in the most difficult times. Now it feels good to allow him into her thoughts now.

As though he can read her mind, Franko asks, "Are you thinking about Jonathan?" Nothing escapes Franko. "Where do you think he has been?"

"I don't know; I never, ever heard from Jonathan. I thought I might." She is glad she can finally say his name aloud, even if it isn't great news.

They walk through the garden and Franko spots large pieces of statuary from Italy, Spain and Turkey. There are even pieces of ruins that might not have been legal to take out of the country where they were found.

"I always wondered just what it was my dad meant to build. He loved to collect and seemed to have some sort of a plan, but he never shared his dreams with me."

"Maybe he meant to build some sort of temple to the gods. What do you think?" muses Franko.

"It's fun to imagine he had that sort of idea within him. I don't think I ever knew him very well. When I married, I didn't pick a total father figure ...... not my father anyway. They say we often marry someone very similar to our fathers, but Bernardo was always so vocal with his ideas, and Jonathan certainly told me about writing his book."

Soon Katherine puts aside thoughts of Jonathan, and begins to concentrate on the gigantic task ahead of her. Together she and Franko return to the house and make a list of all that needs to be done.

"Can I have first picks on the antiques?" Franko already has a long list. "The stained glass lamps, the velvet love seat, the large kitchen cupboard. I know there will be more." He is in his element.

Katherine looks around the house. "Isn't it amazing, how things are so important to people, and after they are gone, it is of no interest to anyone else, just stuff for the trash bin? The antiques are valuable, but most of the things are nothing anyone would want or even be able to use."

By the time the sun begins to set, they are covered in dust and ready to quit for the day. They drive down the road and check into a small inn nearby. Katherine had noticed a vacancy sign on the way up. She has called on her cell phone for a reservation.

They apologize to "Please call me Vivian," the innkeeper, for being so grubby and ask to reserve rooms for the next few days. Vivian shows them to connecting rooms with fireplaces. In contrast to the dusty, dreary house, Katherine's room, with its butterfly theme is a delight. Franko has an equally delightful room decorated in deep purple and white. In the tub Katherine lets the hot water run over her for a long time, rubbing coconut scented shampoo into her hair, rinsing it three times. She scrubs and scrubs, to get the dirt out of her pores. She blows her nose with enthusiasm trying to get rid of the smell of mouse droppings.

Dinner is served at six, and they are relieved that they don't have to go somewhere else to eat. They order a bottle of Shiraz, and sit back, slowly sipping her favorite wine. Now that she is here, it is a relief to be able to unwind. It is midweek and there are few guests, making it unnecessary to socialize. Even Franko is quiet. Normally he can talk enough for both of them. After their dinner of lobster pasta and fresh vegetables, preceded by the house specialty of fresh tomato soup with cognac, and ending with French Silk Pie they are replete. They head up the stairs and briefly hug goodnight. Katherine's flannel nightgown feels good, as the temperature drops during the night.

The caretaker meets them at the property the next morning. Katherine has never met him in person, only talked to him on the phone.

"Hello, I'm Robert." He announces in his Yankee accent. He is a small man, full of energy and vigor. When he smiles, his blue eyes twinkle with mischief. "Bout time you made a decision to sell," he tells her.

Together they go through the house and walk the property. Franko follows along and by the time they finish walking the boundaries, Katherine is bushed. Franko is puffing.

"You both need more exercise," says Robert. "Come sit down on the porch."

"What do you think this place might be worth?" Katherine asks Robert.

A typical closemouthed Yankee, he replies, "I have no idea; I think you should find yourself a good Realtor. They give free appraisals, you know. They do that so they can get your business. You might also want to look for an auctioneer. They come out and tell you the value of what you have. I'll bet those antiques in the house are worth a bundle." He begins to chuckle. "I don't envy you at all."

That evening they talk with Vivian, the innkeeper, and explain what needs to be done. They ask her advice about finding a realtor and an auctioneer. It is then that Vivian tells them about a young couple who had stayed at the inn, and on a hike had discovered her house. They had paid no mind to the Private Property sign…… they walked in anyway and conveniently found the key under the mat. They loved the house, and asked Vivian to please let them know if it ever came up for sale.

Katherine begins to wonder about the coincidence. It feels very right to her. She doesn't want to have a hassle; she just wants the money to send to Silvere in Bangkok. All she can see is the wreck of a house, but others with more imagination, might be able to bring it back to life.

They meet with "Antoinella, from Italy." She is a Realtor and a friend of Vivian's. She has a great head of dark curly hair and a wonderful Italian accent. She shows up at the house the next day, and they sign an agreement. Katherine thinks Bernardo would have enjoyed meeting someone from his country. Antoinella assures Katherine that she will be able to handle the sale of the house. Rick the auctioneer, comes the next day. When Katherine learns the estimated total value of the antiques, she is astounded.

"Oh my, will I be able to afford all this now?" moans Franko, in jest.

"What an academy award performance, maybe you should open your own actor's studio. Of course you can have anything you want, in trade for your labor."

They work hard, cleaning, scrubbing, and straightening. Katherine finds a few things she wants, but not much. She is happy that the proceeds will be high, as it will really help the orphanage.

Antoinella contacts the young couple before Katherine and Franko leave. The couple immediately makes an offer on the house. They plan to run an antique business, so they also make an offer on the antiques. After a day of intense negotiation, Katherine is very happy to get the price she asked for.

"Good for you, Katherine. You stood by your guns. You have changed. I think you're capable of taking care of yourself now." Franko is proud of her.

The sale goes through easily, due to Antoinella's good nature and competence. The young couple is full of enthusiasm, and within three months, Katherine is freed of a huge responsibility that she had needed to address and release for a long time. Her life is improving; it no longer feels so difficult. At home again, she takes a course on Feng Shui, and learns how moving things in one's life clears up many things. When the sale is finalized, she feels a huge blockage release from her life.

This body

grown fragile, floating,

a reed cut from its roots....

If a stream would ask me

to follow,

I'd go, I think.

The Ink Dark Moon

SUMMER RETURNS

Bernardo has been gone for over a year. The numbness has begun to dissipate and Katherine feels as though it will be possible to live fully again. She has been through an experience of grief so deep she could never have imagined it. Through her ordeal, she has changed a great deal. She now feels capable of going on with her life... alone, if that is her future. She feels good about herself.

The twins have finished building their homes on the pineapple plantation. They have retained someone to run the plantation while they continue with their education. They are excited about the little house they have built for Katherine. She promises to come for Christmas. When they meet her at the airport, they see she has come back to life. She is no longer like a delicate flower that might wilt at any moment.

"Close your eyes, Mom." They drive up to her cottage. It is artistically designed, built of teak, surrounded by tropical flowers and palms; a screen veranda runs along the front. It is absolutely charming. Inside the house, huge windows open to the ocean far beyond. The brightly colored pillows on the couch and Hawaiian flowered upholstery bring a happy atmosphere to the whole place. The kitchen is open to the whole house. Deep blue tiles cover the counters below glass-fronted cupboards. It is totally outfitted with things they know Katherine loves to cook with. They lead her into the bedroom. A king size bed greets her. "Oh this is huge!"

"Well Mom, someday you might want to share this house with someone. We want you to have enough room."

Katherine laughs. "I can't imagine."

That night, over dinner at the main house, Katherine lets the twins know how much she appreciates what they have done for her. "I'm so fortunate to have you both. I don't know what I would have done without you. I'm glad I was able to foster your independence, because you have taught me so much. You respected my needs and gave me the time to heal. I love you so much. Here's the first draft of my book."

They sit at the dining room table and begin to see for the first time what Katherine has created with hundreds of photographs.

"How can they be so cruel? Are these young boys sold too? How terrible, those children used by people! Look how old these young girls' eyes look."

"I've sent the proceeds from the sale of my parents' home to Silvere for the orphanage. She wrote and said she was able to add on and refurbish so much. There is even money left for the future. I'll make an endowment from the sale of my book. I know money helps, but what will help more is to find parents, people to adopt these babies." The twins agree.

"I am playing with the idea of going on to Bangkok to show Silvere the book. I think I might take a trip while I am here."

"Mom, that's a great idea." The twins are happy to have their mother back.

****

The weather in Thailand in January is the best it gets. Katherine checks into the same guesthouse where she and Jonathan stayed before. Memories come rushing back. She loves the warm humid weather. Walking the streets of Bangkok, she is reminded of how the Thai people always smile. She remembers the floating nun, and what she had said. It all seems to make sense now. She orders the same meals she and Jonathan shared on her last trip to Bangkok. At last, she allows herself to miss him, but she no longer feels the deep pain she felt before. Opening to a new way of life, she pushes her memories aside and sets out for the orphanage. It looks wonderful. With the money she has sent, Silvere has been able to make major changes to the building, and she is able to house many more children now and hire people to help. She introduces Katherine to the new children who have arrived since she was there before. Happily, all the babies she remembers have been adopted. Their photographs still hang on the wall. All those big brown eyes staring back at her touch her deeply. Tears well up in her eyes, but she tries to hold them back, and instead returns the infants' smiles, and touches those beautiful small brown hands that reach for hers.

Silvere loves the book. She goes through it page by page and is amazed at what Katherine has been able to accomplish after she left Bangkok. "This is beautiful; I've never seen anything like this. I know it will make a difference to anyone who sees it. You have already made a big difference in these children's lives."

They go out for dinner that evening. "The only real solution is a change of culture, tradition," Silvere says.

"I understand that the culture is different in other countries. I can't possibly force any major changes on people even though I believe it is right. I only hope I can make some progress. I believe that focusing on the babies is the best thing I can do. I can do that for the rest of my life, and maybe by that time, other things will change too.

"Katherine, that is true. Each adoption makes a difference. Your book will bring awareness to the world of their needs. I have my doubts that we will ever change the needs of the market for sex. That has been going on since the world began."

Katherine is pulled in two ways; she is of two minds. When she is truthful with herself, she wants to find out what has happened to Jonathan. On the other hand, she doesn't want to interfere if he has a new relationship. She is still puzzled by his disappearance. She knows he has no phone at his house in Chiang Rai house; he always used his cell phone. She decides to call Tony, the fellow who found Jonathan for her in the first place. She can write, but that would take too long, and if Jonathan was no longer at his home, how will a letter find him?

On the phone, Tony recognizes her right away, as soon as she explains briefly who she is. "Oh, Miss Katherine, where are you? When are you coming back to see me?"

She decides not to tell him she is in Bangkok. She doubts that he has caller identifier. "Tony, I've been trying to reach Jonathan. Have you seen him lately?"

"No, Miss Katherine. He came back here after he finished his book and stayed about a month. Since then, I haven't heard from him. Is everything all right? I could drive up north to his house and see if he is there."

"No, Tony, that's all right." She is very disappointed. "I'll try to get back to see you sometime soon. You were so kind to me."

Slowly, she hangs up the phone, still puzzled. If he had died, Tony surely would know. It would have been in the paper. Maybe no news is good news.

Katherine returns to Hawaii, and spends a couple more weeks sightseeing, enjoying the weather. Although they are back in school, they make time for her. She meets more of their friends and feels at home in her little abode.

By February, she is back home. She continues to work on her book. It makes her feel of use now. After many tries, she makes contact with an agent who quickly finds a publisher who offers her a contract. She signs it and is thrilled. She is tying up loose ends. It feels good.

There is one more major thing she must to do. She realizes the twins no longer need a home to come back to. If anything, she will go to them. It is time to consider selling the big house. It is far too large for one person. She can afford to keep it, but there is too much work. It is time to let it go. Katherine contacts a Realtor and the house goes on the market.

Finally, Katherine is able to give herself some freedom. It has taken much time to get to this place. She understands that many people have gone through the process before, but now she also realizes that it is an individual process that has to happen. She is beginning to release her external life with Bernardo. She has accepted that she will never forget him. How could she possibly? He had been a major part of her life for so long. What remains is the richness of their relationship. He was such an amazing man, and he will remain in her heart forever. On the other hand, she is no longer his wife, nor needed as the mother of his children. Changed in profound ways, it is becoming more difficult for Katherine to remember her life in the past.

She has been through a metamorphosis. Walls she built, so carefully in childhood, are disappearing, breaking down. She can almost feel the cracks grow larger, and feel the great breaths of freedom, as she releases her safeguards from the past. The breaking open occurs, and as her inner strength increases, she finds her sense of humor, and a new way of observing the world than in the past.

Her life is no longer structured. She is free to do whatever she pleases. Her inheritance is substantial, and there is no immediate need to earn a living, although at some point, she feels she will want to go to work.

Franko, always ready to give her advice and support, suggests enthusiastically that she take an art therapy course given on Monhegan Island, off the coast of Maine.

"I've never painted,." she says, intrigued.

"Try it. You'll have lots of fun. You don't need to know anything about painting."

"Well,.........painting is sort of like photography, I guess. You know, painting with light."

"You need to do something different, Katherine." Franko assures her again that she does not need to know how to paint to enjoy it. He had been to the class the year before and had a fabulous time. He had learned a lot about himself by the end of his classes.

Katherine makes the reservation for early June. The Island Inn has a room available for the dates she wants to go. She flies from New York to Rockport, Maine. From there, a limo service delivers her to the town where the ferryboat departs for the island, early the next morning. She spends the night in a small motel. It is nothing fancy. The next day a storm has moved in, and it is pouring.

Making her way down the gangplank, she watches as two handsome young fellows carry her luggage on board. The tide is out, so it is a steep walk down the gangplank. The railing is cold and slippery. As she steps from the pier to the ferry, the taller boy holds her hand and smiles at her as the ferry bobs up and down. When she reaches the deck, she feels somewhat dizzy for a moment. It is definitely not a day to travel up on the top deck. She takes a seat on a bench inside, the luggage piled up in front of her.

Everyone is boarded; the doors are closed as the Captain announces the safety regulations. He adds that they offer hot coffee, and warm cinnamon rolls, along with cold drinks up front. "You can buy a map of the island also, so you will know where to hike," he says.

Katherine has never been seasick, but a few people begin to suffer immediately. The woman beside her is very quiet and her eyes are closed.

Once the boat leaves the harbor, the ocean becomes rough, the water washes up over the front of the boat and

Katherine can hardly see anything. After an hour and a half of rough seas, the ferry pulls up to the wharf at Monhegan Island. At first, it had seemed to be a dark shadow in the storm. The tide is high now and it makes it easier to get up the gangplank. The passengers have donned their warmest clothes and they are waiting with shoulders hunched in the rain. Their luggage is tossed aboard a rusty pickup truck, and carted up to the hotel. Before she heads for the hotel, Katherine stops at a little café on the wharf for a cup of hot tea and a snack.

The Island Inn is a very old hotel. It stands proudly on the hill, high above the harbor greeting all new arrivals. It is an elegant old building. Katherine walks slowly up to the hotel. She sees tiny white flowers called Snowdrop in Summer, mixed with flowering thyme, sprinkled with purple blossoms. She feels happier and happier about the fact that she has made the decision to come here. It is a different world, and reminds her of the way the world was when she was growing up.

"Welcome to the Island Inn," the pretty dark-haired girl at the desk announces, as she hands Katherine a registration card to fill out. She gives her a key to her room, along with some breakfast coupons and informs her that her bags are already in the room. Crackling logs in a huge fireplace warms the lobby. Chairs are filled with people sitting in various sections, reading, and waiting out the storm. A family noisily plays Monopoly at a round table. There is no view from the porch. The fog has rolled in and it is as though they are wrapped in thick cotton.

Katherine has been up since early that morning. With the fog and rain outside, she feels ready for a nap. When she enters the room, it is chilly and she cannot find a heater. It is definitely a summer resort. Fortunately, the bed is covered with a large down comforter. She unpacks, still shivering, and finally crawls beneath the comforter. Moments later she falls fast asleep.

It is after five pm when she awakens. Dinner is served between six and eight. She showers and heads downstairs. The fireplace and added bodies waiting for dinner lend a little warmth to the atmosphere, but when the dining room doors open, cold air rushes into the lobby.

A fantastic menu awaits her. The inn does not have liquor license. Franko has advised her of the need, to bring her own bottle of wine with her. A young Polish waiter opens the bottle with finesse and holds it up for her approval. After she nods, he pours it into her glass. She sips the deep red wine and looks at her many choices on the menu. Her mouth watering, she decides upon mussels, a small Caesar salad, and rack of lamb. "Very rare please." She is hungry, and finishes with a piece of the huge chocolate cake she noticed at the table near the entrance. It is drizzled with raspberry liqueur. She returns to her room as soon as she is done. She wants to be ready bright and early for her art class.

The next morning, the rain continues to fall softly, but the sky begins to brighten. During the night, Katherine had awakened and felt aware of the wind and the wildness of the storm. She feels fortunate to have a room in the main building. It seems safe there. The old building has withstood many storms throughout the years. This morning, she dresses in the old clothes she has brought for painting. "Bring nothing you care about," Franko has warned her.

Breakfast is biscuits and gravy, scrambled eggs, bacon, orange juice and strong coffee. She is ready for anything. She takes off down the road, following directions to the teacher's house. There are no public vehicles on the island; she must walk, or forget it. It is a pleasant journey, even in the drizzle. The picturesque road curves around and past another hotel. Near the post office, Katherine spies an empty store for rent.

She finds herself imagining the creation of a store here. "I could move to this charming island." She is happy to find her imagination returning.

She passes The Trailing Ewe, a well-known, casual inn, where everyone eats at the same table. Soon a great colorful fish with huge lips greets her at a gate beside the road. It is the artist's signature work. Franko had discovered him when he had bought one of his fish in an art gallery in New York. When he learned that the artist gave art therapy classes, he had signed up. He loved it. Katherine recalls one of those fish out on his terrace, grinning at her from amongst his plants.

She walks into the covered patio area, up some steps and then knocks on the door.

"Hello!" A tall, energetic man, dressed in a tee shirt and blue jeans, sporting an immense, bushy moustache, greets her.

For a moment, she wonders what she is doing here.

"Come on in and have a seat. You are first. When everyone else gets here, we will get acquainted. I'm Mike." He goes back to grinding coffee beans.

She walks into the living room and looks around. The walls are covered with paintings and artwork. Soon the other students arrive. There are seven budding artists. Mike directs them all to sit in a circle while he explains how the class will proceed. He offers them coffee, perfect with fluffed cream. He explains that this is a different kind of art class. "As a verbal culture we are quite sophisticated in erecting defenses in our verbalizations. However, when engaged in creative acts, such as art making, the artist engages in pure uncensored, unconscious expression. Art therapy provides a safe forum for communication of one's innermost self, since the activity is outwardly directed and the product appears outside oneself. Let go of judgment. Be spontaneous.

There is no right or wrong way to paint"

There is a collective sigh. "If you are inclined, you are welcome to come earlier the next morning and meditate before class"

He gives them instructions about mixing their colors. "Okay, you're on your own for the first hour."

Katherine walks into the studio and chooses a place. Hesitantly, she tacks up a huge piece of paper on the wall, the blank sheet staring her in the face. She wonders how she will ever fill it.

"Remember there is no right or wrong way to paint. Just let yourself go," Mike reminds them.

Katherine takes stock of her area. The brushes are large and she realizes that once she decides to make a stroke, just one, and the paper will begin to change. She opens large jars of paint and takes up her acrylic pallet. She fills it with bright colors. Whoosh, she makes her first stroke. The paint is soft and creamy, luscious. The next stroke is large and bright. It is a sensuous experience, freeing and joyful.

At first, Katherine tries to paint flowers she loves; soft, pink peonies. Soon she finds herself painting with bright purples, pinks and golden yellow. She does a wash of blue over her work. It changes everything. Her work becomes wilder with each painting. She paints in pastels, then with more bright colors, now understanding how children must feel when they are allowed to paint freely. She fills sheet after sheet, hangs them out to dry in the yard, spreading them on the grass after the sun comes out.

The second day she and the others tear their paintings into pieces and make them into a collage. They paint over that. There is no clinging to what they have already created. Katherine wants to keep some of her paintings, but as she tears the paintings apart, the freedom astounds her.

At the end of the first class, she walks down the road and stops at the little convenience store for lunch. A pretty, efficient girl with a bare belly and a ring in her nose runs the lunch counter in back. Katherine orders pizza and takes it outside where she sits with other visitors to the island. They converse about their travels. She wanders around the island, with the map she has bought in hand. The gentle breeze caresses her. The sun is warm. Later in the afternoon, she buys a sweatshirt to keep warm when she sits on the lawn of the Island Inn. It is a magical time and she is coming back to life. There is always someone in the lobby, friendly and ready to talk.

"Most people in the world have never heard of Monhegan Island, let alone been here," a longtime visitor tells her. "It is a perfect part of the past, so many writers and painters have come here for inspiration." Katherine's sadness is finally at bay. She has been forced to move forward with her life. As the days go by, she sees with new eyes. The class teaches her about more than just painting. She now notices how the purple lupines in the fields, give rise to other flowers, greenery, and blue skies, filled with fluffy clouds beyond them. There is much depth in the world when one begins to see.

A young girl comes up to her as she walks along the beach at sunset. She opens her hands and shows Katherine the sea glass she has found when the tide goes out. She explains how the sea makes smooth, bright little pieces out of glass and returns it to the land.

By the end of the third day, Katherine is ready to drop. She did not expect this to happen. She doesn't believe she has exerted much energy in her painting. At least it does not appear to be that way. She asks Mike about it. "You are using a new part of your brain while you paint, Katherine. Although it may not seem like it, because you are enjoying yourself, this is a deep exercise."

She finds herself using different colors than she did in the beginning; bright yellow, and orange and gold. One painting is a giant sun; beings flying toward it. Another painting is of a ring of angels looking down upon earth, dancing for joy. She has developed a primitive style and she quite likes the result. She thinks she will pursue painting when she goes home.

By the time the last day arrives, she hates to say goodbye to her fellow artists. They have grown close. Mike rolls up their paintings so they can easily carry them home.

It has been four days of pure joy for Katherine. This has been her first solo trip to this amazing island. She doubts that she is going to become a fabulous artist, but something good has happened. When she looks at her paintings and tries to see what they say, she feels a great healing has occurred. She understands it is a beginning and now she will be able to go forward with her life. She is reminded of a teaching from her course in Thailand. "The path is the way, not the destination." She has no idea of her destination anymore.

Right on time, the ferry chugs up to the wharf. The sea is calm. Katherine climbs aboard easily and takes a seat on top, so she can look out at the ocean. What a change from the day she arrived, when it had been so dark and stormy. Today she can see the sea gulls on the rocks, chattering, diving for fish. The day is bright and sunny. The whole experience, the darkness and rain in the beginning and now the lovely weather seems to reflect what has happened in her life. Although it is subtle, the impact of this trip will reach far into her future.

I love you the gentlest of Ways,
Who ripened us, as we wrestled with you.

Rainier Maria Rilke.

TAKE FLIGHT

There is one last thing Katherine must do for Bernardo. In his will, Bernardo had specified that he wanted his ashes to be spread around his ancestral home in Tuscany. He wished to be set free in the hills of Tuscany. Until now, Katherine has not been willing to let the last of Bernardo go. She has not been able to grant his wish.

The house is up for sale; she has finally been able to give away all of Bernardo's clothes. It is time for her to walk through the last door. She must close this chapter of her life. She feels strong, and knows she must grant his last request. There is no way she can refuse him. During the art class on Monhegan, when she tore up her paintings and restructured them, something opened in her life. The final part of her healing must occur. It will be an important finale to Bernardo's life of drama, enthusiasm and joy. She cannot let him down.

Once she understands and accepts that she is now ready, she calls the twins and asks if they will accompany her. They demur, "you should do this on your own. He would have wanted it that way." They are adamant. Although it is puzzling, she tries to understand what they are telling her. She accepts their decision.

In August, she flies to Tuscany. Bernardo's family estate is in a valley, below a tiny town built on a hillside. Katherine has not notified the family that she is coming. She knows the house is always open. Servants who live there year round look after it. When Bernardo made out his will, he told her he didn't want his family to interfere with his last wishes; she must do this on her own. On her arrival, she drives by the huge home. Fields of olive trees and grape arbors surround it. None of the family seems to be there. The busy relatives who live and work in Rome normally take their vacations in September. This will be a private affair.

This is a special time. It has to be done right, just as Bernardo would have wanted her to do this. She is glad to be alone, yet unsure of how she will orchestrate the next day. Bernardo had always loved the small village, filled with inviting tiny restaurants, tables set out on the sidewalks. The streets are lined with small shops. Her hotel room overlooks the valley, verdant and green, fields filled with yellow flowers. She can see the family home in the distance.

Bernardo had left Italy when he was young. He knew that he would never work in the family business once he discovered the film industry. Although he enjoyed Italy, he seldom was able to return. After his mother and father died, he no longer stayed in touch with his cousins. His older relatives were all gone, and the younger ones were too busy to be acquainted. That had been fine with him. In the old days, he might have been needed in the family business, but when he decided work in the movies, he was no longer useful to the family. He never explained the family dynamics to Katherine. He tended to live in the moment.

On her first evening in the little village, Katherine walks down to the piazza. She remembers the restaurant where she and Bernardo had eaten dinner when they were last here. She finds the same table where they had eaten. It is empty so she takes a seat. A tall, dark, handsome waiter fluffs up her red napkin with a snap, and places it in her lap.

"I'll start with a glass of your house Chianti." She says remembering that it is the specialty of this area.

People walk past, hand in hand; a musician plays a mandolin, and smiles at her as he strolls by her table. The music plays and she feels a sense of contentment.

"Are you ready to order?" the waiter asks.

"I suppose this will sound silly. I know I won't be able to eat all this, but please bear with me. I want to order all my husband's favorite dishes."

"That is fine. Will he be joining you later?"

"I don't think so."

He takes out his order pad.

"I'll begin with the Ginestrata... sweet and sour cream soup. Right?"

He writes that down.

"He always loved the Carote Al Rafano, the carrots with horseradish. Insalata Verde, the green salad, the Costolette D'Agnello, those wonderful little grilled lamb chops with cucumber. And those Fiordi Zucca Fritta, the fried zucchini flowers. I know it sounds like way too much food, but this is a celebration."

The waiter grins happily. He is sure that he will receive a large tip from this extravagant woman.

"No hurry," she says. "I want to enjoy my wine first."

The waiter lights the candle as the sun begins to set. A soft breeze ruffles the skirt of her dress. Her hair is slightly tousled. She is relaxed; the last act has begun.

Suddenly the hair on the back of her neck tingles. She feels, more than sees, someone out of the corner of her eye. She turns her head to see well. A man's movement seems slightly familiar. He walks toward her. She feels faint. Her heart begins to beat rapidly.

"Can it be? No! I'm just imagining things." She tries to reassure herself.

The next moment she is looking up into his face, his beloved face. "Jonathan, is it really you?" she barely whispers.

"Oh, yes, my darling." He stands before her, waiting, a step away.

She is shaking. "I can't believe it; I want to, I don't want to! I don't know if I'm happy to see you or angry, or what I feel."

In the end, nothing matters. Her heart opens. He holds out his arms and she rushes into them. They hold each other for what seems like hours. Taking a deep breath, Jonathan drinks her in. Katherine, at last, lets herself feel how starved she has been for his love. She dissolves in his familiar scent, and nestles her face in his neck. Her longings burst forth, and she can no longer keep them locked inside.

"Jonathan, what happened? Why didn't you come back? I thought you might be dead." She bursts into bitter tears.

"Oh, my darling, I must explain. This has been terrible. He strokes her hair, trying to comfort and calm her. I have kept the most difficult promise I ever made. I had no idea things would turn out as they have."

"What do you mean?" she asks, looking into his eyes.

"Please, let's sit down, and I'll try to explain." They sit. "I hope and pray that you will understand and forgive me. I wanted to be with you, with all my heart and soul …ever since Bernardo died. So many times, I have been close to giving in and come to comfort you. I hope you will be able to understand and forgive me. "

She is puzzled. The sun begins to set behind the clouds. Flames of orange illuminate their faces. It is as though they have come back to life from somewhere beyond. He takes a letter from his inside coat pocket. The waiter returns with another glass and pours Jonathans some wine. As he walks away, he smiles. He is sure the husband has arrived, in spite of what Katherine has told him.

"Please tell me more." she begs Jonathan.

"Oh Katherine, I have let you down. I wasn't there for you when you needed me. I feel I have been untrue to you in some way. You are my best friend, the woman I love dearly.

You need to read this letter from Bernardo. I hope it will explain everything. Sometimes it seemed that my loyalties were confused, but now that it is over, I hope it has been the right thing."

Trying to understand what he is saying, Katherine offers, "Jonathan, it has been so long. If there is someone else, I understand."

He smiles at her words. "Oh, no, my dear. It is nothing like that! It is that I have lived up to my word, and done the most honorable and painful thing I could ever have done at the same time. Please, let me explain a little first."

He takes her hands in his. "When the movie rights for my book sold, I could hardly believe it was Bernardo who bought them. I wonder if somewhere in his subconscious mind, he realized that it was you that I based my character on. I was never sure that he knew but at times, he seemed to. Once he began to know and trust me, he asked for my help. He had been bright enough to call me in the first place. He wanted to get the script right. Nobody realized he was planning his last film

"Remember when he and I met? We got along remarkably well. Why not? We had great similarities, especially in our attraction and love for you. We had both fallen in love with the same woman. As we grew closer, Bernardo told me that he did not believe that he had long to live. He made me promise not to tell you. He was worried about you, not himself. We talked so much of the time, and often it was not about the script. He had come to the realization that he had been selfish in not letting you develop to your own fullness, your independence. Selfishly, he wanted you all for himself. He admitted that in his way, being a director, a teacher of life, he loved to create situations for you to enjoy, roles for you to play. In the end, he felt that he had crippled you somehow. He was very happy that you had taken it upon yourself to go to Chiang Rai on your own. He knew he needed to set you free, and he hoped that when he did, you would return to him. You did."

"It wasn't his fault. I never seemed to find it important until that last year," she protests.

Jonathan quiets her. "Let me go on." She nods. The waiter quietly brings the salad and sets it on the table. Neither of them is aware.

"When I arrived at your home, I believe he must have sensed closeness between us, no matter how hard we tried to keep it from him. His intuition was remarkable. It must have been what made him a great director. I thought we were so careful. Right before I left for home, he told me what he had sensed. He was grateful that you had returned home after Chiang Mai, and stayed with him after whatever had happened to you. I never explained, so he never knew what had really happened. He just imagined what might have happened to you. He said that he couldn't be sure he would have come home if the tables had been reversed."

She laughs ruefully. "That's for sure."

The waiter brings the dinner and the bread silently and quietly walks away.

Although they are not hungry yet, they breathe in the wonderful aromas.

"What is all this?" He gestures to the several dishes.

Katherine quickly explains her madness. "Please go on."

"Perhaps knowing he was coming to the end of his life, he had become more generous. He admitted to me his jealous ways, his life of selfishness. He wanted to do whatever he could to make your life without him as happy as possible." Jonathan smiles. "He loved you very much, you know."

"Yes, I realize that. He was special, a different person, and my life would never have been so full if he had been anyone else. I accepted Bernardo, as he was when I married him. I understood our marriage would be different. Even the last year, while I was learning to make my own way, I could never fault him. But still, I don't understand."

Jonathan moves his chair close to Katherine. "He asked me to watch over you if anything happened to him. At the same time, he begged me to stay out of sight until you got your bearings. He wanted you to realize that you could be strong on your own. He gave me a letter to open in case of his death. I had to promise him I would do what he asked. That was the hardest thing I have ever done. I wanted only to come to you, to take you in my arms and share your sorrow and grief. As soon as I heard that he was gone, I opened the letter to me. He asked that I give you the time and the freedom to handle this on your own. You needed to grow your own strength and be free of him" He hands her the letter. "Here, please read this."

Katherine opens the letter. It is written on Bernardo's stationary, with his letterhead; dated a few weeks before his death.

Dear Katherine,

Please, forgive me for what I have put you through by the time you receive this letter. I hope you can understand. I have asked Jonathan to promise to watch over you, from afar, until the time that you are able and ready to dispose of my ashes. That will be the signal that he must come to you. He had no idea what I was asking when he promised to follow my instructions. I of course have no idea how long that will take. I knew that you needed to be strong enough to live for yourself, and to release all the obligations that I will have left for you to take care of. The accountants, and agent and everyone will have done all the necessary work. I also gave him letters for the twins asking for their support and asking that they stay in touch with Jonathan so he will know where you are, and when to give you this letter. Please understand and forgive them all, if you feel betrayed. You know how much they love you. You have always been our strength, the center of our lives in the important ways. I know that. I loved our life together. You have been the greatest gift that God could have given me. Who knows where I am now, but I give you my blessings in all the happiness that comes into your life from now on. You deserve it.

I love you forever,

Bernardo

"Oh my God!" Katherine cries out. "In a way, he was asking you to take care of me, showing that he understood our love and that it was all right."

Jonathan nods. "I believe so."

She shakes her head. "Can you believe it? To the very end, he is still directing in his own way. It could not have turned out any other way, being the person he was. Isn't it amazing?"

"Now what do we do?"

"Well my dear, I think we might just partake of this wonderful meal you have ordered before it all grows cold. Let's celebrate in his honor or would you say, along with him."

"That's perfect. Tomorrow we can fulfill his last wish." They raise their glasses, filled with red wine, and toast, "To Bernardo."

The following day, they drive to the villa together. It is a hot day. Dust flies from the road as they pass many beautiful old houses surrounded by fields. It is the end of summer and they can see farmers in the field, harvesting their crops. They drive down the road toward the house. Wild flowers border the road. An old dog lies on the front steps of a farm. In a yard, a small herd of goats wander about. A goat is being milked by a large woman, dressed in peasant type clothes, a bandana on her head. She waves to them and they wave back.

A tall grove of cypress trees borders the entrance to the house. "How grand!" exclaims Jonathan.

"Yes," Katherine agrees. "Bernardo always said his family had illusions of grandeur." They park the car to the side of the house and remove Bernardo's urn. A woman comes to the door. She recognizes Katherine, but appears to understand what is happening, so she nods here head and walks back inside.

A slight breeze blows. They walk behind the house, and head toward the fields and flowerbeds. "This is it." Katherine dips her hand into the urn and takes some of Bernardo's ashes out. She holds them to her heart for a moment and then scatters some of them in the garden, some into the breeze, and some into the grape vines beneath the olive trees. She continues until the urn is empty. Bernardo is now mingled with his own history.

"Now Bernardo is a part of everything," she says tearily. "He must be happy, wherever he is now. We have followed his last wishes. Bernardo has once again cast us in our roles. I hope we have played them to perfection, as far as he is concerned."

Jonathan begins to laugh. He leads her over to a garden, bright with yellow daisies and blooming lavender.

"I am sure that is the truth. He has directed his last story and now his entire being will fertilize these gardens. If he has anything to do with it, it will be a spectacular and astonishing, lovely production." He pauses for a moment.

"But, you know what?"

Katherine looks into his eyes. "What?"

"From now on, we're going to write the script."

-----FINI-----

This is how I would die
Into the Love I have for you
As pieces of Cloud Dissolve in Sunlight

Rumi

Acknowledgments

For Pat, my husband and partner in life. Thanks for all the time, patience effort and expense, putting up with my writing and me. Thanks for taking me on your adventures giving me inspiration and all sorts of ideas for this book.

For fifteen years The Common Writers: A Group of eclectic beings braved the winter weather and each week came to my house in Snowville to share their work. We gained courage from our sharing, and that made all better writers. Calvert, Joanne, Ben, Luigi, Natalie, Walter Staples, Joan Sherman, Kathy, Bob, Jeanne, Dave, and many more who came through our door all those years. You kept our house in order.

Chris Gillette; The first person to actually read the somewhat finished copy. She kept asking for the finished book.

Ashley (She left us and is a better place), helped edit both my books. Hope she is happy with her kitties.

Janet and Bob, great friends who supported my poetry rights from the Japanese poets.

My friends at the Conway Public Library, Betty, Kate, Margaret and more helped me find all I needed along with valued friendship.

More of my friends read and helped me so I hope they all will understand how much I appreciate their support in so many ways. Including the Snowville Drinking, Eaton Readers, the Conway Public Library Readers lead by Kate.

A NOTE TO MY READERS

The ideas for this book took birth while I was sitting in the lobby of the Krungshri River Hotel in Auyuttha, Thailand. I had promised my husband, if he took me on the location of Mortal Kombat, Annihilation to London and Thailand, I would finish my first book Hairdresser to the Stars. I fulfilled my promise and as I read the finished version I realized how many people, and adventures it took to actually tell this story. The characters kept growing and learning.

I love to share my life and so my husband loves to tell about the remark Winston Churchill made to a woman. "Madame, do you ever have an unexpressed thought?" I think that describes me. I have learned so much in life and always want to share the good things.

I am a connector or a facilitator. I love to point people toward what will make them happy and grow.

I spent much of my life working in the movie business, I do write as though the book is a film. I looked for people to cast as my main characters. The first one that appeared was Jonathon Pryce, the British Actor. He charmed me first in Brazil, then Carrington, and finally in Evita. Something about his characters called to me and he inspired Jonathon. I have never met him, but admire him. I always hoped he could play that part when the book is made into a film. I have taken such a long time that I am not sure if he is the right age any longer. So am casting in my mind again. Clive Owens might do. But I shall have to leave it up to the filmmakers.

If it takes too long it might be Johnny Depp or Leonardo diCapprio in the leading part. I love their work.

The main character Katherine is such a combination of people that I never could settle on one perfect person. She is so many people I have read about and known. Bernardo seemed to be a combination of the many directors I have met in my career. They are one focused bunch of people with vision and the good ones are capable of bringing actors beyond the script.

My life in Snowville, New England for thirty years has given me roots, and friends I would never have found elsewhere. I am thankful for the opportunity to have experienced that. Although we have moved to Ajijic, Mexico, to be in the warm weather, our little town of Eaton Center will always be a part of my heart. Thank heavens for email. You too can write to me. Look up my web page on Google, it is under construction.